FALLING MOON
THE SAGA OF MOONBABY

MICHAEL SULLIVAN EDDY

Requests for permission should be addressed to Pack Mule Publishing
info@packmulepublishing.com

This is a work of fiction. Names, characters, businesses, places, events,
and incidents are either the products of the author's imagination or
used in a fictitious manner. Any resemblance to actual persons, living
or dead, or actual events is purely coincidental.

Eddy, Michael Sullivan.
Falling Moon
The Saga of Moonbaby
ISBN: 978-0-9914947-0-5

*I dedicate this book to God first for guiding me
and giving me this story.*

I also thank my wife Jane for putting up with me through this time.

chapter one

Cold, Wet, and Tired

Under a cold steady drizzle, a line of cars and trucks sit and wait for U.S. customs at the border of Canada. With so many cars in just a couple of lines, it seems more like the DMV.

Jack grips the wheel in frustration as he fumes over all these stupid new border procedures. *Why are they looking at everyone instead of just looking at the specific types of people who are the ones who are going to commit the crimes?* Jack remembers when he was a kid and his parents took him to Canada, it was like crossing from one state to another. You never even noticed unless you read the sign, "Welcome to Canada" or "Welcome to the United States". It was barely more than a sign back then.

Jack cranes his neck to see up the long row of cars to the agents who seem to be taking their time over every vehicle. *Really, we are only going to Canada,* Jack thinks. *This country is going to hell in a hand basket with all the rules and regulations to supposedly protect us!* He realizes that he did not just think it, he said it aloud. His wife looks at him puzzled and then shakes her head because she knows what he was thinking and decides not to say anything.

The line is like a toll plaza that has stopped taking tolls and won't let anyone go by. Through the lines of cars, officials with hats, badges, and guns are walking around interviewing the occupants. Why are you coming to Canada? What is the purpose of your visit?

Jack thinks back to when it was just to go, maybe get lunch, go shopping, visit a park. Used to be you needed no real reason, like taking a

Sunday ride. That all changed since September 11. Somehow, we all got fearful, though there was good reason. Jack stares blankly out the window. *How far are we willing to go for safety?*

Jack had read a story in the paper about how they are now using drones to spy on terrorists, but not just foreign terrorists, U.S. citizens suspected of terrorist activities. It all started with two wars and the all-encompassing "War on Terror." It seemed to Jack like it was okay with Americans as long as it was happening in the Middle East to people they didn't know. The government was just protecting us from another 9/11 and you had nothing to be afraid of if you were not a terrorist.

But it got more intrusive as they started to use certain tactics here on American soil, investigating U.S. citizens. Jack could see a uniformed official motioning for a family to get out of their mini-van. He thought about something he'd read that there was a special order that said the government could kill one of our own citizens with a drone as long as it was in a foreign country, but now they are doing it here on American soil! Jack didn't know if that had happened yet or not. There was nothing in the news about it. Though the news was in the tank for the President for so long, he wondered if they would even report it if it had happened. Jack did not think so and besides, the government was good at covering up that sort of thing anyway.

Jack looked around at the line of non-moving vehicles. No drones here, just people who'd better be in no hurry.

An oil tanker is idling in another line for all commercial vehicles, about four back. It looks normal, some Canadian oil company logo on the side. On closer inspection there is an outlet that doesn't serve to let oil in or out. It is well concealed and easily missed. A compartment large enough for one or two people. Moonbaby is in there. She is wet, cold, and very tired. Her bones ached; it's been days since she slept in a bed and she can't remember a time when her whole body hurt. She was never the type to rough it; oh, her parents took them camping occasionally when she was a kid, but Moon never really liked that. No AC, bugs, and sand sticking to you everywhere. The only bathrooms had to be shared with God knows what type of people. She could shower but never seemed to get the sand out of all the cracks. It was not something she enjoyed. That is why this really sucked even more beside the fact that most of her money was gone and some nasty people wanted her dead.

The compartment is rank with a mixture of rust, oil, and old body odor. The smell came primarily from the rags that are the only padding on the floor. It's rough and hard to breathe; she has a paper mask on, the kind you see the Chinese wearing in news reports out of Beijing. *How did this ever happen? I'm not a bad person, I'm educated, I pay my taxes, never been in any trouble except maybe a speeding ticket or two. How is it I'm running from my own government?* If it wasn't really happening it would be something out of a sci-fi novel or a movie like...what was that Condor movie? The Robert Redford one.

Moon would laugh if it weren't all so surreal. If she could be in this place then anyone could. This happens to people no one ever hears about. But the government was out of control and coming after her. How is that? She was an attorney and respected jurist. Her family was in the entertainment business and Democrats to boot. *We are not bad people, we fix the planet. We help the poor. I even volunteered and spent one Thanksgiving feeding the homeless.* So how is it she is now a hunted criminal?

What little money she has left is in a backpack. When the shit hit the fan she'd had to go with what she could carry. She has a watch, well, a Rolex and that was kind of her ace in the hole. That last thing to give up for freedom if she has to.

Was it just weeks or even days since she'd been making her way in Hollywood. *My problems started not that long ago,* she thought but she realized that it all began long before it got to her.

The country was supposed to be in a time of hope and change. Back during the previous administration, Congress voted in laws that were supposed to keep us safe. People really weren't paying attention, not that many paid attention any other time, it's just that we were losing more freedom. At the time, Moon thought that getting rid of one administration and trading for another would fix everything. But it didn't. Things got worse, more and more regulations and rules created a freedom-reduced safety, curbing business and personal freedom.

Was this why she was stuck in this filthy place? Moon sat on the metal floor not really knowing how she was going to save herself much less get her life back to the way it used to be. She starts to nod off and thinks about a time when life was good and she was in ignorant bliss of the things going on.

chapter two

Home Sweet Home

It's Christmas morning back when life was fun and uncomplicated. As uncomplicated as the life and world of a Hollywood entertainment lawyer could be. Moon gets out of bed; it looks like another beautiful California day.

Moonbaby Franklin is a beautiful five foot seven inches of muscle and bone. She is very athletic mainly because she loves to run. She has beautiful dark eyes and brunette hair that is kissed by the sun with blonde streaks. Many people, mostly women, think she highlights it but she doesn't. The sun has always affected her hair in this very natural way. Still, people think otherwise but they are not the people who know her. Those who know her also know that she is brutally honest, sometimes to a fault. She tells the truth about herself and anyone else. She can keep her mouth shut otherwise she couldn't be in the law business but it prevented her from being a defense attorney. She would have to defend people that she knew were guilty and she could not do that.

Moon has tanned skin, high cheekbones, but not a gaunt face as you see on some models. She has full cheeks without being fat and full lips without looking as if a surgeon made them. She has well-defined arms that look as if she was a rower and when she is in a bathing suit, you can see the vein that runs on top of her six-pack abs. This tells you that fat just does not have the chance to stick to her.

She is a highly intelligent and inquisitive person so that is an advantage in the practice of law. It also helps being in entertainment law, though sometimes she wonders how some people in the business are so stupid and successful at the same time.

5

Moon goes out to the kitchen and makes some coffee. She puts on some flip-flops and walks out to get the paper; she wonders *Why do I even read the paper as it is usually behind in the news.* She figures it's something to do while she drinks her coffee. She looks down the street and everything's quiet. It's early still and people are not up and out yet. She loves this time of day, as it seems she has it all to herself.

Moon goes back to her bedroom and dresses for her run. She runs most every morning even when she feels bad. She enjoys running that much. You know the kind of person who doesn't do it because it's good for them but would run even if it were bad. She likes the solitude of running alone.

She lives in the Hollywood Hills and running the ups and downs can be quite challenging physically. It can get hard on the joints but today there was no problem except for a nagging pain in her neck.

Moon is a little hung over from the night before as her best friend Jan took her out drinking. Christmas Eve and Jan wanted to go out, *well what the hell* she thought. She broke up with Butthead, that's not really his name but she still can't seem to say it even though it's been about three months. She knows why she doesn't want to be alone but Jan seems to need company even more than Moon does. Christmas Eve is an odd time for Jan to want to go out. Having children and the attachment she has to them no mother could surpass but a divorce decree could.

The children were spending Christmas Eve with their father; Jan was alone for the first time in years. She was the one really feeling like drowning her sorrows in a night out so she dragged Moon along. Moon called a limo service to pick her up. They drove over to Jan's house, then on to Jar.

Jar is a nice place. Moon felt like meat so this was the spot. Steaks and martinis, a great start to the night. The chef at Jar does much more but they are known for their beef. The head chef has an active lifestyle like Moon's. She met her on a mountain bike trail once and Moon has loved the restaurant ever since.

Jan was in a mood that made it almost seem like Jan of their college days. Moon thought she was going to have to hear a bunch of sad tales of broken hearts and promises but instead Jan was more like *let me loose for the night.* She was the kind of Jan Moon remembered: free, fun, and unencumbered. Moon asked about the kids. "The kids are great, they are with their father and he's doing fine." Jan pursed her lips a little. "Can we talk about something else?" Moon pretty much got the message that Jan

6

didn't want to talk about that or any problems either of them had.

Dinner came and they ate and talked endlessly about old days and the possibility of new and better days ahead. After all, we just got the man we always wanted in the White House and we are looking for that hope and change to come. Well, Moon got the man she wanted; Jan was just nice enough not to complain about it. Jan threw back the last of her latest martini, "Let's not talk about politics either tonight. Let's talk about free sex and men, or women if you like." She made herself laugh. Maybe it was the martini.

It was later that became a blur. Moon was a little shocked that Jan drank as much as she did. As a reporter for KTTV, Jan was very concerned about how she appeared in public. The night turned into too many drinks, too many stops for drinks, and they weren't 21 anymore. Moon realized she couldn't drink like they did back in school.

Jan really needed a release and if Moon was being honest with herself, she did too. Now Moon sat drinking her coffee and stalling the start of the day, she's not yet feeling like facing people which is contrary to her personality as she is very good with people. Today is different; it's Christmas and that means the people are her family. Her parents and her sister. Moon doesn't have any children of her own but her sister Aspen does and she will be at their parents'. The kids will be up early looking for evidence of Santa Claus. Christmas with the kids.

On to the home front to face the family. She thought she could get more coffee on the way and maybe her head would feel better. She gathered up the gifts she bought. She had to admit to herself that she really liked shopping for the kids though she didn't have time in her life for kids of her own.

Her niece and nephew were easy to buy for. They would love her then go home. Moon figured it would be different when you had a partner you could trust who was in it with you. Aspen had that; her husband Sam was a trustworthy guy who worked hard but was there at all the soccer games and Christmas pageants and around the house to relieve the pressure. Moon was jealous of her sister at times that she had found such a man. *I might have actually had that man with Butthead but that was not to be.*

Moon's parents live in a secluded spot for being in the hills of LA. Her parents moved from the beach well after she got out of law school. Charles and Anita seemed like such proper people now but when Moon was a kid they were far from proper. They were wild, free love, anti-establishment types but who had educations. They were not anti-money and they'd been successful in many ventures. They also felt God blessed them and that made them very spiritual which rubbed off on their daughters. They were not Bible bangers but they were true believers and they lived it.

Moon understood the idea of God and what that might mean to her in the world but she never felt his presence personally. Her parents would say that is because she has God inside her and while she understood that, she didn't feel it.

Anita came to the door. Moon gave her Mom a big hug. Charles popped up behind his wife, "Where's my hug!" Moon's Dad always gave her the biggest hugs; it was as if he was never going to let go of her. She missed that. The kids ran up to Auntie Moon all excited; they knew there would be another round of gifts now that she was here. One by one she got a *big hug, big kiss, hug kiss, my you're getting big,* Moon retracts a little and thinks, *oh, and you're a little sticky.*

As the day went on, all the presents were unwrapped and there were hugs all around, kids off playing with toys and checking out each other's loot. Moon looked around the dinner table, *Christmas is almost over. How fast the time seems to go. We work and rush through life to get to these moments and then they are over sooner than they should be.* Moon was contemplating her life and how it seemed to be blowing by her as if she were a spectator.

She loves her job and loves the life that seems to have chosen her, but so much seems to be missing. Moon always gets this way around her family mostly because of her sister and the life that she has reminds Moon of how different they are. Dinner was great, the kids are already up from the table and fussing over their Christmas loot for the fifth time.

Nice to be young and unconcerned about life and its trials and tribulations. Children are like that; sometimes Moon thinks she'd like to go back to that time of her life again. Although as a child, she was never that way. Not really a normal kid, Moon questioned just about everything that she encountered. She was twelve going on thirty and enjoyed childhood but more as an adult would have. *How complicated it all seems to get later with house payments, bosses, dating, blah. It sometimes gets to be too much.*

Moon made her way around the house, "I think it is time to go." Her

Mom always made her feel as if she was leaving too early but Moon said she was tired and needed to go home. As she drove off, she did feel a twinge of regret as she saw the house getting smaller in the rear view mirror.

Back in her own home, Moon can truly unwind. She bought the house last year, moving from a downtown condominium. It was a time like now when the day was about done and she could sit and let her mind go blank staring off into the distance. *It will be good to get the holidays over with and back into a routine.* Work was always slow this time of year because people were traveling on vacation or visiting family. She really would rather get back to work and her routine than deal with this chaotic party time of year. It starts with Thanksgiving then Christmas and finally ends with New Year's.

chapter three

Work of the Past

Moon felt more home at the office than at home, not home like her house, more home as in *I'm productive* and that is how she lived her life.

Work was good; Moon enjoyed doing what she did. She wasn't helping the downtrodden but she did do some pro-bono work that involved young people and getting them back on the right path. A friend in the District Attorney's office got her involved. Stan Davis was an Assistant D.A. and the primary youth court prosecutor. They met back at UCLA and had been in a study group together. After graduation, she moved on to Bamberger, Sullivan, and Wright and he went to the D.A.'s office.

Stan was a good fellow and they were close friends through school though Moon always felt the pressure to move the friendship to another level. Once they moved their separate ways, Stan got married and the pressure was off. They became colleagues in their work and when he called her to suggest that she volunteer for the youth court she said okay.

As Moon walks into the office, Jennifer almost jumps out of her seat to tell Moon about her appointments for the morning. Jennifer was a very efficient and helpful secretary but she loved to tell Moon how much work she had and seemed to relish it even more if it was bad news. Maybe it just seemed that way first thing in the morning.

Moon was not a happy person in the morning; she took time to warm up to the world until she took her run then she was full of life. Jennifer was the opposite. She charged out of bed, ready to greet the day first thing or this is how Moon imagined her to be. She really didn't know that much about Jennifer's personal life but she was happy and energetic by the time she got to the office.

Moon was working on a case when Jennifer's voice warbled out of the phone intercom, "The Sheikh of Whatsisname or some such on line two." A call from a Sheikh was not what Moon would expect. They're not the type of people who tend to involve themselves in her business. Moon punched the blinking red light and hit the speaker button.

"Elizabeth Franklin...Yes...hello?"

The woman on the other end sounded maybe Arabic, definitely proper. "The Sheikh will be right with you. Please hold, madam."

The next voice on the line was a British accent, more of the unexpected. "Good morning, Ms. Franklin. I am Sheikh Mohammed Waseem. It is my understanding you are one of the most prominent entertainment attorneys in the Los Angeles area."

Moon was flattered and a bit disarmed. Everything about this call intrigued her. "Well, thank you! How can I help you, uh...sheikh...sir?"

The Sheikh explained he was in the oil business and owns a theater company in London but now would like to start a Hollywood studio or acquire a production company already in operation. He would also like some legal advice on operating a studio in America. Moon spoke with him at length and made an appointment to conference after she looked into his requests.

The Sheikh was born in Doha, Qatar, in 1968 as Mohammed Abdallah Waseem, a great grandson of the founder of Waseem Petroleum, an international oil concern. He grew up just outside the city on a compound where he lived with an extended family of aunts, uncles, and cousins. They all went to private elementary school with other privileged Arabs. He was the eldest of eight children by a nephew of an Emir. As a boy, he was a good student and enjoyed reading about foreign lands, stories of mystery, and science fiction.

The young Mohammed's interests disturbed his parents as they would have liked him to have less of the Western culture's influence and all the perversion that came with it. They wanted him to study the Quran and other books of Islam but Mohammed was not interested. Oh, he went through the motions and believed in God but he didn't really want to live the way his parents did or as the teachings of Islam would have dictated.

He loved movies. American movies were not easy to come by as the government controlled what got to the public and elements of Western culture just did not make it to his part of the world. Mohammed shared his fascination for all things American with his cousin, Kadyn. Kaydn was the only son of Mohammed's uncle's tenth wife. He and Kadyn grew up in the same family complex so they went to the same school and they lived close to one another. The boys both loved going behind their parents' backs to catch anything from Hollywood that got past the government's censors.

Mohammed liked science fiction while Kadyn loved courtroom dramas. He would get old Perry Mason episodes and watch them on tape. Mohammed and Kadyn would trade off going to movies of the genre each of them preferred. Really though, they both loved movies so much that it didn't take much convincing for either of them to watch the other's favorites. Kadyn and Mohammed were inseparable all the way through high school but that is when it started to become apparent they'd be taking separate paths.

In his last year of high school, Mohammed began a campaign to go to college in the United States. He wanted to go to Embry Riddle Aeronautical University in Daytona Beach, Florida. He based his choice on two reasons: one, he really liked planes and two, spring break. He thought spring break in Daytona was just about year-round and there would be girls, girls, and more girls. Really not very typical of a teenage boy, well in Qatar, it was not supposed to be. His parents did not really suspect that girls were his motive and he wasn't telling them.

Mohammed was a very good-looking young man and as he grew older, he turned into a very handsome man who could catch the attention of any woman he wanted. He got excellent grades and scored in the top one percent on standardized tests. His parents could not argue with the fact that he'd been a superior student so when he got the letter of acceptance from Embry Riddle, they agreed to send him. On to America he went, joining the freshman class of future pilots in 1986. Kadyn, on the other hand, wanted to go off to college and then to law school. The cousins went their separate ways but both were on a path of becoming Westernized.

The Qatar military was willing to let an American aeronautical university train Mohammed to fly. Kaydn's pre-law curriculum didn't get him off the hook for military service. Barely a year into his college career, he was called to pull a stint in the Qatar Armed Forces. He wasn't happy about it but it wasn't long after returning home that Kadyn seemed to come back to following an Islamic way of life. After completing military service, he wanted to resume his education in the U.S. but by then he had developed different reasons for wanting to study American law.

Mohammed immersed himself in his American education. While his family approved of flight training, they did not suspect his experiences at university were establishing a foundation of Western influence upon his life.

When he arrived in Daytona, Mohammed was a little naïve as any young man from the Arab world would be when he first set up in the U.S. Though he had read everything he could about life in America, how he was living was not what he'd expected. It did not take him long, however, to get used to the freedom. It took a toll on his first semester grades but he recovered very well and that was never a problem again.

Daytona Beach can be a melting pot of people from around the U.S. and the world and Embry Riddle attracts students from all over the globe. In the late 1980s, Americans still associated Arabs with wealth and oil and Peter O'Toole. Mohammed found he was quite good at making new friends and he fit in well with all the different types of people he met.

So began Mohammed's transformation into "Moe" as his new American friends called him in Daytona. Mohammed sounded so formal and to Americans it sounded funny, like if all Christian men were named Jesus. His parents would have been appalled but his new name let Mohammed feel more like he fit in. Americans accepted Moe as his name and willingly accepted him as well.

Moe excelled at flight school and made many American friends. He was very unhappy that graduation meant an end to his time in the U.S. He tried to get his parents to agree to let him stay on for graduate school but they had other plans. So back home he went, back to a life that he frankly wasn't comfortable with anymore.

Moe's American flight training landed him in an elite unit of the Royal Air Force as an officer. He flew jet fighters for about a year before his superiors singled him out for the Sandhurst Military Academy in England. Little did they realize that by sending him back to live among westerners they were ensuring Moe would complete the minimum military service he could get away with.

Moe loved England almost as much as America. He studied military tactics while making many friends and enjoying life in a free and open society. He also developed a new passion.

London has some of the finest theater in the world and Moe became very enamored with it. He'd always loved movies but as he was getting older, he became fascinated with how live theater connected to the audience. Unlike at the movies, a theater audience plays a role, extending their approval to an ongoing event.

Moe's transformation into a fully assimilated Westerner was complete after his stay in England. He was more American and British than Arab and that was okay with him; it would not be okay with his family. He stressed over the prospect of having to keep up appearances when he was back home so no one would suspect how fully he'd changed. His family would expect he'd only "play along" with the conventions of the West while he was there but he wasn't supposed to have allowed it to taint him. He struggled to suppress the Western manners and comfortable demeanor that had become second nature. He hadn't even realized how his speech had acquired a unique cadence that blended an American meter with a mellifluous British inflection. Londoners heard him as a foreigner but back home he caught hell daily for speaking Arabic as if he'd learned it from Rosetta Stone.

Moon hung up the phone and turned her attention back to the work she'd been doing before Mr. Waseem's call. As their conversation had progressed, he did not seem to be too different from any other super-wealthy person she dealt with in the entertainment business though she had not worked with anyone from the Middle East before. Oh, she knew some people that came from that part of the world but they were Americans now. She had not had any business dealings with any non-Americanized Arabs.

Moon asked Jennifer to look at the calendar and schedule a conference call about an acquisition. She also needed to talk to her friend Tom Berkowitz about what might be for sale in production companies.

Companies of this type don't advertise that they're on the market as that usually panics employees and stops projects in development. Well-connected and discreet people like Mr. Berkowitz are the only way to find potential prospects. It was very convenient that Moon knew Tom; she really doesn't find property as part of her normal job as she usually spends her time after the fact preparing the contracts of sales and mergers. She also represents studios in developing contracts with actors. That can keep her very busy but she said she would look into this for Mr. Waseem and that is what she is doing.

Moon caught Tom as usual, rushing between appointments.

"Your timing's pretty good," Tom said. "There might be a well-established operation on the market that could be purchased for the right price. Who's the buyer?"

Moon didn't want to give away too many details, "It's someone who will pay cash so I don't see a problem." She didn't know this as clearly as she would have liked but Moon assumed money was not going to be an issue in this transaction. As she hung up the phone, she was relieved Tom hadn't started asking questions she couldn't answer yet. It was Monday and she'd have the week to get her ducks in a row but now was not the time, it was time to get out of the office and on to the gym.

Three days a week she went to a boot camp gym along with the daily running she did. She had been going there for a couple of years and it really helped to tone her up. Running kept her in good shape but her upper body was not as strong and she knew that as you get older the more weight resistance exercise you could do, the better off you were going to be at fifty or sixty.

Class was intense but it made time go by faster. The trainer, Danny, had a reputation for working his groups the hardest and Moon liked it that way. Before she knew it, the class was over and people were packing up. Moon was stuffing her damp towel into her bag when she realized Danny was standing behind her. "Are you going to join us for drinks tonight? A lot of us are going." His smile seemed a bit flirtatious. Moon liked the idea of being invited but claimed she had other things to do. Tonight her plans were nothing more than a date with a sautéed fish.

The road to Moon's house wound its way up a steep grade but she never gets tired of the drive. Some people might find it tiring after awhile but it's why she bought a house up in the Hills. She liked taking the road less traveled, at least by anyone who doesn't live up there. It could be a pain if you're in a hurry but you had just better not be and then it's a pleasure with all the twists and turns.

Settling in for the evening, Moon remembers the mail, grabs a beer, and walks out to the mailbox. She takes a minute to sort through the stack of restaurant coupons and bills when she notices a car parked two doors down in front of the Johnsons' house. She thinks they should still be in France. *Hmmm. Maybe they are back now and someone is visiting?* In the waning light it looks as if someone is in the car but it's really hard to tell. Better stop staring. Go back inside.

Settling down with her beer, dinner, and laptop, she does a search for this Mohammed Abdallah Waseem. Much later, she will think back to how quickly this seemingly minor event got the wrong people's attention. She would never have believed that the government could work this fast.

chapter four

We Are Watching You

It was five o'clock when Agent Richard Washington got the call to go by a woman's house and check things out. It seemed like anyone could be a subject for Homeland Security surveillance these days. This time it was some lawyer who lived in the Hills and Richard really didn't think anything of it except that it ruined his plans for an evening with his girlfriend. He'd be a good little soldier and do what he was told.

Homes in the Hollywood Hills were often set close along the twisty, switchback roads. Sometimes big walls were right at the road if they had some land to them. It wasn't easy for Richard to find the house or to pick a spot where he could get a good view of it without being obvious.

He sat there for what seemed like an eternity thinking maybe this woman was not coming home. He also had to endure the various neighbors giving him suspicious looks as they were arriving home. Finally, he sees this nice BMW pulling up to the driveway and into the garage. This should be the subject; he has a description of her vehicle and it matched. He gets out of his car, looks around, walks back to his trunk. He takes out what looks like a toy flying machine. It has six fan-type blades and a center fuselage. The fuselage could hold many types of payloads about the size of a brick, not that heavy but a camera or a small supply canister would fit. Really it looks like any number of battery-powered toys you could buy for $19.95, but it's not. It's a carbon fiber spy drone with a high-def camera that can be flown over long distances and controlled without the need for line of sight direction.

Richard sets it down on the roof of his car and gets back in. He pulls out a hand-held controller that looks like the same type you'd expect to come with that toy from Radio Shack. Over his head he can hear the drone as it lifts off the roof of the car. Richard deftly guides it toward the subject's house, focusing the on-board camera to look for windows. He's able to zoom in on a living room but no one's in it so he systematically circles the house. Then he spots her. She's in a towel. She drops it to the floor and takes some panties from a drawer. *This is not too bad of an assignment now, this lady's pretty hot.* Richard finds himself a bit distracted by the subject's long, shapely legs and tight bottom. He zooms in on her breasts; they're not large but they are very nicely shaped. He feels a little like a pervert and guilty for staring at her this long. You're a professional. Do your job. Richard maneuvers the drone to pull it back from the window.

Moon is scrutinizing her biceps in the mirror to determine if that boot camp class is having an effect when something reflects a spot of glare in her eye. She quickly grabs the towel to cover herself and walks to the window. She sees nothing but the backyard and up the hill behind her. Oh well nothing there, she finishes getting dressed.

Outside, Richard doesn't realize the close call he just missed when he sees the subject coming out of her house. He gains control of himself and the flying machine as he quickly directs it into a steep vertical climb. She walks to the mailbox and surveys the street up and down. She stands there looking at the car; can she see Richard inside? He scrunches down in the car seat and watches Moon from the controller. The drone is hovering far above her head, taking pictures of her at a distance that she doesn't notice. No, she can't see him, the light is too dim and the streetlights are too far away to illuminate the inside of the vehicle. Still she is just standing there looking. After a moment that seemed far too long for Richard's nerves, she turns and walks back inside. He's got the drone hovering over the subject's house so he backs the car just down the hill and out of her sight if she comes out again.

Richard flies the drone back out and further away so he can get a good overall look of the house and the grounds. He can zoom in on any window from so far away, the subject won't be able to see the unit.

Moon goes back to trying to enjoy her dinner but something about that car is bothering her. She feels silly and hopes the neighbors don't see her looking but she can't resist going to check again. The car is gone. *Okay, you're just being stupid now.* She looks around some more and everything is as it always is, nice and quiet. She goes in and gets back on the laptop then decides that she will let Jennifer do her job. She sits down in front of the TV to numb her mind and go to sleep.

Richard recorded a good overall view of the subject's home, inside and out, as well as some detailed footage of her. *Very detailed, heh-heh.* He got perfect shots for facial recognition and she could even be identified by the birthmark on that tight little butt of hers. He gets the drone back in the trunk and heads for home. He'll write his report tomorrow; it won't be much as this lady doesn't look to be doing anything different from any other single person in America.

Even before Richard gets home he already has a message that he has to go back in the morning and continue surveillance of the subject until further notice. Richard can't help thinking it seems like a waste of time. There looks to be nothing going on with this woman; she's just another person making her own way and, from the looks of her house and car, she's doing pretty well. So why does his boss have him risking exposure when there is no apparent danger? Sometimes Richard wonders why the Department of Homeland Security even exists if a lot of what they do is monitor U.S. citizens. He figures if they stop a terrorist attack on American soil, he can justify it that way.

The next morning Richard gets up early and drives over to Moon's house to sit, watch, and expect to find nothing. He is out just as the sun is coming up, there is little traffic and the roads are clear. He's tired, as sleep did not come easy last night. He'd gotten home late and went to bed thinking he had to get up early, so that was all he could think of every time he closed his eyes. He thinks he dozed off about 1am and awoke at 5am so he got about four hours. That's not enough, he risks falling asleep. Stakeouts are boring enough without the complication of a sleepless night and he didn't expect this to be anything but boring.

Richard got situated and waited for a sign of life at the house. What he didn't know was Moon got an early start and was already running. She was coming up the hill towards her house when she realizes she's running straight for the same car as last night, parked in the same spot.

What's this guy doing? Moon walks up behind the car, wiping the sweat off her face. She taps on the passenger side window and muffles a little giggle when the man inside jumps. Richard tries to pretend he wasn't startled and drops the drone controller. He fakes a bout of coughing and throat-clearing as it hits the floorboard. Richard can't think fast enough; he has no idea what to think. He definitely hadn't planned on this.

"Good morning!" The lady at the window is way too perky for such an early hour. She knocks on the window again and Richard figures he'd better roll it down because she won't be going away. "Are you here to see the Robertsons?"

Richard stammers a bit and decides to pretend he's half asleep. The lady at the window points at the house. "The Robertsons. They won't be home for a few more days."

"Yeah...yeah, the Robertsons. Um, I'm supposed to meet someone here about doing some work on the house. A contractor with a key. We're remodeling the kitchen," Richard mumbles, impressed with himself that he came up with a cover story.

Moon flashes a friendly smile. "Oh, okay. I just thought maybe you didn't know they were out of town. Since you were sitting here last night too and you're back again first thing this morning."

Damn it, Richard thought. *She's messing with me and she seems to be enjoying it.* "Thanks, I appreciate it. But you know, I, uh, was supposed to meet that contractor and get instructions, so..."

"You could call him," Moon suggested. "Save yourself some time."

"Yeah, right. Hey, will do. Thanks." Richard would really like to get rid of her by this point. He figured they'd chatted enough that he could roll the window up and maybe she'll think she's imposed on a stranger for long enough. He let out a deep breath when she turned and trotted off. Richard managed a bit of a smile as she looked back and waved. *Come on, lady. Go the hell home already.*

Richard knew he couldn't risk staying there another minute. If she saw him still parked there when she left for work, it would look even more suspicious and when lawyers get suspicious they start investigating.

Richard did learn two things about his surveillance subject: she's an early riser and she's got balls. She is a bold one walking up to a strange man in a car and speaking directly to him. A lot of women wouldn't do that; they would go inside and look through the windows and maybe call the police, especially in a nice neighborhood like this one.

Moon kicked off her running shoes when she got in the door. That was a total bullshit story. *What is that guy really doing here, stalking the neighborhood?* She laughed to herself as she thought about how flustered she made him. She spoon-fed him a story and he was so quick to go with it. *Total bullshit.* Whoever this guy is, he didn't do his homework and he didn't have a plan.

Richard couldn't decide if he should drive home for a nap or go throw down the biggest coffee in town and get himself completely awake. He opted for the Starbucks drive-thru and pulled in at the end of a rush hour line. *What could she do? Talk to those people when they get home and ask if they are having work done? Nah, people don't know their neighbors anymore. She was messing with me. As far as she knows, my story was the right one and I have a reason to be there.* Richard started to feel a bit smug. He didn't want to think a surveillance subject had gotten the best of him. Yeah, this won't be a problem.

Moon showered and dressed and headed out to the office. She forgot to eat breakfast. She was bothered by the sudden presence of this man in her neighborhood. She couldn't help thinking he might be there because of her.

Moon was anxious to get to the office and start looking into the situation. That wasn't going to happen as traffic was at a standstill for some early morning accident. It looked like an eighteen-wheeler was ruining some poor soul's day. If she was going to be stuck there, she might as well use the time. She got out her phone and looked up Frank Cahill, a private investigator she's used for celebrity divorce cases and even stalkers. Her call went to voicemail. "Frank, it's Moon, how ya been? Look, I might have a little problem. This one's for me. I need you to run a license plate number."

Traffic kept stopping and starting, it gave her something to do. Moon could feel a bit agitated if she had to keep sitting there. *Why was this person hanging out on my street? Was he trying to watch me? What case could I be working on that someone would want me investigated?* She could not think of any. She was only working on some contracts she was writing for a couple of studios on upcoming movies. There was a merger between two small production companies but nothing that would involve her personal life. *Maybe it was Butthead?*

No, why would he care and bother to have her watched. That was finished long ago, still, it was the only path that she could follow out of this. She would have to call him. She checked her contacts and yes, there he was; she had never deleted him. She sighed in remembrance as she pushed the call button and it started to ring. *What the hell am I going to say to him? I don't want him to know why I'm really calling so I need an excuse. Shit, quick, quick hang up!* She fumbled with the phone to cancel the call. She had not thought this out very well.

It looked like daylight at the end of the jam so she put down the phone and concentrated on driving. Too many nuts driving in and out of traffic trying to get one second ahead of her and everyone else. She didn't need to add to the accident list today.

Her phone rang. It was Bruce, aka Butthead. The call must have gone through before she cancelled it and now he is calling. *Crap,* she thought, she wasn't ready for this and wouldn't have thought he would call her back anyway.

He knows she is there, she just used the phone even if it was by mistake. *Yes, that was it!* She will say sorry it was a mistake, she was driving and she pushed the wrong button.

"Hello, Butt...Bruce what's going on?" She can't believe she almost called him Butthead. "Sorry about the call, I'm in the car and I hit the wrong contact."

Bruce really didn't mind, "No problem, so what is going on with you these days? It's a nice surprise to hear from you."

Okay, he bought it. Maybe she can get him talking a little and he'll give away a clue that he's stalking her. He did say it was nice to hear from me. They talked about current events and some family stuff, Christmas and what not. It seemed like no time that she was at the office parking garage and they were still chatting.

"You know, it's really good to hear your voice again. I'm glad things are going so well for you." Bruce sounded like he meant it.

Damn, did he have to be so nice about it? Moon hoped maybe he was feeling a little guilty. After all, it was his fault they were not together. She ended the conversation with the same pleasantries and said good-bye.

She parked the car and sat there in thought. It was nice to talk with Bruce again and that bothered her, she thought she had no feelings left, but she decided that he wasn't the reason for Stalker Guy. *So what's really going on?*

Jennifer was already in when Moon breezed past her desk without looking up, the wheels spinning in her head.

"Yo, hello? Like, good morning? Are we a grumpy Gus today?" Moon thought how Jennifer's persistently perky morning attitude could be a pain sometimes.

"No, sorry," Moon apologized. "Just a lot on my mind. Any calls?" There was one call in particular she was eager to get.

Jennifer grabbed her tablet and plopped herself down in front of

Moon's desk. "Frank called. He said he'll have that information, whatever it is that you wanted by lunch."

Oh fantastic. Moon felt a little relieved. "Did you find out anything about our new client from the Middle East?"

Jennifer opened a few windows on the tablet. "I'm working on it now but there isn't much except that his family is related to the Qatar Royal family...ooooh, our first royal client, huh? How do you say that? CAT-ARE? Cat, are you under there? Here, kitty!" Jen giggled. She could crack herself up. "And he's in the oil business. Duh, right? Well his family is anyway and he heads one of the business divisions of Waseem Petroleum. On the Board of Directors. Worth in the BILL-yons."

Yeah what a shocker, Moon thought. *What rich Arab isn't in the oil business? I could have told her that without even looking.*

Jennifer swiped through more screens on the tablet. "Oh this is cool! He owns a theater company in London! Royal and artsy!"

"He told me about the theater company when we talked," Moon realized she'd deflated Jen's excitement. It made her feel a little bad. "Look, it all sounds good. Call our security company and run a routine background check and credit rating."

Jen slumped down in the chair. "Don't be surprised if the Sheikh's credit rating is 5000 or something," Moon managed to coax a giggle out of Jennifer who perked back up. She dug around in her attaché for her wallet. "And could you run down to Jamba and get me a smoothie? I didn't get breakfast." Moon handed Jen a few bills. "Get whatever you want and be sure to put something in the tip jar. Especially if it's the cute guy."

Jennifer's usual smile was back as she bounded her way out of the office. "Thanks, Moonshine! Back in a flash!"

Moon had trouble staying focused all morning. She got anxious every time Jennifer buzzed her with a call.

A little before lunch, the phone intercom beeped. "Frank's holding on line one."

Moon could barely pick up the receiver fast enough. "Frank! What did you find?"

"Well good morning and hello to you too, young lady!" Frank Cahill was a retired LAPD cop who still had very good connections to the police. He knew most of the chiefs of police in all the small communities that made up the area that most people would just call LA. He also had some connections with Hollywood and he served as a consultant for a few of the better police dramas.

Frank did work from time to time digging around in people's pasts or checking out the employees of production companies to vet them for a new client's business. He also tailed people in divorce cases when the firm's client might be on the hook for a hefty settlement. Frank was good at being very discreet which was absolutely invaluable when your client list features famous names. In this day of paparazzi and rag magazines that would pay for gossip and photos it was good to have a man like Frank on your team. He'd earned the trust of many high-profile names and executives in the entertainment field.

"I'm going to take a guess something's got you worried. Well you tell me all about it, sweetie."

"Yes, I'm sorry, Frank. Hello and good morning!" Hearing Frank's voice was already helping to calm Moon down. "You're right. I am a little worried about something."

"You said in your message that this was about you. It's not for one of your clients?" Frank asked.

"No, not a client." Moon let out a sigh. "I think I'm being watched. There's been some guy in a car hanging around in my neighborhood."

"And you live in the high-rent district! Hell, anything out of place around there is gonna get noticed right quick. But what makes you think this guy is after you?"

"Call it a gut feeling, call it paranoia," Moon admitted. "He's been parked in a spot with a view of my house. But when I went to go talk to him..."

Frank interrupted her, "Hold it, hold it, you talked to this guy?"

"Yeah. It was kind of an accident," Moon said. "He was on my street last night and when I went for my run this morning, I turned up the hill on my way home and practically ran right into his car. He was just sitting there, out on my own street in broad daylight. I figured what could he do. Thought I'd try to check him out."

"So what'd ya say to him? What'd he say to you?" Frank asked.

"I tested him with a bullshit story, he fell for it. And I seemed to rattle him a little, like maybe he thought he'd been made," Moon recalled. "I mean, if he were a PI, there to get some dirt on one of my neighbors... well...what would you do?"

"Hell, I wouldn't let anybody trip me up with a line of bullshit, that's for sure!" Frank laughed. "But if I was out on a job, I wouldn't let anybody start sniffin' around me. I'd say something to scare 'em off and right quick too."

"So what did you find out about that plate?" Moon asked. "Any clue who this creep is?"

"Well, creepy might be the case here. I hate to tell ya, hon, I couldn't find a registration," Frank admitted.

"Oh come on, how can that be?" Moon complained.

"Now don't get upset," Frank tried to reassure her. "There's a few more places I can keep lookin'. But this is a little irregular. You got any unusual new clients? Any business that's outside the typical blockbuster movie stars and hippie-dippie creative types?"

"I do have a prospective new client but we don't even have a business agreement in place yet," Moon said. "I only talked to him on the phone yesterday afternoon. But get this. He's an honest-to-god sheikh from the Middle East. Oil business, related to Arabian royalty, the whole bit."

"Aw hell that's gotta be it!" Frank exclaimed. "Since 9/11 I don't care if you're the Sultan of freakin' Brunei, out at the disco with Paris Hilton. This sheikh of yours is probably on some watch list. Hell, these billionaire Arabs, the government's gonna profile for any new bin Laden."

"That crossed my mind but I figured there's nothing the government does that fast," Moon said. "Seriously, I just spoke to the man and literally hours later, this guy is outside my home."

"Yeah but this could be why I didn't find the plate right off," Frank replied. "If this guy is from the CIA or Homeland Security... driving one of their vehicles."

"Oh thanks for that!" Moon whined. "Way to make a private citizen feel safe in her own home!"

"Aw, don't get yourself upset, sweetie," Frank tried to reassure her. "Maybe it's him. Maybe this sheikh is just super careful who he does business with and it's one of his own people checkin' you out. But it could be completely something else. A PI hired by opposing counsel, looking for a weakness in some open case. You work some big money deals."

"Yeah. That's true." Moon wanted to believe there could be all kinds of explanations.

"Hey didn't you wring eight figures outta some action movie has-been for his ex-wife? Maybe he's still pissed."

"FRANK!" Moon bolted up from her chair. Jennifer poked her head around the door. Moon waved her away.

"Aw hell, I'm sorry, sweetie!" Frank said sheepishly. "Yeah, that wouldn't be very good would it. I don't know what I was thinkin'. I'm sure that's not it."

Moon sighed a deep breath. "Can you just find out who's in that car?"

"You know I will," Frank insisted. "Don't worry that pretty head o'yours. Hey I bet this sheikh just wants to find out if you gotta boyfriend. But you gotta make sure you're the only wife, ya know what I'm sayin'?"

"I think you just cracked the case!" Moon laughed.

"Alright sweetie, let me get back on this plate. I'll call you as soon as I've got something." And send me whatever you've got on this Sheikh."

"Thanks, Frank," Moon said. "I'll have Jennifer email you what we've been able to find out. You don't know how much I appreciate this."

Moon hung up the phone. She did feel better. It was most likely something that she was working on already. *Some night-school lawyer trying to get some kind of edge on me. Well good luck with that, I live a really boring and uneventful life.*

Jennifer popped her head in. "Hey Moonpie, everything okay? Can I bring you some lunch?"

"I'm good, thanks." Her secretary had a way of keeping Moon's stress level down through her busy workdays. "I'll be leaving soon for a charity lunch downtown."

"Oh so that means I have the rest of the day off?" Jennifer held up her hands. "Kidding! I'll keep researching our Sheikh Waseem."

Moon swapped out her attaché for a handbag. Today's charity lunch was just another in a long list. In fact, she had to say no to what seemed to be daily requests for her presence at various events. She had to appear at the partnership charities, but she'd gotten involved early in her career with other foundations for professional reasons and now her schedule is chock full of philanthropic functions.

She stepped out of the elevator and seemed to be alone in the parking garage. Her car beeped as she unlocked it and she heard the door locks pop up. Wait. Something didn't sound right. *Was that some kind of buzzing noise?* She froze in her tracks, trying to hone in on it. *There it is again!* It seemed to be over her right shoulder. She turned quickly; she found herself looking square into the lens of a camera that was looking back. In a flash it veered to the right and buzzed out of sight.

What the hell was that thing? It looked like a toy but Moon was sure it was very sophisticated. She did not know why she thought that but this was her impression. She wanted to see if she could find and follow this thing. If the person behind the camera knew she'd seen them, maybe they've taken it in. She'd have to move fast.

Out the parking garage and on to the street, she turned right as that was the easiest way to avoid crossing traffic. Her plan was to circle the building and maybe she could catch whoever it was putting the thing away or if it might be still in the air, though she doubted it.

She must have circled the building five or six times and saw nothing but people walking or driving. Damn it, she knew what she saw! *Well this is too weird. This has got to be Stalker Guy looking for me. Why is someone spying on me?* The last thing she was concerned about now was some damn lunch. *But I'll be around a lot of people. I'll be completely safe.* She turned the car and headed off to the event.

The luncheon was like all the others. The standard meal, salad and beef or chicken that was overcooked and dry. The speaker was actually pretty good. He talked about improving education without spending more money. But this was a fundraiser. What they wanted was more money, right? As she looked around the room, Moon could tell some people did not agree with the speaker's proposals but most were like her. They thought there might be some good ideas here and that's what the event was about, raising money for inner city schools.

Moon left a check for the firm's usual donation. She felt a little uneasy about leaving the building. All the way back to the office she tried to drive while looking out the sunroof, scanning the sky. *This is utterly ridiculous! There's no technology to follow me all around with some toy-looking thing.* Still, she could not stop looking up. A couple of times, she almost rear-ended the car in front of her. When she nearly ran a red light, squealing brakes and the blare of car horns brought her back to reality. *I'm a good lawyer but I'm not this important.* She laughed at how silly she could be and got back to the office without causing a pile up.

High in the sky, so very high that the naked eye could not see, a much bigger flying machine had a lock on the black BMW and precisely recorded its location coordinates as it pulled into the parking garage.

chapter five

Bureaucrats

The espresso shots in his Venti Americano were clearing Richard's head but his thoughts were starting to buzz. *She didn't call the cops when she got back home. That neighborhood, they would have been there in two minutes. Did she really buy the story? She's involved in something or Hargrove wouldn't have me watching her, but what?*

Richard's boss was Cole Brennan Hargrove, an upper-level manager in the Department of Homeland Security. He was a mid-level manager of surveillance in the CIA for ten years before coming to the DHS. He was there through the development of the drone system. Now he has agents like Richard using them to spy on people.

Drones have been around a long time but not until recently have they become armed and dangerous. They did not play a real role until advanced engineering made it possible to control them without the need for line of sight control. Now they can fly further and even be navigated from halfway around the world.

Cole helped developed new uses for drones and learned to avoid explaining to authorities the new ways to use them. He was one of the first to think the smaller ones could be armed. He became well-versed in the use of drones and how they could serve his personal and professional agendas. Advancing drones from surveillance to actually taking out targets had helped his agency gain power and control from the military.

Cole distrusted the people he answered to as he thought they were plotting to replace him. He thought the men and women under him didn't like him and he would have been right, of course they never did anything well either. He wasn't right about everything except that the people who answered to him didn't like him. In fact there was actual visceral hatred for him. When he left the CIA, they almost threw a party but they didn't want him to come to it as they really wanted it to be a good riddance party.

Cole was not a happy person and moving to Homeland Security did not improve this, in fact, it just made things worse. He didn't see it as a move up. He was at Director level now which sounded impressive but he thought he should be the Secretary of the entire agency. Instead, he was back in line about where he was at the CIA. He did have a little more power because the Executive Director immediately above him was lazy and pretty much let him do what he wanted as long as whatever Cole was doing made the guy look good. He also had to move out to Los Angeles which did not make him happy, as he had to sell his house. His two kids and ex-wife were back in Virginia, though he rarely saw his children even when he lived close to them and if he never saw his ex-wife that would be too soon for him.

Decisions Cole made at work were not always made for the good of the government or the people he was tasked to protect or even the agency he worked for. No, most of the time he made decisions based on how they might advance his career so they weren't always the best. In the next few days and months, Cole would be making one bad decision after another just to cover his own ass. Richard was to be on the front line in all these bad decisions and they were going to start now.

Moon had gotten Richard flustered but he figured he'd have a good chance of staying out of sight while keeping an eye on her at her office. The building was in a pretty busy area downtown but still he thought if he looked too obvious, someone might get suspicious as to what his intentions were.

It seems today that more people are taking notice of others and what they are doing. The tragedy of September 11 awoke people and they realized they needed to pay more attention and they were. Police went on more false calls than ever before from people who thought they saw something suspicious.

Richard went into the lobby of the building and found Moon's law firm in the directory. He was a little surprised he could go right upstairs without signing in at the desk. Some buildings still allow that, not many but some. He went up to the floor below Moon's to determine which side of the building her firm's suite number would be facing. Now he knew which direction he could point the drone. The telephoto lens would let him fly it far enough away that no one in Moon's office would notice it.

Richard got set up in an alley down the street and brought out the little toy. He turned back to the car to see a bike messenger had been watching him.

"Hey dude, what is that thing? Did you build it?" the kid shouted over to him.

Richard stayed focused on his task. "I'm just testing it."

The messenger seemed determined to check things out. "Why dont-cha take it around the corner to Pershing? Plenty of room to maneuver over there."

Richard decided to treat the situation like a minor aggravation. Besides, he felt more aggravated than like he'd been discovered. It didn't take any effort to add an edge to the tone of his voice, "I'm just testing the vertical stabilizers." He wasn't sure what he'd said but it sounded good.

The kid started walking his bike toward Richard. "Hey is it for a movie? Is it, like, some new Tony Stark shit?"

Richard turned and gave the kid a solid glare. "Yeah, it's some shit. Now don't you have some urgent contract to deliver or some shit?" The kid flipped him the finger and popped his bike over a curb. Richard had the alley to himself.

He steered the drone toward Moon's building. He hovered it about a block away and zoomed in to a ninth floor window. He scanned across that whole side of the building until he spotted Moon's office.

Her back was to the window and she was working away on her computer. Richard zoomed the camera in as far as it can go; it was very challenging to keep the unit under control but he was getting very good at it. He could not really make out what she was working on so he pulled the zoom back to a more manageable level. A woman came into the office. This was a good opportunity to test the directional microphone and see if he could pull in their conversation. He grabbed the headphones and fine-tuned a digital setting on the controller. The voices were a little muffled but he seemed to be picking them up.

The conversation sounded like typical office business. The other woman's name is Jennifer, that was clear. *Probably the secretary.* Richard grabbed one side of the headphone and pushed it in tight against his ear. The lawyer seems very concerned about getting a particular call. *Contracts signed, yeah so what.* Wait, something about a sheet? A sheikh?

Some Arab guy? *Okay, that could be an issue if she's doing business with an Arab.* Richard tried to get the volume up on the audio but the higher he went, the more ambient sound and even street noise he'd pick up. He listened as closely as he could.

Theater? A theater company? Oh this is nothing. Did she just say the name? Sure, gotta be Mohammed somebody. *Abba-daba, what? Woz something? Wozeen?* Richard could make out about every third word. It seemed to depend on what they said, some words he could make out more easily than others. *Wow, there's a phone call she's really stressing over.*

Richard watched Moon bang away at her keyboard and look through files. *A lawyer's day sure looks boring.* Okay, cell phone call. Charity. Beverly Hilton. *Hung up already, that's nothing.*

He looked at his watch and decided to see if the lawyer would go to lunch, then he'd pack up. Wait, she's got a call. *HOLY SHIT DID SHE JUST SAY 'GUY IN A CAR'?* Richard pounded on the controller, trying to up the amplification but he only pulled in more noise. He strained to listen as closely as he could. *Bullshit story.* He made that out. She was talking about him. This was bad. Really, really bad. *Who could she be talking to?* Something about the neighbors. *OH SHIT SHE GOT THE LICENSE PLATE.* No wait. She's back to the Arab guy. Royalty. She's pissed about something. The secretary's back. *THAT CAR.* She definitely said *THAT CAR.* This is really, really bad.

Richard was certain that was the call Moon had been waiting for. *She's checking out the car. Yeah, a lawyer would do that.* His mind raced. He would have to edit the footage. *They'll fast forward through it anyway and they'll see it's just some lawyer sitting at her desk. This could not get back to Hargrove.*

The two women were still talking. *Lunch. Charity lunch, that's where she's going.* Okay this is good. He could get some footage of her leaving the office and he knows where she's going. This is good. It wraps up the morning. And he's got her talking about some Arab. That'll be the big payoff. Richard thought it through and felt like maybe his blood pressure was coming back down a little.

The parking levels were on the lower floors. Richard would have to bring the drone down between the buildings. He knew he'd risk exposure but he'd try to grab some quick footage. He didn't have enough time to search for Moon's car so he brought the unit down and did a broad pan and scan. He was able to pull it back and get a view of the elevators on each parking level. He kept the unit focused and steady. The elevator doors opened. *There she is!* Richard saw Moon striding across the garage. He struggled to keep the camera focused on her while trying to determine which direction she'd be heading. *Does she have to walk so damn fast?* He swung the drone around the corner of the building and suddenly, there she was, right there looking straight at him from the screen of his controller. It startled him as if they'd made eye contact.

Richard nearly panicked; he pulled the drone up into a straight vertical climb when the controller screen blinked. *Shit! I can't crash this thing in downtown LA!* Besides costing about three years' pay, Hargrove would have his ass if that night's news was all about the strange device that nearly killed a downtown pedestrian when it fell out of nowhere and smashed into the sidewalk. He smacked the side of the controller because that always works. The drone flickered back into view. *Thank you sweet Jesus!* He wanted to get the thing back and into the car trunk as quickly he could manage.

"Damn, this is not worth it! This woman is not worth the time and effort!" Richard shouted aloud to himself as he tried to drive out of downtown. So she's got an Arab client who's in the theater or something, that's no crime. There's no indication she's a national security threat and by trying to follow her in her neighborhood and downtown, it's too easy to get spotted. Richard was worried and a bit angry. *This assignment is too risky and I'm not finding anything worth a damn.* This woman is very resourceful and intelligent. If she thinks something's going on, she won't let it go.

Richard had pissed off the bike messenger. Cameron was like all his brothers who lived on razor-thin wheels; no samurai of the streets would tolerate disrespect on his own turf. He stuck around to watch from the corner of the adjacent building. It seemed too weird that this dude would lurk around the dumpsters instead of testing this thing, whatever it was, in an open space. After all, there are plazas all around this section of downtown, just a few steps away. *Was this dude trying to hide?*

When Richard set the drone aloft, Cameron had no trouble keeping up with it. He was one of the top "alley cat" bike racers and could weave his way through any urban obstacle including a crowded sidewalk. He chased this flying machine around the block until it began to hover along the side of one particular building. He was able to get a really good look.

It was pretty cool but it was just floating around up there. Maybe the dude really was just testing it? Some people take smoke breaks, maybe this guy plays with toys. Cameron pulled out his iPhone and shot some video. Better get going; he had a full sack of documents and deadlines to beat.

Typical for his day, Cameron made several deliveries and found himself back on West Fourth. He was pushing his way out of a revolving door when a flash caught his eye. Across the street, a lot closer to the ground this time. The flying thing was maybe just three stories up and it seemed to be traveling toward him. The video quality would be really good from this angle and he could zoom in to capture some detail, maybe close enough to figure out what this thing was.

Cameron dodged his way across the street. He was practically right underneath the thing when it shot up into the air. Damn. This is no toy from Hobbyking. He stood stunned for a second when he saw the flying machine take off from so high up and so fast he wasn't sure even he could keep up with it but he'd sure try. Cameron sped off on his bike.

Moon's handbag went flying into the dashboard when she slammed on the brakes. *Damn messengers! How can any of them still be alive?* She couldn't blame the biker completely; she'd been trying to drive around the block while looking up through her sunroof. Whatever that thing was she'd seen in the parking garage, it was nowhere to be found now.

Richard headed back to the office. He wasn't part of the Public Affairs office in San Pedro. It had a receptionist, some small offices for clerical staff, and an official Director of State & Local Programs for California. That was the public face of the agency.

Other divisions like his were headquartered in nondescript buildings. Richard's office was in a strip shopping center that looked as if it was out of business and abandoned, like a commercial location so undesirable, there wasn't even a sign to lease the space. This was where the real work happened. Investigators like Richard and others who followed the most dangerous suspects operated out of divisions focused on gathering intelligence and conducting electronic surveillance.

This facility was the repository for many other toys like the one Richard was flying around. There was even a warehouse full, connected by an underground hallway to the administrative offices. In fact, most of it was underground in much the same way Disney World has its control centers and operational facilities underground to keep it all hidden from the public. But even more sophisticated than the Magic Kingdom, the warehouse at this Homeland Security location had a retractable roof so the largest unmanned aerial vehicles could be launched.

Richard pulled the car into what looked like a commercial storage unit. The windows were painted over but all anyone could have seen were a few cars in storage or that would be what they thought. Richard parked and walked through a series of doors and down an elevator that required a magnetic keycard. He signed in at the guard's station and placed his thumb on a sensor to open the last door into a large room of cubicles.

The few agents at their desks were working silently. Richard found his desk and logged into the computer network. When he wrote up his report this afternoon, he'd leave out the parts about being seen by two people, one of them being the surveillance subject. Again.

To complete the file, he'd have to submit his report to a group of computer and financial geeks that would be studying the subject's bank accounts, cell phone calls, computer search records, and any possible paper trails. He knew they weren't going to find anything; his instincts told him there was nothing here. He was right most of the time about his gut feelings which was why he was such a good investigator.

Richard had actually started to like Moon as she seemed to be a woman who would be interesting to know, but that was never going to be a possibility. She certainly had a killer body; the images he'd seen of her that night in her bedroom he would not soon forget. So finish this and get home and move on to the next person of interest, that was his plan. Little did he know that this would be far from the end of it.

chapter six

Out of the Kiddy Pool

Moon ended her day about the same way as always, she went to the gym to get in some exercise before going home. After the boot camp class, Danny hit her up again to join everybody at the Mexican Cantina for drinks.

"We always have a great time. When are you going to quit being a loser and join us?" Danny ribbed her, "Come on, you have to make up for that time you said you'd show and you didn't!"

"Guilty as charged!" Moon put her hands up in surrender. "I'll come!" Danny slapped her a high five. She could run home quickly and get cleaned up then stop by the grocery store later. *Good plan,* she thought. *Why not, get out and have some fun.* The people in the class weren't her friends as she knew little at most about them but some could become friends and she really ought to make time to add new people to her life.

When Moon made it to the bar, she looked around for someone she could recognize. She spotted a woman about fifty who always stayed in the back corner of the gym. She had said hello to her before but had not really talked much; Moon thought maybe her name was Pat.

Moon decided to take the chance, "Hey Pat!"

"Elizabeth! I'm glad you came! Grab a seat." Pat pulled a stool closer. "Are you doing tequila straight or margaritas tonight?"

"I think I'll opt for a margarita, if we can get the bartender's attention." Moon wouldn't settle for a house Margarita, she was very specific about how she'd want the bartender to make it as she hated the sugary mix that usually got passed off as a margarita, especially in these chain Mexican restaurants. She'd insist on top shelf Blue Agave Tequila like Don Julio.

The house stuff was for people who didn't know what it was supposed to taste like. She'd try not to make a big deal of it in case that's what Pat was drinking. Changing the subject would be a good idea. "Pat, feel free to call me 'Moon.' My first name is actually 'Moonbaby.' Friends call me that. Elizabeth is my middle name."

She started using Elizabeth in college and on into law school. As a lawyer, the name 'Moon' or 'Moonbaby' would not have been very professional, or so she thought. Her parents understood her rationale but still they would always call her 'Moon' and secretly wished she would always use that name but, as an adult, she could choose what she wanted to be called. She could use any name she wanted. People changing their names or going by something different than what they were born with was a Hollywood standard.

"That's so unique and lovely!" Pat gushed. "My name is really so plain and boring." Pat reached out and slapped Moon's knee. "I could be a little envious! It suits you!"

People from the boot camp class were starting to flow in. Danny finally turned up among the last to arrive. Moon wondered how she could get ready faster. The evening went by eating chips and guacamole. Moon had a second drink but it was getting time to go as she rarely went out like this on a work night.

It was fun though to see people in a different light and get to know them a little better. She said her goodbyes and headed for her car. She didn't notice there seemed to be just one other person walking through the parking lot.

Moon unlocked her car and was reaching for the door when she thought she heard a footstep directly behind her. She turned and found herself face to face with a bearded man in a plain dark suit.

"You better watch what you are doing as it could get you into much trouble," He looked maybe Middle Eastern or Indian, his words were halting and stilted with a slight accent Moon couldn't place.

Moon tensed up, ready for some kind of an attack. "What the hell? Who the hell are you?" she screamed. The man looked at her for a moment, his face completely expressionless. He turned and walked toward the restaurant.

Moon jumped into her car and hit the locks. She cranked the engine as quickly as she could and nearly peeled out of the parking space. She looked in the rear view and saw a group of people standing at the cantina's front door. *Where did he go? Inside? Around back?* She wasn't going to go looking.

Moon pulled out her phone and fumbled for Frank's speed dial. She was pissed it went to voicemail. "Frank! It's Moon. Shit's gettin' real! Call me! I don't care how late!"

She pulled into her driveway and didn't get out of the car until the garage door was all the way down. She rushed into the house and tested the security system to be sure the panic button mode was activated. Her cell phone rang and flashed Frank's name, she felt a little less alone.

"Frank! You're not going to believe what happened tonight! I can't believe what happened! I'm still shaking!"

"Hey slow down!" Frank tried to be comforting, "What's going on, sweetie? Are you alright? Where are you?"

Moon sat down on the edge of her living room couch and tried to collect herself, "I'm okay. I'm at home. I'm all locked in." Her breath started coming back, "I was at a restaurant, getting into my car and there was this man, he was right behind me! So close, he could have grabbed me, he could have carjacked me, he could have had a gun!"

"So what did he do? What happened?" Frank asked.

"He just snuck up behind me and told me I could be in trouble because of what I was doing, whatever that's supposed to mean." Moon was getting over her fear and anger and exasperation were setting in. "Tell me you found something on that car."

"Yeah, I'm sorry I was going to call you tomorrow. I just finished doing some digging around today," Frank explained. "I don't have good news, actually I have next to no news. That car is from a government motor pool alright but I can't find which agency. So I tried to find any government connection to any case you had ongoing. I turned up nothin'. Plenty of swimmin' pools and movie stars in your line of business but nothing with a direct line to any government agency. Not state, not Federal."

Moon felt a little relieved but not much. "That sounds about right. So why should somebody from a government agency be stalking me?"

"Proves you were right about the guy's bullshit story, not that I ever doubted ya. There's no building permits in your neighborhood anyways. I ran a quick search on that." Frank said.

"Damn, Frank," Moon said. "You really think of the details!"

"Oh that ain't everything, not by a long shot," Frank said. "I figured

I'd look anywhere I could so I dug into current police investigations and found nothing about you. I checked with some other PIs and you're not on their radar. I even called in some favors that I was tryin' to save and guess what. Bupkis! Lady, you are clean as Ivory soap!"

"That's good to know but where does this leave me? A government stalker on my street, some creep in a parking lot. Oh and there's more! I saw something weird at my office. I have no idea what it was, there was some kind of device, it was, like, flying...hovering...in the air between the buildings."

"What the hell?" Frank groaned. "Any film crews around there this week?"

"No, I thought of that because it definitely had a camera lens on it." Moon said. "Nearest permit was over at the Bradbury that day, typical. Nothing around my building."

"Well there's just one thing. It's the only thing but I'll be damned if I can figure out why anybody's got their panties in a bunch over this mister Sheikh o'Araby."

"Did you find something Jennifer and I missed?" Moon asked.

Frank continued, "There is a report with the FBI and State Department about this...uh, Sheikh Mister Mohammed Abdullah Waseem but that was just after September 11 and he was cleared. Not on any watch lists. Everything you sent me checked out."

"Jennifer is nothing if not thorough in her research and I double-checked everything myself," Moon replied.

"He seems pretty above-board but I'm still suspicious of some of these towel heads," Frank grumbled. "Watch out how you associate with them."

Moon bristled at the comment, "It's called a turban, Frank. Don't be racist!" Her phone beeped. "Frank, I've got another call. Given how weird today's been I better take it. I'll talk to you soon. And THANK YOU!" Moon hit the flash button and tried to sound calm and cool though she didn't recognize the number and didn't know what to expect, "Elizabeth Franklin."

The voice was familiar, "The Sheikh will be right with you. Please hold, madam." Moon's mind raced. *Holy crap it's him. Is he calling to see if I'm still alive?*

Moon gripped the phone tightly. She felt the tension creeping back over her. The sound of the Sheikh's silky British baritone calmed her a bit, "Good evening. Please forgive the late hour. I was traveling today

42

and I've lost track of the time zones. I'm terribly sorry. How are you this evening, Ms. Franklin?"

"Good evening, Mr. Waseem," Moon mustered her most professional voice. "In my line of work late night calls are not that unusual. You didn't attempt to deliver a message to me earlier this evening, by any chance?"

"I beg your pardon?" The Sheikh seemed genuinely confused.

Moon decided not to press it but couldn't help dropping a hint of snark, "To what do I owe the pleasure at this late hour, sir?"

"I'd like to discuss our business arrangements and it's essential that we meet in person. I will send my private jet to transport you to Hawaii for a meeting tomorrow."

Moon was taken aback, "Such short notice would be highly irregular. Why don't we meet here in LA at your next available opportunity? I can arrange for a business suite at the airport. You wouldn't even have to come into the city."

"That would be very accommodating of you, Ms. Franklin, but I'm afraid that is not possible at this time." The Sheikh would not be deterred. "I will pay your hourly rate for the full duration of the trip as well as a retainer to confirm our business relationship."

Moon felt like she'd have to go if she wanted to hold on to this client. "I'll need to go over my calendar with my secretary and check with my colleagues. I could get back to you by mid-morning."

The Sheikh was a step ahead, "I've already arranged for a jet to be at LAX to take off at any time tomorrow that will accommodate your schedule. I will send a car to your office address at noon. If you're not able to make the trip, please have your secretary inform the driver."

Moon had to try not to stammer, "Uh, Mr. Waseem, you're saying you'd have a jet sitting at LAX, waiting for me all day? I may have commitments that can't be rescheduled."

"It's quite alright. I consider these arrangements to be suitable. I will hope to make your acquaintance in person tomorrow evening. Once again, please forgive the late hour. Good night." And with that, the Sheikh abruptly hung up.

Moon could only stare at the phone for a moment. She was impressed but maybe a little nervous. Why go to such lengths to meet her? She got out her laptop and logged into the office network to look up her schedule. There didn't seem to be anything over the next two days that couldn't be postponed. Besides, her curiosity was overtaking her nerves.

She wanted to meet this mystery man in the flesh.

Moon got into bed but could only stare at the ceiling. She was still too keyed up to sleep. She remembered what she had buried at the back of her shoe closet. She got up and dug around a stack of boxes to find an aluminum case. It had been a long time but she was able to recall the three-digit combination to the lock.

Her father had purchased the Glock for her a long time back when she started out on her own. She told him she would never need such a thing but he made her take it anyway. She used to go target shooting with him and as a child that was fun but she never wanted to think she'd ever need a gun. Until now. The Glock still looked brand new. She loaded the magazine and put it on her nightstand. She fell asleep, worried she'd dream about being watched.

The next morning Moon felt like she'd need the whole pot of coffee to get going. She started to go out to get the paper and paused a moment. This was stupid, she felt nervous to go outside? She stepped out. Quiet like always. The paper in its usual spot on the drive. She couldn't resist looking down the street. No strange cars.

Moon packed an overnight bag for Hawaii and felt a little worried. Her office would know where she was going and who she was supposed to be with. What could this Sheikh do? She looked at the gun on the nightstand. *If I'm on a private jet, could I take it with me?* She headed into the office early to prepare for what she already knew would be a long, long day.

Richard was barely in the office before he got a message that the boss wanted to see him, ASAP, that meant now. *Wonderful,* he thought, *I haven't even sat down and I have to deal with Hargrove.*

Cole was sitting at his desk waiting for Richard without making it look like he was waiting. He never had anything to do but read reports and then schedule assignments and go to meetings. Sometimes he even had to go and listen to the Secretary of Homeland Security give speeches. His job was fairly clerical. Mostly he reviewed and scheduled priority targets. He got out in the field on special occasions but only when he wanted to or if he had to resolve a problem one of his agents caused.

Richard walked into Cole's office with a smile and a friendly good morning even though there was no real friendliness in him, but there was none from Cole either. He sat down before Cole invited him to sit. He tried to take control of the conversation before Cole could get a word out, "Be warned. I haven't had any coffee. What could be this urgent that it couldn't wait a few minutes?"

Cole knew what he was doing and took a stern tone, "I read your report about the Franklin case."

Richard feigned indifference, "There was nothing to it. She's just a lawyer. Lot of Hollywood clients. Gets a lot of exercise. Eats fish." Richard shrugged his shoulders.

"Really? Nothing to it?" Cole acted like he was shocked. "So there is nothing more to tell other than what you have said in the report?"

Richard wouldn't crack, "Nope I put everything in the report."

Cole leaned back in his chair, "Okay fine. That'll be all. I'll let you know your next assignment."

His suspicions were up but Richard played along, "I will look forward to it." He left Cole with the least smile he could muster.

Richard could not help but think Cole knew something. *What could he possibly know? There's nothing! What was he trying to get me to say?*

Richard got back to his desk, opened the report, and read it again. It was complete and told most of the story, at least the story he was supposed to be writing about. Sure, there were a couple of details he'd left out but why would he write about them? They'd serve no purpose except to give Cole ammunition to yell at him.

Later that day Richard got an email from an unidentified account. This was not completely out of the norm as they all used unidentified email accounts from time to time. The email contained an embedded video. It launched automatically and Richard felt his stomach drop. He watched footage of the drone hovering alongside the parking garage of Moon's office building. There was an audio track, "Shit! Where'd that thing go!" He recognized the bike messenger's voice off camera at the point when Richard knew he'd pulled the drone out of Moon's view.

"The Latest Hollywood Sensation! 200 Hits on YouTube!" blinked at him in red letters on the screen. Richard felt almost sick as his official ID photo faded in. It had been animated to look like his mouth was moving.

"Shit where'd that thing go? Shit where'd that thing go?" kept repeating in a loop.

ShitShitShit. Either Cole already knows about this or one of the Geeks is out to taunt him with it before dropping the bomb to the boss. *He can't know about this already or I'd have an extra asshole by now.*

Americans were so angry to learn the NSA might be listening to everyone's phone calls. They'd be just as mad to find out the technology existed to scan every video and photo posted to YouTube, Facebook, Tumblr, all over the Internet.

Richard would have to find out which of the Geeks wanted to torment him. He crossed the building to their dirty little world. He did not like going down there. It was a place filled with Hot Pocket wrappers, Mountain Dew cans, and virgins. Richard chuckled to himself; he really didn't know what the Geeks' sexual status was, he just imagined that it could not be very extensive because they never left their computers. This made them assets to the agency except their people skills were something less than desirable.

Richard walked in the room and no one looked up from their desks. He could have walked in with his sidearm drawn and mowed them all down and none of them would even know they were dead. Richard tapped on the window of a small glass office. He had to knock pretty hard before the hunched figure inside looked up.

The head of the department was Michelangelo, his parents were creative Christians and his father loved the Ninja turtles. Everybody called him Michael. Richard didn't care about his name or how he got it, he just wanted information.

Michael demonstrated the usual geek disdain for what they called IRL communication, In Real Life. "What could you possibly need that could not have been requested by email?"

"I need information now and not in email form," Richard said. "I need a copy of the Franklin report, the part this department generated."

"Why didn't you ask your supervisor for it?" Michael asked.

"You know I report directly to Hargrove. Nobody wants to talk to him," Richard replied.

Michael understood that. He did not like most people that much anyway but Cole, even less. Every time he had to talk to Cole, Michael would get the feeling he was being molested.

"This would be highly improper to put it on paper and not to go through normal channels." Michael said.

Richard agreed, "Look I know, I just want to confirm some of the speculations I have about the case that I didn't find in field surveillance."

Michael stared at Richard as if he were trying to make up his mind, "Alright, but I'm only doing this because there's really nothing in this report. Read it and shred it when you're done. I really don't care anymore about a case that's over, at least as far as my department is concerned."

Richard turned on the charm, "Oh thank you so much! You guys really do such a great job down here!" He gushed nervously, not sure if maybe Michael had sent the video himself.

Michael took a stack of paper from the printer and handed it to Richard, "Double cheese and sausage."

"Excuse me?" Richard reached for the report but Michael wasn't letting it go.

"From Gino's. The pizza you're going to go upstairs and order to be delivered to entrance 4B."

Richard caught on quickly, "Of course! Absolutely! You got it! And with my compliments!"

Michael released the report to Richard's hand, "Two liters of Dew."

Richard tucked the report inside his lapel. He felt like he was carrying contraband. He'd get back to his desk, get the pizza ordered, and log out. He wanted to get somewhere he could not be watched, somewhere he could read the report without interruption.

He did not want Cole to know he had the entire report. This was no problem for him as his real office was the car anyway. Until he had a new assignment he could come and go pretty much as he saw fit. A new assignment would put him back out in the field and that was fine with him. He couldn't run into Cole if he wasn't in the office.

chapter seven

Information Misunderstood

Moon banged away at the keyboard, re-arranging the next forty eight hours. She did not know if this was the right decision, flying off on a moment's notice to Hawaii, though she has had to do it before. It is not a regular occurrence but there have been times she would have to fly out to a movie site and arbitrate a dispute that was holding up production. Technology has alleviated that problem some but there are still times when she just has to be there. She was sure Mr. Bamberger would tell her she should go.

Harold Bamberger was the firm's senior partner. Even though she was the firm's most recent partner, he still felt a little fatherly toward Moon. Maybe because she'd seemed so young when he'd hired her.

Harold stood up and walked around the desk when Moon came in, "How is my favorite partner?" Moon blushed a little about the way Harold would fuss over her. It never seemed inappropriate that he'd always give her a hug.

The firm had been in the movie and entertainment business for fifty years. The original founder had been Wright and Sullivan was long retired so Harold was able to move his name to the first on the door. He joined the firm straight out of UCLA. He'd been there during that golden era of television in the 1970s, helping new production companies start up. It was by chance that Moon had interviewed to be a summer associate but she knew she'd found a mentor when Harold personally extended an offer.

Harold was equally fond of Moon as a jurist and as a person; she was one of the most honest people he knew. That was a problem when she first started working for him as she tended to admit everything. He had to teach her that holding back was not lying and not everyone had to know everything she did. Moon had become one of the firm's best and most thorough lawyers even if her mouth got her in trouble occasionally.

"What's on your mind today?" Harold asked.

"I have an unusual new client and he's made an unusual request," Moon explained. She poured out everything she knew about the Sheikh but she left out the weird incidents. She felt this was one of those times when not everyone had to know everything she did.

Harold listened intently and leaned back in his chair, "This is what our business is all about. Important people, demanding our time, when they want it, on their terms. It sounds like this Sheikh might just be very important to you and the firm."

"There's no question the business could be extensive if he does buy a studio," Moon replied.

"Go! Lay the foundation for years of business to come." Harold peered over his glasses. "A client like that could get your name on the door."

Moon headed back to her office. Harold's advice seemed to lay it out in such simple terms. She was feeling better about it but she wondered if he would have given her the same advice if she had told him everything. She still isn't certain if the stalking and the Sheikh are connected so no need to open that can of beans yet.

Moon went back to her office for her laptop and attaché and to fill Jennifer in on the sudden change of plans.

"Hawaii? I'm sure you're going to need an assistant," Jennifer said, hopefully.

"You know if I thought I was going to need you, I'd bring you," Moon replied. "But I don't even know what this meeting is going to be about."

"But Moondoggie, that's my point! Be prepared for anything!" Jennifer made praying hands, "Please?"

"It's going to be all business and no fun this time," Moon said. "And I'm only going to be there tonight and tomorrow. It's going to be exhausting! Now I need you to help me get out of here."

Jennifer quickly gathered together all the files Moon would need. She got Moon's office in order and confirmed what she'd cover for the week. She ticked off her instructions to her boss, "Okay, I'll be downstairs at noon to give the driver directions to your house and no hiding in the trunk, got it!"

"Next trip, I promise," Moon raced out the door.

At home, Moon checked and re-checked every door and window lock and the settings on the security system until the doorbell rang. She looked through the peephole and saw a man in a driver's uniform and a limousine in the drive. She stepped outside and handed him her bag; she was nervous trying to set the alarm and get the door locked up.

Moon had been so absorbed in scrolling through emails on her phone that she hadn't noticed they'd been driving in the opposite direction from the airport. When she looked up, the only thing that kept her from having a panic attack was the fact that they were on a major road; in fact, they were on Franklin Avenue, a thoroughfare she liked to joke was her personal street.

Moon was trying to get the driver's attention when they turned into what appeared to be the back entrance of a studio complex. *They're going to tie me up and release a hostage video to the media, all in stunning HD.* The limo pulled up to a helipad where a pilot appeared to be waiting, at the ready, for a passenger. The door opened and the driver extended his hand, "The helicopter will transport you to LAX, madam."

As she looked around, Moon realized she was at the back of Prospect Studios. She'd come here for business with Disney before and knew there was a helipad on the grounds but had never been to this area of the complex. *Wow, this is impressive.*

Moon stood there trying to be casual about it all as the pilot loaded her bag into the helicopter. He helped her into a seat and strapped her in. In just minutes she was looking down at all the cars crowding the freeways. She let out a sigh feeling lucky she was up here and not down there. She again thought this was impressive, not that she hadn't flown in a helicopter before but this seemed different.

The flight was very short and they landed right next to a hangar with a private jet, not just any jet, but a 727. *Whoa. Mostly it's the studios that own aircraft like this, not individuals. Well, maybe George Lucas and Oprah.* Moon was losing her sense of worry and becoming extremely intrigued for whoever it was she'd be meeting.

An impossibly gorgeous Asian flight attendant directed Moon up the steps into the plane. She found herself stunned yet again as she gazed around the jet's interior that looked like the lobby of the W Hotel in Hollywood. The flight attendant directed her to an enormous leather chair and strapped her in.

"I am Hatsu, I am here to meet your every need today. We have com-prete kitchen and chef on board," Hatsu waved her hand like a spokes-model. "We prepare anything you rike. What is your choice for runch today?"

Bottled water and a small plate of sliced fruit were already laid out on the end table next to Moon's seat. "Just this will be fine," Moon said as she took a bite of a huge strawberry. She was still dealing with being a bit overwhelmed. *Oil money definitely beats movie money, that's for sure.*

Moon could hear the engines starting when the pilot came on the speaker. She thought it seemed odd he spoke as if this were a commercial flight full of passengers, "The weather looks clear all the way to Hawaii. We'll be in the air five and half hours so settle back and get comfortable."

Moon closed her eyes as they taxied down the runway and she quickly fell asleep. She'd had such a restless night but her surroundings now were so relaxing, she was out like a light.

She wasn't sure how long she'd been asleep when she awoke with a blanket over her and nothing but ocean to be seen out the window. Moon didn't want to think Hatsu had been watching her sleep so that she could leap to her service the second Moon opened her eyes. But there she was, holding out a steaming hot towel on tongs. Moon wiped her eyes and realized she'd actually slept well and felt refreshed.

Hatsu waved her hand like a spokesmodel again, "You are free to move about the cabin as you rike."

Moon thought she'd take a look around. *I bet the bathroom is just as spectacular as everything else.* She felt like she was sneaking around as she passed a bedroom with a neatly-made double bed and what appeared to be a fully-appointed conference room, complete with video screen.

Sure enough, the bathroom would rival anything in a luxury hotel with a huge sink, small shower, a selection of toiletries, and even a hair dryer. Moon took her time freshening up and re-applying her makeup before she went back to her seat. She'd just pulled out her laptop when Hatsu was once again looming over her. "This prane offers WiFi." This time Hatsu's spokesmodel move was to open her hands as if she were in-forming Moon she'd just won the laptop that was propped on her knees.

"Wow, that's great!" Moon exclaimed. "Will my phone work?"

Hatsu removed a wireless handset from the wall and presented it to Moon with a flourish. "Prease to use the aircraft terephone system. It is compret-ry private for your co-vee-yess."

Her office knew where she was but Moon had not told her parents she'd be gone for a couple of days. She dialed the phone and heard various clicks and beeps.

Moon's mom answered the phone, "Hi honey! The connection sounds fuzzy. Are you driving in the Hills?"

"You'll never believe it, I'm on a private jet going to Hawaii to meet a client!" Moon couldn't help gushing a little.

Anita wanted to know all about the client but Moon couldn't provide any details, "Mom, you know that is confidential but I can tell you he is very rich."

Anita knew better than to keep pressing Moon for information so they talked about the helicopter ride and the luxurious plane, "I gotta go, Mom. I just wanted you and Dad to know where I am and I'll call you as soon as I get home, a couple of days tops."

Her mother did not always like how secretive Moon had to be but she knew her daughter was a smart girl who could always take care of herself. Anita and Charles stopped worrying about their eldest long ago but like any parents, wanted to keep up on what their children were doing.

Moon needed to call Tom. With the Hawaii trip coming up so quickly, she hadn't had time to touch base.

As usual, Tom was quick to answer his cellphone. When he found out Moon was on her way to meet the potential studio buyer, he went into full sales mode.

"That studio is the perfect property! If your buyer moves fast, he can keep all the production crews and staff," Tom said. "Tell him one of their television shows just got picked up by the History Channel."

"Look, this is only the first in-person meeting," Moon replied. "I'm not even sure what he wants to discuss but I've got everything you sent me and I'm ready to present it."

"I know you're the best! If there's a deal to be made, you'll close it!"

"I'll call you as soon as I'm back in town. If anything comes up, Jennifer can reach me." Moon noticed more of those beeps and clicks as the call disconnected. *Weird airplane phone.*

Hatsu brought some sashimi that tasted as if they had a line in the Pacific. Moon spent the rest of the flight feeling like the queen of her own tiny nation in the air. She was a little sad when the pilot announced they'd be landing in 30 minutes.

In Honolulu, a car was waiting on the tarmac, just steps away from the plane. Moon was sorry to have to tell Hatsu goodbye but she wondered if that was the plane, what could the house be like?

The driver extended an "Aloha" but he did not present Moon with a lei. She felt a little silly that she'd notice such a thing, *Hmm, a detail overlooked? We'll forgive this one.* The drive took them through Honolulu and after a while, the scenery began to look more like the Hawaii everyone thinks of from movies and TV. The houses got farther apart and it became apparent that they were in a very wealthy neighborhood, something like the best part of Beverly Hills.

Moon had been to Hawaii before but the colors still amazed her. *It's beautiful like the Hills but not the same green.* The green of the grass and trees seemed like something out of a dream or maybe they were added to the surroundings like CGI special effects.

As they approached a large gate, the driver pressed a button over his head and it swung open. Moon found herself impressed for the hundredth time or so today. Okay, this is not just some limo service; this is the property's driver and car. Lush Hawaiian foliage crowded both sides of a long private drive. The limo pulled into a courtyard that spread out from a main house surrounded by four other buildings that also looked like residences. The most striking feature of the main home were massive windows that spanned its full height and looked as if they would completely open to the world.

A man stood in the doorway of the main house and came out to the limo. Moon noticed that his suit was of a quality that far exceeded what she'd expect to see as a uniform for the help. He escorted her into the house and directed her to follow him.

He ushered Moon into an expansive suite, "The Sheikh will join you for dinner at 8:00. You may rest and relax until then. If you require anything at all, simply press this," he pointed to a small button on the wall next to light switch at the door.

Moon looked at her watch and realized she would have some time to kill. She had gotten used to the idea of asking for anything she wanted, "Is there a workout room?"

The man stepped out to the hall and made a flourish with his arms as if he'd taken lessons from Hatsu, "Of course, madam. You'll find a fully-equipped gymnasium at the end of this hallway. My name is Usef. Please request anything you require."

Usef seemed to vanish in much the same way as Hatsu had been magically materializing on the plane. Moon figured the Sheikh must be highly selective in the people he hires and this meeting itself could be her job interview. As she started looking around the room, it was as much to take in as the whole day had been. The décor reminded her of a hotel suite the Weinsteins had rented for an all-day contract negotiation. She estimated the main room looked to be as large as her entire living room with the space of her kitchen and study added. The bathroom included a bidet and a steambath. Moon felt overwhelmed with a desire to twirl around in the center of it all like she was in a dream. She crumpled in a heap on the huge couch, taking it all in.

Richard left the office and headed for the nearest Del Taco; he was hungry and did not care what he ate. Richard was not into health food. He sat outside at a table as far away from people as he could so he could focus on reading the report. He still felt paranoid about somebody seeing him but of course there would be no one here who mattered.

The report was standard; the Geeks had looked into bank accounts, credit reports, and phone calls. They had a way to crack into it all and not be recorded as a hard hit. This lawyer had a good-sized savings account especially for someone of her age. She had a normal checking account, though what she pays a month on her mortgage is about what Richard gets paid a month. *She must be a very valuable lawyer for her firm,* Richard thought. She had an account with a stockbroker and what he assumed was a very nice retirement account.

There were some notations about an offshore account that the Geeks had been unable to penetrate. It would have required an excessive intrusion that the bank could have noticed. They analyzed her income and compared it to her tax returns. They estimated there could be a sizeable amount of money in that offshore account but it did not appear she was doing anything that could have constituted tax fraud.

Richard was a little confused by a section of the report that was all numbers and letters. He guessed that it was IP addresses and codes for bank access. Overall, there didn't seem to be anything about the subject's finances that was much different from professionals in her tax bracket.

Richard scanned through the cell and office phone records. Recent calls from the Middle East could be troubling though it was not a crime to communicate with someone in the Middle East. It is also not a crime to provide professional services to citizens of a foreign country or a foreign-based company conducting legal business in the U.S.

The Middle Eastern phone records were traced to a major oil concern of which only one known person of interest could be connected, a Kadyn Waseem. *Waseem! That's the Arab guy's name!* More significant, this Waseem was a member of the immediate family who held interest in the oil company. Richard realized he'd be profiled as another possible bin Laden, a potentially radicalized Muslim with access to extensive financial resources. Moon could have been doing business with anyone associated with the family's oil corporation but this one connection would set off the alarms.

Richard put it all together. *It WAS a connection to the Arab guy and it was his work that nailed it. This has to be what got this Elizabeth Franklin on the radar. It's the kind of thing that Homeland Security looked at all the time. Most turned out to be nothing but this was how we caught people planning terrorist activity on U.S. soil.*

It was a fair trade in Richard's opinion to keep people safe. The innocent ones never even knew someone had looked into their affairs, so no harm no foul. Though he also knew if the media or the ACLU ever found out about everything Homeland Security did, they'd definitely pitch a stink. The agency is protected by most of the new laws and executive orders of the recent past but they still pushed the line a lot. That was Richard's opinion and he did not express it to others. He did his job and he kept his mouth shut. He had a plan to do his 25 years, collect his pension, and live out the rest of his life quietly.

The rest of the report referred to the Waseem family and the surveillance that was currently in process on key members. There was an extensive profile on a Mohammed Abdallah. *Yes! There's my Mohammed! Did I nail him or what?* It looks to Richard that this Mohammed seems to be the subject of the most extensive surveillance currently being conducted on any member of the family because of his business dealings in the U.S. He was also a first cousin to Kadyn which put him too close for comfort to the guy on the watchlist as far as Homeland Security would be concerned.

Most of the big families in the Middle East had someone falling off to the radical side and it was hard to separate them. The wealthy Sheikhs would have so many wives each there could be hundreds of children to try to keep track of. Richard found in this Kadyn Waseem's file that he was the son of his father's tenth wife. *Damn, he could have half brothers and sisters he didn't even know, much less one particular cousin.*

Richard felt pretty good about the job he'd done. They'd found the Waseem name in the phone records and he delivered the name "Mohammed" to them. *This Arab guy does something with theater. He probably doesn't even know the cousin. It's over, at least for me it is, and there is nothing about my screw-ups so I'm covered.* Richard decided this called for a Combo #9. He could really go for some chili cheddar fries. Until his phone rang and his appetite was gone.

Flipping through the pages of the Franklin report was only making Cole seethe. He was sure Richard had missed something. *That dumb bastard. He can't seem to do anything without screwing it up.*

Cole called down to Michelangelo. *What a stupid name. Who would name their kid Michelangelo? Someone who wanted their kid beat up every day.* Michael did that on his own, becoming a computer nerd and locking himself up in a basement most of his life.

The call sounded like it picked up but Cole could only hear something vaguely like a grunt on the other end.

"Pick up the phone! Who's there? Pick up the goddamn phone!" Cole hollered.

Michaelangelo finished his bite of pizza and got around to responding. He would have been happy to make Hargrove wait until he'd finished the whole slice. "Yeah, what?"

"The Franklin report. I want that information on the subject's offshore bank account!" Cole ordered.

"I told you how difficult that would be," Michael said. "That level of intrusion will get noticed. Just get a court order."

"Here's your court order, DO IT NOW!" Cole barked. "That's an order. Am I making myself clear?"

"Very." Michael give the phone receiver the finger before he hung up.

Cole rang his secretary and demanded she get Richard back in his office.

The secretary brought up the list of agent status on her screen, "Mr. Hargrove, it looks like Agent Washington is logged out of the office. Would you like me to get him on the line?"

"Don't bother I'll talk to him soon enough, now get back to work," Cole grumbled.

Cole was sure the office incompetents had failed the assignment and there was a lot more they could have found. *They just don't want to do the work.* Cole dialed Richard's cell.

Richard answered his cell phone knowing who it was but simply said hello.

Cole was peeved, "Don't act as if you didn't know who was calling."

Richard resisted the urge to ask How would you like me to answer it, asshole? "I'm just sitting here looking forward to hearing from my boss about my next assignment."

"Cut the crap," Cole snapped. "There isn't a next job. You didn't finish the last one right."

Richard let out an exasperated breath loud enough for Cole to hear, "The Franklin case? Well what was all that about in your office this morning?"

Cole wasn't the type to provide an explanation, he just gave orders, "Do what you're told and do it right this time. I need something on the subject and I don't want to hear excuses, got me?"

Richard knew better than to complain, "Okay you're the boss."

Cole yelled into the phone, "That's one thing you got right!"

Richard heard Cole slam the phone down. *Okay, fine. I will keep following Ms. Franklin if that's what you want me to do. It's going to be a waste of time but what the hell I'm getting paid and she isn't bad on the eyes.*

Richard figured he would pick back up on the surveillance tomorrow. Today he would go hit some balls at the range and go home early. Maybe call his girl and see if he could get a little.

chapter eight

Paradise Lost

Moon got up off the couch, unpacked her things, hung up a dress for later, and changed into some workout clothes. Lucky for her she always packs something to run in.

The hallway to the gym seems very long. She doesn't know if it's someone's primary residence but she'll get the address and look up who is on the deed when she's back at the office.

Moon wasn't really all that surprised that the gym looked like it could be a Gold's that opened just yesterday. Fully-outfitted with every kind of professional equipment, all so shiny and new she felt funny about sweating all over it. The view from the elliptical was so incredible she got lost in the first thirty minutes just staring out over the garden.

As Moon walked back to her room she passed by an open door. A man and woman were arguing in a foreign language; Moon assumed it must be Arabic. The woman was fully shrouded in a burqa. The man glared at Moon and slammed the door as she passed. She would not have expected to be the only visitor, still it was disconcerting to see a woman being yelled it and not saying a word back but just seeming to take it.

Moon could never get used to seeing the way some Islamic women shroud themselves completely, even with a screen over their eyes. She supposed that they were used to it and it was their choice to live this way, it just was not a way Moon could envision living.

Moon felt energized after the workout having that long day of traveling, even if it was the most luxurious way to travel. As she was showering, she thought she heard someone in the bedroom. She peeked out of the shower but no one was there. She heard a door shut from down the hall. She couldn't shake the feeling that someone had been in her room.

She'd brought one of her favorite Alexander McQueen dresses and figured she'd choose the accessories if she needed to go with a boardroom or cocktail party look. The dress was a little above the knee with a slight slit on the side. It was a deep dark red, not quite burgundy or garnet but a deep rich red and when she sat down just enough of her brown, athletic, and shapely thigh would show. Moon's look tonight would be a little more than boardroom but she wanted to impress and she knew this would do it.

Moon was ready ahead of 8:00 and she figured Usef would materialize at her door on cue. Of course, he did. He stood in the hall outside Moon's suite as if at attention, "I'm here to escort you to the dining room, madam."

"Great! Let's go to this party!" She couldn't resist trying to get the stoic servant to crack a smile.

"I'm terribly sorry, madam," Usef said, "It is only a dinner and there will be no other guests besides yourself."

Moon laughed, "I understand. I was just lightening things up." Usef turned and walked silently down the hall.

A beautiful table was laid out poolside. The lights danced off the water and lit up the foliage in the garden. Moon had been to quite a few luxurious Hollywood events but the crash of ocean waves beyond the lush tropical blooms made for one of the most spectacular settings for dinner that she had ever seen.

A tuxedoed waiter pulled out a chair and offered Moon a drink. She wanted to keep testing what she could ask for so she ordered a Ketel One martini; the waiter bowed in acknowledgement. *I guess I'll be getting that,* she figured. She was admiring the landscaping when she realized that a tall figure was emerging from the shadows.

Moon looked up from her chair and found herself trying not to let her mouth drop open. *Was this the Sheikh?* She thought he must be at least six foot three, maybe four, with a waist so trim and tight she imagined the chiseled abs underneath the silk shirt that tightened slightly to reveal a deep cut between his biceps and shoulders.

Moon remembered reading in the Sheikh's profile that he was in his forties but he easily could pass for early thirties. His jet-black hair was trim on the sides and back but tousled over his eyes. As Moon stood to meet him, she was struck by his dark piercing eyes framed by thick, perfectly groomed eyebrows. His full lips would look almost cherubic if not for the dusting of elegant stubble across his jaw. *With blue eyes this guy could be David Gandy.* Moon had to fight the urge not to swoon.

She didn't know that Sheikh Waseem was finding himself just as taken with her. He found it difficult to maintain a sense of professional composure when he desperately wanted to get a good look at the smooth muscular thigh that peeked out of her dress.

He extended his hand, "Ms. Franklin, the pleasure is all mine."

Moon recognized the smooth accent, tinged with British sophistication. "Mr. Waseem, or do I address you as sheikh?" Moon reached out but there was no handshake; the Sheikh squeezed her hand gently and held it for what would be considered a few seconds beyond propriety. Their mutual gaze never wavered as they took their seats in unison.

A smile broke out across the Sheikh's face, "Please, you must indulge me. Do call me 'Moe.' It is what all my friends and personal associates call me."

Moon felt the tension dissipating, "Only on one condition. My first name is not really Elizabeth. You must call me Moon or even Moonbaby. That is my real name!"

Moe was utterly delighted, "I thought Moe was an interesting and abnormal name but I think you must have me beat." With that they were both laughing and feeling totally at ease.

"You would not believe the many reactions I've gotten to my name," Moon said. "I use Elizabeth in my work of course but friends and family call me Moon. My father loves to call me his Moonbaby."

"I hope this means we are already friends," Moe said as he tipped his glass to Moon.

Moon smiled, "In my line of work I find that as time goes on, I hope we can stay friends."

Moon raised her glass to his, "I will call you Moe and you will call me Moon until the time we see we haven't a future, how about that?"

Moe seemed to revel in the moment, "That is a lovely toast from a lovely lady. Now, I want to get down to the business of learning everything about you! Who is the brilliant but beautiful attorney at law, Moonbaby Elizabeth Franklin?"

They lost themselves in conversation. Moon talked about growing up with hippie parents and why she got into entertainment law. Moe spoke of how the world of Hollywood was his refuge when he was a boy and how that lead him to pursue an American education. They realized they shared a unique bond, each of them seeking to work in the arts but from the business side instead of performing.

Moe leaned in closer to Moon, "As much as I love the theater, I want to reach people around the world. Film can do that. I want to make a difference in people's lives by touching their hearts with a universal message."

Moon thought that Moe seemed to radiate passion as he spoke about his dream for making films in Hollywood. She was fascinated by him.

When their dinner was served, Moon thought it seemed time to steer the conversation toward business, "I've handled deals like this so many times before but now that you've shared your vision with me, it doesn't seem like business anymore. This production company sounds like the fulfillment of a dream for you."

Moe wanted to tell her she seemed like a dream, "The particulars of finances and contracts can wait. Right now I am getting to know my new business partner."

Moon turned a bit coy, "Is this how you operate with all your business partners? You must have so many."

Moe appreciated the challenge, "As a matter of fact yes, more or less. I think it's essential to get to know a person extremely well if they are to be a close associate. A man like me has to choose his partners and colleagues carefully."

Moe continued, "I must feel absolute confidence for those in whom I place my trust. I admit I am feeling very comfortable with you now."

"I have to ask. How was it that you came by my name and contacted me?" Moon inquired.

"A gentleman in London. A fellow theatrical producer. Only you did not represent him. You were opposing counsel but he was so impressed with your skill that even though you made him pay dearly, he was envious of his adversary for having found you."

Moon found herself a bit flustered, "Wow. I think even I'm impressed with my reputation! This may be difficult to live up to."

"There are no doubts in my mind that I have found the right lawyer and colleague. Tomorrow morning, ten o'clock. We'll discuss the business details." Moe's smile was so disarming that Moon felt as if she had known this man for years.

"I'm sure you'll see I have everything in order," Moon said.

"I'm sure you will. But for now, tell me. Have you ever had real Turkish coffee? Brewed by an actual Turk in the traditional manner?" Moe snapped his fingers to summon the waiter.

Usef had been keeping his distance discreetly all evening. He appeared behind Moe and bent down to whisper something in his ear. Moe stood up rather abruptly. "I regret I must bid you good night." As Moon stood, he took her hand and pressed it to his lips. Moon did not want him to let go.

Moe continued to hold Moon's hand. "Until we speak again," he said as he turned and walked slowly into the house.

Moon sighed a little. She knew that she would not be able to sleep for awhile. She walked out towards the garden and the beach, deeply breathing in the warm Hawaiian air. She slipped off her shoes and dug her toes into the soft sand. She thought about how she'd met some of the most famous and glamorous people in the world but never had she been so captivated. *Oh my god, that man. THAT MAN!* Her head was spinning. She smiled at the thought of the work ahead requiring them to spend long hours together. She looked up into the sky at her namesake and realized she could hear her heart pounding.

Moon turned towards the house and stopped in her tracks. Usef was up at the pool deck looking down at her on the beach. She made her way back up to the lawn and stared back at him as she put her shoes on. She felt emboldened after having spent such an intimate evening with the master of the house, "Are you watching me, Usef?"

"Of course, madam," Usef replied with a matter of fact tone. "Your safety is my responsibility."

Moon was a little surprised, "What on earth could possibly bother me here? It seems to be the Sheikh's own private paradise. But tell you what. I'll let you walk me to my room but only because I like you."

Usef bowed his head, "It would be my duty and pleasure, madam."

Settled into her room, Moon tried to calm herself down by arranging the documents she had for Moe. She was able to drift off to sleep, confident that he'd be very impressed with the deal she has to present to him but mostly she hoped she might dream about him.

Moon woke up in the darkness and thought she felt entirely too awake for having slept only a few hours. The clock on the nightstand read 5:12; her watch said it was after seven. Back home it was later than the usual time she awoke. She decided not to disrupt her body's schedule and figured she could watch the dawn break on the beach and take a run.

Moon tried to be very quiet as she walked through the still house. It was so large she had no idea where the Sheikh might be sleeping or even if he might be in one of the other homes. She knew she could get out to the garden and down to the beach if she found the pool deck again. She walked to the edge of the lawn and was removing her trainers when she thought she heard something off in the darkness.

"Madam! Please, you must not go down there! Madam!" Usef called to her in a sort of loud whisper as he made his way down the grass. "I must ask you to return to the house please, madam."

"You may ask but I don't think I'll be going thanks," Moon replied as she pulled off her socks.

"I understand you are likely to be accustomed to be awake at this hour but here we are still in darkness and so I must ask you for your own safety that you return to the house. You are welcome to use the gymnasium. You would not be disturbing anyone." Usef clasped his hands together and kept his head down as if he were begging.

Moon was not daunted in the least, "There's not a soul out here and I think for my own safety I'm perfectly fine so if you'd like to try to catch me and drag me back in, I'll be running that way."

She turned when Usef's tone caught her by surprise. "Madam, PLEASE!" he shouted. He lowered his gaze and pointed to Moon's right. "In that direction, you will find a path that encircles the grounds. Feel free to enter the orchid hothouse you'll find at the southwest corner of the property."

Moon would have argued a little but she decided a run around the grounds could be interesting. She wondered how many homes he might own or lease in various locations around the world. It turned out to be a wonderful path for running as it meandered uphill and down. She took a break at the orchid hothouse and found a hose to grab a drink.

The sun was coming up by the time Moon made it back to the pool deck. She wasn't surprised to find Usef waiting for her, "The orchids are beautiful, are they not?"

Moon decided not to wonder if he'd been watching her. A property like this had to have an extensive security system. *Heck, Moe might have his own police force.* "So what's a girl gotta do to get some breakfast around here?" She felt quite facetious as she was sure she could get Eggs Benedict and a Bloody Mary if she wanted it.

"The chef will have breakfast served by the time you have dressed,"

Usef returned to spokesmodel mode as he waved to a room off the patio. "I will send a maid to pack your bag as you enjoy breakfast. I've been instructed to inform you that you'll be departing the island later this morning."

"That's okay I'll take care of my own bag," Moon said as she headed to her room. She realized she'd forgotten all about how nervous she'd been at the prospect of coming and wished she could stay for a few days.

Moon couldn't resist trying out the Japanese-style soaking tub and the marble shower with six water jets. She was sorry she didn't have time to take a good long steambath. She didn't think anyone would mind if she took one of the bottles of lotion; it made her legs feel fabulously smooth.

Moon gathered up her overnight bag and arranged the studio paperwork in her attaché. She had a notepad and pens ready for notes and a tablet to log in to the office if needed. She headed out to the dining room. She wasn't sure she was back where Usef had pointed out. A chef in a toque stood alongside a table laden with platters.

"How many sumo wrestlers are you expecting?" Moon asked as she surveyed the spread.

"Madam, I have prepared for you this morning a lobster benedict with avocado mousse. If you prefer pancakes, may I recommend sliced bananas, ohelo berries, or lychee from our orchard. The French toast is made with my own sourdough bread freshly baked this morning."

Moon shifted nervously from foot to foot. "Um. I don't want to insult you or anything but, um." The chef looked at her eagerly. Moon thought perhaps if she asked for something special it would make him happy. "You know what. That's some gorgeous fruit. I've never even heard of some of this stuff. Could you make me a fruit smoothie? Whatever you choose. I'm sure it will be fabulous."

"Oh yes, madam! At once!" The chef disappeared through a pair of steel doors. He did seem pretty cheered up.

A small table facing the ocean view was laid out with a single place setting and a copy of the Hawaii Tribune Herald. A flat screen TV filled a corner of the room. She looked around the TV stand and found the remote. She flipped around the channels looking for cable news but happened on the local morning news. Robbers tried to break into a Honolulu jewelry store during the night. Moon wondered, *Where does a criminal try to run when you're stuck on an island in the Pacific?*

The chef arrived with a tall ribbed glass like the kind at old-fashioned ice cream parlors. The slightly pink smoothie was festooned with a striped plastic straw and mango slices. The chef seemed to be waiting for her to try it. Moon swirled the straw around and took a big drink.

The news anchor was saying something about Homeland Security and a possible person of interest on the island when the broadcast suddenly clicked off.

"Your breakfast is to your liking, madam?" Usef was standing behind her. Moon looked over and noticed the remote was not where she had set it down.

"Yes it's great but you know I was watching that," Moon grumbled.

"When you've finished your breakfast I have arranged a workspace for you to review your documents and contact your office if needed." Usef turned and walked away. He seemed to put something in his pocket. Moon turned her attention back to the newspaper.

The chef brought out a large metal cup with the rest of the smoothie and Moon happily finished all of it. Practically on cue, Usef turned up to escort her to an office where she could go over her notes and connect to WiFi.

Moon got so involved with catching up on her email that she hadn't noticed it was nearly 11:00. She thought it seemed very odd she'd have to look for Usef; he always seemed to be right there. She figured if she ventured too far out of the office, he'd find her. She turned down a hallway she'd yet to explore when Usef appeared right behind her.

"Mr. Waseem is an hour late," Moon said, pointing to her watch.

"There has been a change of plans and the Sheikh sends his deepest regrets," Usef said as he went into a deeper bow than usual. "He will not be able to meet with you today. I have been instructed to have a limousine drive you to the airport. A first class ticket has been reserved for you for a 2:00 flight to Los Angeles on United Airlines."

Moon was quite disturbed, partly by the prospect of flying commercial. She peppered Usef with questions he either couldn't or wouldn't answer. He would only say that the Sheikh had something unforeseen come up and he would contact her about the business deal if she would leave the documents for his review.

It seemed pointless to keep trying to get anything out of Usef. Moon decided to resign herself to what was happening. "Okay fine, when do I leave?"

"The car will be here in a half hour's time. Please leave the wiring instructions for your fee," Usef said as he handed her a small note pad.

"I don't know what it's going to be," Moon replied. "I'll have to calculate my hours and prepare a bill."

"That will not be necessary," Usef insisted. "The Sheikh has authorized me to wire a sum he's certain will more than adequately compensate you for your time as well as the time spent in preparation for this visit."

Moon was just about to protest when she considered what she'd experienced in the past twenty-four hours. *If it's not enough I'm sure he's good for it and if it's too much we'll consider it a retainer.*

Moon sighed in exasperation as she took the notepad and wrote down the firm's bank and account number. Usef seemed relieved, "Thank you so much madam and please accept my apologies on behalf of the Sheikh. He expressed to me that he did so regret not being able to see you this morning." Moon was too disappointed to even come up a snotty retort.

Usef had brought her overnight bag to the entry hall and asked Moon to sit and wait for the car. She sat there thinking it had been a waste of her time and Moe's money to leave without having the intended business meeting. *Maybe his real priority was to meet me in person* she wondered. *And we certainly did hit it off.* She decided to feel okay with the whole thing but she would be curious to find out how much money Moe would think one dinner conversation would be worth.

Moon looked at her watch and realized it was long past the half hour Usef said it would take for the car to arrive. *It's their car and driver, what's the hold up?* It occurred to her that she never did see those two people again. *Why would a couple be here unless they are family?* The Waseem family is so large there could be any number of family members here, any time. They don't all have to be as Westernized as Moe is.

Moon was pacing around the entry hall when Usef rushed up, absent his usual eerily calm demeanor. He seemed almost frantic, "Plans have changed madam! I have arranged for a charter jet out of Maui. You must leave immediately."

Moon saw the limousine pull up to the door. Usef grabbed her bag and began pulling her by the arm outside. The driver got out of the car and opened the passenger door. The two of them seemed determined to get Moon into the car as quickly as possible. She decided everything had gotten just a little too weird.

Moon dug in her heels at the car door, "Just hold it one minute. I'm not getting into this car without an explanation. What is going on here?"

"Nothing madam, nothing at all," Usef tried to sound calm but he was literally breathless. "The Sheikh was so embarrassed that you would have to fly commercial that he demanded I make special arrangements just for you. Only the best for you, madam, now please get in the car."

Moon was trying to decide if she should continue the protest when the driver stepped forward as if he would grab her and stuff her into the limo. "Okay but you tell Moe, uh, I mean Mr. Waseem that I was not happy about this and I find this rather...irregular. You tell him this is not how I do business!"

"Absolutely madam," Usef gushed. "I will voice your displeasure to the Sheikh but please get into the car now and I thank you so much."

Moon stepped halfway into the car and blocked Usef from closing the door. "Okay look. Either I get a call from Mr. Waseem personally while I am in this car or I will not be getting on that plane. Is that clear? A personal call from him, not some assistant or anybody else, you got that? I will speak directly to Mr. Waseem or I will NOT be leaving this island!"

Usef and the driver stood momentarily stunned. "I will take care of it madam. On my honor I will contact the Sheikh right now if you will please just get in the car," Usef begged. The driver shot Moon a glare that told her she was pushing it. She was barely in before the door slammed shut. The driver squealed the tires taking off out of the compound.

The driver who had been so friendly and personable yesterday was racing through side streets today, seemingly trying to avoid the main roads. He'd also put up the glass partition. Moon leaned forward and banged on it. "My phone isn't ringing! Nobody's calling me! I need this phone to ring NOW! Now, damn it!"

The car took a corner so sharply Moon slid across the car seat. Her phone rang. She didn't want to be angry with Moe but she didn't know what to expect and she was very worked up. She took a deep breath and tried to answer calmly.

"I'm so sorry about all this. I truly am so sorry." The connection was very bad but the sound of Moe's voice melted her anger immediately.

"This is all a little strange. I'm your attorney now. You should tell me what's happening," Moon tried to sound concerned instead of mad.

"You're right. You deserve to know who you are dealing with. I have a very large family as you know. Some of them can be very opinionated and they think I should not make investments outside of Qatar or outside of the oil business at all," Moe sounded very straight-forward.

"That doesn't surprise me," Moon said. "But you don't seem like a man who can be deterred from what you want. Has something happened?"

"Well," Moe seemed to be choosing his words carefully. "I was contacted by a particular family member and I felt I needed to address the situation immediately. It is true though that I changed my mind about putting you on a commercial flight. I want my own hand-picked staff to be responsible for getting you back to Los Angeles safely."

In a weird way, Moon rather liked what she was hearing but she wanted an explanation. "I appreciate the personal concern, but Usef was freaking out back at the house. He acted like something was very wrong."

"Usef has worked for me for 15 years," Moe explained. "He knows there is a level of request I will make that he must move heaven and earth to accomplish it and with the greatest expediency. He knew that today was one of those times. He has never let me down."

Moon was a little skeptical. "Hmm. Well, he didn't strike me as the excitable type so it was really weird when he seemed to be practically in a panic."

"I met Usef when I was in the military," Moe explained. "He continues to think of me as his commanding officer and I know in my heart that man would give his life in his service to me. I believe this because sometimes he will act like it. I'm sure that's what you saw today."

Moon wasn't sure she was buying it completely but part of her wanted to believe anything Moe said.

"I am truly sorry to have to bother you with my family's problems," Moe seemed to be pouring his heart out. "It hurts me to have you think something less of me and I will make it up to you and regain your trust."

Moe had been so candid last night. Moon was hearing the passion and concern in his voice again. She decided she'd give him the benefit of the doubt for now. "Alright. You look over the file I left and I'll call you tomorrow."

"I will look forward to hearing your voice again," Moe said. "I won't rest until I know you've been delivered safely back to your home."

"Thank you. I believe you mean that." Moon thought she heard Moe say something. "Hey, this connection is really bad. Are you there? Hello?" She heard clicks and beeps and could tell the call was dropped.

The driver pulled into a small airstrip beside a Cessna prop jet. Moon was a bit surprised when he did not immediately come open her door. He walked out to the meet the pilot. The two touched their hands to their hearts and then warmly embraced. They talked for a moment and looked in her direction. They hugged again before they both walked over to the car. The pilot took Moon's bag and offered his hand to help her up a step into the plane. She turned and looked back. The driver touched his hand to his heart and bowed his head to her. She wasn't sure what to do so she simply waved and shouted out a thank you.

The pilot shouted something to the driver in Arabic before climbing into the plane. He strapped her in and explained in a thick accent that he would also be piloting the second leg and plane of the flight from the Maui airport to Los Angeles. Moon noticed that something about him made her think Moe might also know him from the military. He seemed to cut that kind of dashing figure like Tom Cruise in "Top Gun." Only much taller.

As the plane climbed into the sky, Moon had a sense that she should feel very safe as this pilot's passenger. She looked out the window at the clouds and started replaying her conversations with Frank in her mind. Maybe the incidents had all been related directly to Moe as he had suggested. But instead of Moe himself, maybe it had been a family member of his trying to check her out and even scare her off, thinking they could foil his business deal. It's not like he couldn't get another lawyer. And he certainly had all the money in the world.

But the guy in the car, he was from the government. Probably anything this Waseem family does could attract attention. *That's got to be it,* Moon thought. She looked up at the pilot, manning the controls, and for the moment she felt that nothing and no one could hurt her.

chapter nine

Back Home

Richard reached over his girlfriend to turn off the alarm. Maria did not stir; he looked at her sleeping and smiled, thinking about last night. He really had no expectations that she would even come over but when he called she seemed all for it.

For an evening he was happy and he even forgot about his crappy boss and job for a few hours. He told her in a whisper he had to get going early and she could leave whenever she wanted. She reached out with her hand a moment and patted him and went back to sleep.

As he headed out to leave, Richard was a little surprised he didn't have any messages from the office. He got in his car and decided that he would ride up to Moon's house and start there. She was probably just getting in from her run about now so he could watch her house and not risk being spotted on the street. He didn't see the point of going but he'd log the time and Hargrove should stay off his back.

He made a stop at Starbucks and got a coffee on his way. He wonders why he stops there because he does not like all that fancy latté stuff. He just likes black coffee but he does like their black coffee.

Richard swapped out his usual vehicle from the motor pool and arrived at Moon's about seven. He made sure to set up in a different location this time, hoping she wouldn't notice a random car in the neighborhood, even if she happened to see it. The location was not as good but he could still see most of the house so it was a trade off.

He sat there watching and thinking of how people like this get involved in unsavory business, though he really didn't believe there was anything wrong with Ms. Franklin, he just had to do his job. He sat there and soon it was eight o'clock, then eight thirty and no movement. Suddenly his phone rang and it was Cole, he thought about not answering, but he did anyway.

"So genius, do things look pretty quiet around the subject's house?" Cole seemed like he was trying to bait him.

"Well, yeah, pretty quiet," Richard replied, trying to sound cooperative. "No movement yet this morning."

"There's a reason for that numbskull, the subject may have left the country," Cole said. "I want you to get into that house and see what you can find."

"Do we have a warrant to enter the premises?" Richard asked.

"Yeah, national security, that's your warrant," Cole yelled. "Get in that house and find what that woman is hiding!"

Richard saw no reason for taking a risk like this but it was easier to just say yes and get on with it. He decided to give the neighborhood time to get out and get to work. *Everybody who lives around here is probably a location scout or associate producer.* Besides, it was early but he could use a something to eat.

Richard swung by a drive-thru for breakfast then home and threw a toolbox in the car. He had a pair of coveralls he used when he wanted to look like a workman. By the time he got back to Moon's neighborhood, even the stay-at-home moms would be at the park with their kids. He went ahead and parked in front of Moon's house. He grabbed the toolbox and walked right up to the front door.

Richard made short work of the front door locks; he was more concerned about the security system. He slipped into the house and quickly found the keypad next to the door. The Geeks had rigged a small circuit board with leads that could interrupt an electrical system without shorting it out. Pretty much everyone set their systems to 30 seconds. He knew he had to work fast to pry the keypad cover off, get the device clipped into the electronics, and get it disarmed.

Richard wanted to get around the house quickly and efficiently, hitting all the usual places where people keep important documents and anything they think is sensitive or valuable. He looked for an office or even just a desk where he might find a computer or file cabinet. He found what looked like a den but there was no desktop computer. *Nobody buys desktops anymore. They all have laptops and tablets and carry them everywhere.* He could not find a file cabinet or even a drawer filled with any kind of paperwork or documents. No one without a desktop computer would have an old antiquated box to store a lot of paper.

Richard was careful not to disturb anything. The subject should never suspect anyone was there. If he disturbed something he tried to move it back the way he found it. He moved through each room as a ghost would, moving silently on to the master bedroom and the walk-in closet. The subject lived quite well; her bedroom was bigger than his living room and the closet was about as big as his bedroom. Sometimes people don't hide things in the closet, it seems too obvious but he'd give it a thorough search.

Moon had a ton of clothes and enough shoes to open a store. Mostly suits and a few dresses, they were not what Richard would have expected. He thought a lawyer who worked with Hollywood clients would have more fancy clothing. Most of it looked like professional work clothes. There were a few jeans hanging up and some t-shirts. They looked like the kind that cost a lot more than you would buy from Old Navy or Walmart. He dug around in some drawers and looked in various boxes but the closet seemed to contain nothing but clothes and personal effects. He stepped back out of the closet to check the chest of drawers and nightstand. He found Moon's Glock quickly but thought it was odd. He didn't see her as a gun owner but there it was, right in her nightstand and loaded. He moved on through the rest of her drawers, finding nothing but workout clothes, undergarments, and casual wear. She did seem to fold things very neatly.

The rest of the house went about the same way. Richard found nothing interesting except that while her furniture was very nice, the walls were almost bare. He went into the garage only to find her BMW, a few boxes, and a stack of milk crates with a lot of old books. The typical miscellaneous garage crap was scattered around along with a recycling container with a few beer bottles in it.

Richard stood in the garage and tried to organize his thoughts. What was this woman all about? By the looks of her home, she is a health nut and she doesn't seem to care much about fashion even though she works in the movie and television business. Something about her was starting to intrigue him and he felt he was thinking too much about her personally. It did not matter what she drove or how she dressed to the investigation or to him for that matter. He thought maybe he was even getting a little enamored with her. *So what*, he thought. *If I am, it's not going to get in the way of my investigation. I always thought that there was nothing here and so far, I'm correct.*

Richard decided he'd seen as much as there was to see. It seemed like a good opportunity to call it an early day. When his cell phone rang, he hoped it wasn't new orders. It was Michaelangelo. The Geeks had found his subject. She'd been in Hawaii and was heading home today.

"What the hell? I'm standing in her garage right now! Are you saying she could have walked in on me? When did you figure this out?"

"Don't sweat it!" Michael said. "She's still there. Besides, whatever plane she gets on will be getting diverted. She won't make it home until sometime tonight. Oh and you're welcome!" Michael replied, smugly.

Richard hung up the phone. *This shit is not worth it for me or the agency. This woman is not involved in any plot or illegal activity that anyone is going to find and yet they keep risking exposure.*

Moon was once again the only passenger on a private jet. The pilot was joined by a co-pilot at the Maui airport and a flight attendant who was attentive but not quite up to Hatsu's level. She really didn't care about the accommodations by this point. Moon slept off and on for most of the flight. It was just the middle of the day but the sheer stress had been exhausting. She still needed to process the day's events and how she felt about it all but for right now she couldn't muster the strength.

As she drifted in and out, Moon's thoughts were clearly focused on Moe. She dreamed of him but he kept changing into a boy, then an old man, and back again. She saw Moe through this cycle again and again, then she would find herself walking the hills in her own neighborhood but not able to find her house. She would see Moe again and she would be at the beach.

The pilot announced they were beginning their descent to land. Moon noticed she never had changed her watch while she'd been away but she realized the flight took longer than it should have. She looked out the window and did not recognize the skyline. She called over the flight attendant. "Where are we? That's not LA."

"We are landing in Seattle. We were diverted due to weather," the attendant explained.

Moon was puzzled. "That's weird. Since when does Seattle have better weather than LA? And why would we go north of San Francisco?"

"I really do not know, ma'am," she replied. "I just know that we'll be returning to Hawaii immediately after refueling."

"Oh you are kidding me!" Moon tried to contain her aggravation. "You know, I have had about enough drama for one day without being dumped in Seattle!"

"I'm so sorry, ma'am," the flight attendant seemed rather confused herself.

Moon looked out the window as the jet taxied to the far end of a terminal. She pulled out her phone and started searching for flights. *It's a damn good thing I slept so long this afternoon. Who knows when this day is going to end?*

She was able to get a flight on United with a couple of hours before she'd finally be able to head home. The ticket agent handed her a boarding pass, "Your flight will be boarding at gate six in concourse A."

Moon was relieved to have a ticket for home in her hand. "Has the weather around LAX cleared up?" she asked.

The ticket agent looked rather puzzled. "I'm sorry, ma'am?"

The confusing and bizarre events of the day did not seem to be coming to an end. Moon wanted an explanation, "I was on a charter flight to LA and we were diverted here because of weather."

The ticket agent looked at his screen, "No ma'am. We haven't had any weather delays all day." He looked up at her with an obsequious smile. "You'll have a clear view of the stars to guide you all the way to LA! Enjoy your flight, ma'am."

Moon stumbled away from the counter. Feelings of anxiety started to creep back over her. *Why would an aircraft be diverted for bad weather that did not exist? And who would have the power to do that?* She walked to the gate in a daze, playing and re-playing her conversation with Moe in her head. *Could those family members Moe talked about be behind this?*

This was getting weirder and weirder by the moment, she could not wait to speak to Moe and get some answers. Moon settled in at the gate to wait for boarding. She flipped through her voicemails. Jennifer. Wants to know how the business meeting went and when she would be back. Mom. Hopes she's having fun and we love you. Harold's secretary. Harold wants a callback, asap, no reason given. Moon hit Harold's direct line. She thought she could still catch him.

"Oh no, what an ordeal!" Harold was shocked to hear of Moon's day. "I think I can cheer you up. What do you know about 500 billable hours?"

Moon couldn't handle much more. "What? I've spent all day being confused. Don't confuse me anymore."

"Two hundred and fifty thousand dollars was wired in to the firm's account today. I know your new client said he'd pay you time and travel but you've only been gone since Wednesday," Harold said.

Moon was speechless for a moment. "I didn't even give them a bill. The client's assistant said they were wiring money. He wouldn't tell me how much."

"Very well done," Harold said.

Moon did not agree, "No. I don't appreciate this. It has a look of impropriety."

"Oh don't worry about it," Harold insisted. "We work with very high-dollar value cases. This just proves the client is serious."

Moon also knew Harold would never turn down a dollar, let alone a quarter million.

Moon was too exhausted to get into it. "Look, whatever. We'll discuss it tomorrow."

Moon hung up the phone and found herself thinking of the past week and how her life seemed to be taking an unusual turn and she couldn't do anything about it. Well, no, there is always something she can do. She decided right there and then she will get things figured out and take control of it.

The flight from Seattle was uneventful. Not a cloud down the entire California coast. She'd never been so happy to look out an airplane window and see the Encounter Restaurant. Its parabolic arches made for an unusual association with being home. Rush hour was long over by the time she was in a cab and as soon as she saw her house she felt lifted. Moon had actually started to feel better the minute she entered the familiar environs of her neighborhood. It was good to be home, she was always a homebody anyway. She usually liked to travel but this was a trip she never could have anticipated.

Moon put her key in the door and nearly panicked when she realized the deadbolt wasn't locked. She unlocked the doorknob and immediately noticed no beeping. She was a little scared to step in and check the security system keypad so she tried to stay outside and lean around the doorway. It was off. *Okay. This is scary.* Moon looked around her street. She could see the TV on at her next door neighbors and the people across the street had just pulled into their driveway. *You're not alone, just go inside.* She left the front door open and made her way around the house, turning on every light she passed. Everything seemed normal.

Nothing out of place. *Am I crazy? I was paranoid about locking everything up before I left.*

Moon brought in her bag and went to check the mail. No strange cars on her street. Looks like the Johnsons are back. All seemed right with the world.

Moon was still a little creeped out but with the day she'd had, it would be difficult to feel anything else. She felt safe back in her own home, in her own bed. She stared off into the darkness and tried to add up all the pieces of the recent events. Some just didn't add up. Was Moe being completely honest with her or was he hiding something? Not being completely honest is not always lying but she would hope that as his attorney he wouldn't keep secrets from her. She thought about that. *Was anyone completely open with someone else? Does anyone tell all their secrets?*

Richard decided that going to Moon's house and watching the conventional way wasn't getting him what he needed or at least whatever it was Cole wanted him to find. He decided he'd go to the operations center and check out a different drone, one that had much more capability.

chapter ten

Family Troubles

Moe had a wonderful time with Moon that night. She was much more then he would have expected. She was intelligent as he would have thought but she was also very beautiful and that was a surprise.

Moon was the kind of beauty that intimidated men enough to repel rather than to attract. Men approached women they thought they had a chance with but Moon looked as if no human male could measure up. A woman like Moon presented an exciting challenge. Something Moe found particularly attractive was the way she seemed to understand who he was and where he came from even though they were raised in vastly different environments.

He was a little worried his personal feelings could get in the way of business. While they were talking, he had to keep reminding himself that this was business and she was there as his attorney.

Moe took great pains to personally interview each person who would work with him in any capacity. Besides looking for people of good character and with the appropriate skills and knowledge, he believed that he should know something of their background. He believed that where you came from was important in predicting where you would go. He supposed that this was true everywhere but in today's world of terrorism, who you associate with could be misconstrued. Moe was very careful about that. He tried to view it as simply an inconvenience that as a businessman from the Middle East he may be subjected to greater scrutiny. He accepted that this had become a fact of life in the world today and if he tried to fight it, he could have a government like the United

States making his life extremely difficult. He already had difficulty with an errant cousin so he needed no more trouble.

This was the situation that had shown up on the news. Moe's cousin Kadyn was determined to stop his investments in the U.S. This was not only pointless and irrational but also dangerous to both of them. Moe thought Kadyn no longer cared for his own safety and didn't even realize that he put the lives of his entire family at risk.

Despite how his cousin had changed, Moe still cared for him very much but he wasn't about to let this misguided family member mess things up for him or the family.

And now Kadyn was in Hawaii, trying to interfere with what he thought was going on with his cousin's new American lawyer. From his years at Sandhurst, Moe had been able to assemble a small team of elite soldiers from around the world. He had them in the islands looking for his cousin. They located him before he'd been able to reach Moon. The news came just as he was getting to know his new business associate.

The last thing Moe wanted to do was end the evening with Moon. He had no choice but to excuse himself and find out what was happening.

Usef delivered the urgent update that Kadyn was being held.

"Instruct the team to get him to the plane," Moe said, "We have to get him out of here now."

"What are your instructions for Ms. Franklin?" Usef asked.

"I'll need to speak to Captain Al Sayed. Be prepared to carry out whatever I determine will be necessary."

"I'll hope for the best, sir," Usef said.

"Do not hope but do the best," Moe replied. Usef bowed his head in acknowledgment.

Moe drove himself to the airplane hangar where his team would be holding his cousin but all he could do was think about how much this ruined his night with Moon. He also did not want any possible deal on the production company to fall through. He wanted this type of acquisition for many years and he was so close now, he cursed Kadyn. It broke his heart how the cousin he'd always loved could have become radicalized. Moe never understood the obsession some of his people had with pushing their religion on others. It could have been his Western education, but that really wasn't it. He always wanted freedom in his life and he extended that wish for freedom to everyone.

Moe had assumed a senior role in the family so he found himself dealing with the crazies. Moe just hoped he could get Kadyn back home without incident.

Moe's mind wandered to Moon and he started to fantasize about her. As he approached the hangar, he had to remind himself to stay focused and on task.

Moe pulled up to the jet. He was met by two of his men. "Is he under control?" Moe asked as he climbed the stairs into the plane.

Daoud Al Sayed had been a captain in the Qatar Special Forces Battalion. Now he led a security team for Moe. "Your cousin has been sedated and strapped in," he reported.

Moe looked to the back of the plane. A crumpled figure was strapped into a plane seat, his feet in manacles. His long beard looked matted and filthy and there were streaks of blood on his thobe.

Moe stood over his cousin and could only feel anger. "He put up a fight this time?" Moe asked.

A soldier stepped forward, "He didn't make it easy, sir. But there were no shots fired, no weapons. He did not have any weapons on him."

"Tell the pilot to take off." Moe ordered.

Moe and his team all strapped themselves in. Soon the plane was over the Pacific.

They'd been in the air about two hours when the robed figure began to stir. As he regained consciousness, Kadyn thrashed against his restraints and screamed in Arabic.

Moe stood over his cousin. Kadyn spit at him. "Infidel! Corrupted by the great satan America! You bring shame to our family!"

Moe resisted the urge to throw a punch. "It is you who bring shame upon our family and our name!"

"Death to you if you will not bow on your knees to Allah! Allahu akbar!" Kadyn screamed.

"You wish death to me, my cousin, my brother, my blood. But I will show you mercy!" Moe fell to his knees. "You want me on my knees? I am begging you on my knees. You must stop what you are doing!" Moe reached up and kissed his cousin on the cheek. Kadyn became calm.

"What are you going to do to me, brother?" Kadyn asked quietly.

"It is all up to you what happens next." Moe said. "If you speak the truth with complete honesty and with no hesitation then you will see home again and live a long life if Allah permits. But if you do not," he warned, "You will never see the land of our fathers again."

Kadyn sunk down in his seat and looked at his bonds. He knew that Moe was not bluffing. He knew enough about his cousin that he may be Westernized, but Moe always told the truth and would do what he thought he needed to. A twisted smile crept over Kadyn's face, "You cannot stop what Allah decrees. Allahu akbar!"

Moe gripped his fists tightly. He was growing more angry by the minute but he tried to remember playing with Kadyn when they were boys. He leaned into Kadyn's face so closely they almost touched, "Thinking about you when you were a child and the cousin I loved as my brother is the only thing that is keeping me from throwing you out of this plane!" Kaydn spit in Moe's face.

Moe stood up, "Sajjad, bring the injection."

Kadyn began to thrash against his restraints again. "NO! NO! Death to the infidels! You will die with the great satan America!" Two soldiers grabbed his arms as the third held down his knees. A large hypodermic was stabbed into his arm.

Within minutes, Kadyn was woozy but compliant. Moe asked him a series of questions to find out what he had been doing in Hawaii. The plan had been to kidnap Moon and threaten anyone associated with her. He would do the same to anyone else involved in Moe's business dealings in America. Kadyn also spoke of a co-conspirator but Moe could not get sufficient details to identify this person or find out exactly where they were before Kadyn fell unconscious again.

Moe slumped into a chair. He felt every nerve on edge. He got Usef on the phone. Moon was still under a threat; he had to get her off the island and safely back home. He had Usef arrange two possible ways she could fly home, one commercial and one private. They'd assess the threat level tomorrow and determine which to use.

"Contact Captain Al-Mohannadi immediately and have him fly into Maui. He can take the Cessna between the islands. Iqbal is to drive. Tell them both they are to be armed."

"It will be done, sir," Usef said.

"Protect her at all costs, my friend. Until she is on a plane tomorrow, she is in your hands," Moe said.

"With my life, sir," Usef said. Moe knew he meant it.

"This co-conspirator, we do not have much information about him yet but I will wring it out of Kadyn with my bare hands if that's what it takes," Moe said.

The flight was long and arduous. Moe was able to get a little sleep before they had to stop in Singapore for refueling at the private hangar he maintained at Changi International. He wasn't surprised when Usef called him about Moon's confusion and anger. He knew she was a headstrong woman and she would be unlikely to accept being ordered around without an explanation. The most difficult part was having to talk to her and make it sound like what was going on was just slightly more than an embarrassing inconvenience. He knew at some point he'd have to tell her the whole truth about Kadyn. He hoped he would never have to warn her she should fear for her life.

When they finally landed in Doha, Kadyn was more subdued. Being there made him feel like they were on his turf now and Moe had become the outsider. Moe knew he could only take care of this at home. He would wear a thobe and speak to his father and his uncle. He was the namesake of Kadyn's father, Mohammed bin Awad Waseem, and Moe believed if he demonstrated proper respect and with his father's help, he could win his uncle's support in managing Kadyn. As long as he did not flaunt his Western manners while he was at home, his father and uncle generally approved of Moe's overseas business ventures as they were always profitable.

Moe had not been back home for long when Usef called with disturbing news that Kadyn's accomplice had been picked up by Homeland Security. He was being described in the American media as an Al Qaeda operative. This was not good; a mere mention of the Waseem family name by this suspected terrorist and their entire global enterprise could be in jeopardy. Kadyn was fearful of his father; he was already considered a failure and a disgrace as a son. The wrath of his entire family could have him wishing the Americans had sent him to Guantanamo instead.

Moe would have the usual uncomfortable conversation with his father. He approved of how successfully Moe had diversified his business portfolio but he would have preferred that his son focus his financial interests in the Middle East. Moe loved his father and did not want to argue so he would usually say that he saw opportunity throughout the world but his heart would always be in Qatar. He did an excellent job of managing a refinery division of Waseem Petroleum and he sat on the Board of Directors so that made it difficult for his father to have any real reason to be disappointed.

Money in Moe's family was almost an abstract concept. He really did not do anything for the money but he always showed a passion for everything he did.

Being at home was increasingly difficult for Moe. Each time he felt a little more like a stranger in a strange land. He was not married and in his home culture he was well over the age to have done so. There had been whispers among his family that he might be gay but a man of his station would have accepted an arranged marriage long ago to avoid suspicion. Moe had actually managed to escape an arranged marriage years earlier which upset his mother greatly. Lucky for Moe, one of his younger brothers was actually quite taken with the young lady and he was able to convince his mother that they would make a better match.

Moe was just independent-minded and had not found a woman that he could see staying with for the rest of his life. He was not particularly paternal either so having children was not a priority, a fact that distressed his mother even though she already had two dozen grandchildren.

Moe was greatly concerned about Moon. He hoped that with Kadyn in Doha and his accomplice in custody in Honolulu, she was out of harm's way. But with everything that happened, he did not want her to think badly of him or that she'd lost trust in him. He cared about the business deal, but now he also cared what she thought of him.

This was something new. Never before had Moe actually worried what a woman would think of him. He wasn't egotistical or vain and he never flaunted his money but still he'd never been dumped or even rejected. Women had always been like an exciting challenge or a pursuit. For the first time he felt he might have to prove himself to a woman to win her over. He felt desperate to speak to Moon again soon, desperate to see her in person and prove to her that he was worthy of her trust.

Moe thought it felt odd being home. He had not been back for awhile. He spends most of his time in London because the theater was his primary interest but lately he'd had to attend to more of the petroleum business. After he returned home from the military, his parents had given him a home in the family compound. Being here was like living in a village that was isolated from the outside world. Servants did all the maintenance and shopping. Some of his relatives hardly ever left the grounds.

Moe resolved to spend his time in Doha doting over his mother. He knew how much she missed him. But Moon would be on his mind every minute and he thought about how he'd have to buy a home in LA if he was going to own a production company there.

chapter eleven

Investigations

Richard did some of his own digging into the Waseem family. What he found was fairly typical for that part of the world if being a huge family of polygamous billionaires could be typical. There did not seem to be any extreme jihadists among the family members but among that many people there will always be some who lean toward the radical side. The CIA had done an investigation on the family back in the nineties and again after 9/11. All the prominent Arab families were being investigated during that time. In the case of the Waseems, the findings pretty much cleared the whole family of any suspicion.

To continue his investigation of Moon, Richard requested time with a much higher altitude drone that had an HD camera. He really did not request this level of equipment very often because it was launched from a covert airbase and controlled by a drone pilot. This was the only way he could be sure to avoid being spotted again. Cole had not found out about the previous incidents and Richard wanted to keep it that way.

He would be in communication with the pilot and could see all the drone saw in real time. The drone was launched and autopiloted itself towards Moon's house using GPS coordinates. Richard was able to view the live video feed and control the camera. The real benefit of this drone was that it could remain over fifteen thousand feet away and still be able to zoom in on a book in someone's hands. It took a little getting used to the idea that this drone was so powerful. The images were so precise it was difficult for Richard to believe the drone could be far enough away to not be seen.

He panned out and saw a wide view of the neighborhood. After a minute or two he saw someone running up the hill. It was Moon, out for her usual run. She was looking good as always and Richard had to remind himself this was not what he was supposed to be doing so he directed the pilot to just stay there and watch.

Moon arrived at home and stayed outside for a while, stretching, drinking water, toweling off. Richard was a little disturbed when she appeared to be fixated on something up in the sky. She didn't seem to be looking in the direction of the drone or they'd be having another of those "eye to eye" moments like back at the parking garage. Richard panned around and caught sight of a traffic helicopter buzzing Moon's neighborhood. That had to be it. She did keep looking at the sky but the pilot assured him that the drone was so high even if the subject looked in the right direction, it would look like a bird.

Richard couldn't shake the feeling that Ms. Franklin was looking at them and this was bothersome. This woman was a thorn in his side and she keeps spotting him. The pilot told him he was paranoid and that everything was fine but they were running out of time and there seemed to be nothing to watch now.

Richard hadn't expected to see much anyway. He really just wanted to learn and play some more with drones. He had only used the smaller one he could control and he was eager to try out the highly sophisticated ones. It was fun but it really did not take the place of the old tried and true methods for surveillance. Richard would just have to go back to conventional ways of following the subject. He would have to get a GPS device on her car; he would wait until he could get into the parking garage at her office. This would be better as he could just follow her at a distance and the device would store and download everywhere she went. He should have done this from the beginning; he just thought it would be over by now.

Richard went looking for Moon's car when she was back at work the following week. He parked on the street and walked into the parking garage. There were cameras but he was not concerned with them as no one ever looks at them unless there is a problem and he was not going to create one today. His plan was to slip in and slip out but he hadn't counted on how many black BMWs there would be. He had to walk each row of cars looking for the license plate. He flipped the device on and it sprung to life instantly. When he found the car, all he had to do was reach high up into the rear passenger fender and attach it with a magnetic mount. He breathed a sigh of relief as he thought he finally would be able to do his job without the subject bugging him.

As Moon expected, Bamberger wanted to see her first thing Monday. She'd spent the weekend thinking about what to let him in on about Hawaii. Obviously she wouldn't bring up anything about what she felt personally, that was going to stay private. She would tell him about the man and the business deal only. But they never did get to discuss the deal. It's not unusual for an important businessman to be called away and have to cancel a meeting. As Harold pointed out himself, the money indicates the client is serious. Moon was sure all Bamberger wanted to know was how much of the money she expected to receive.

Bamberger went straight to the subject, "The partnership agreement covers billable hours and retainers. I assume you're considering this a retainer payment?"

Moon felt a little defensive. "I really had no idea how large of a transaction this would be and I still haven't been able to reach the client but I will."

"Alright, well you decide how much of your time this much of a retainer covers and we'll see if the other partners think that's fair. Agreed?" Harold asked.

"I'll speak to the client as soon as I can. I think he's overseas and I may have to go through some channels to locate him but I know who I can call," Moon replied.

Bamberger asked a few more questions about the future with her client and time lines but Moon could only give him a little information. She promised to keep him in the loop and he seemed satisfied with that.

Moon laughed a little to herself as she left his office because when Bamberger was done with you, he was done. It reminded her of the computer in "Tron", when it was done it said, "End of line." With Harold, you knew the conversation was over whether you wanted it to be or not. For now, she had a lot to catch up on and she'd try to resume a normal workweek, if there was such a thing in Hollywood.

Richard sat back in his car patting himself on the back for doing what was a routine car GPS tagging. He was happy because anything involving Ms. Franklin had been anything but routine so far. Now he could go anywhere to monitor her car's position and she wouldn't be leaving the office for several hours anyway. He decided he was free for a while so he thought he'd go get some errands done, maybe a little grocery shopping and normal life stuff he usually doesn't get to do in the middle of the day.

Moon's day was typical. She spoke to several clients and cleared her desk of all she could. She was feeling caught up but she was the most concerned about Moe and how soon she would be able to speak to him.

Moon called the number that was supposed to be for his office and got a messaging service. They couldn't tell her anything about how or when the Sheikh could be reached directly. She was forced to dictate a message to the attendant, "I'm not going to do any more business this way until I get a number that I can reach you directly. I'm sorry but I gave you my cell number and as your attorney, I should have yours."

Moon was feeling aggravated so she called her mother to calm down. She soft-pedaled the story of Hawaii and only told her Mom all the good stuff. No need at this point to upset the apple cart when there may never be a cart at all. She said it was all business and acted as if she does this all the time. Still, Anita always had a strong mother's intuition. She had a sense Moon was holding something back but she also knew when not to press her daughter for more information and this was one of those times.

Moon hadn't talked to her sister since last week and she knew Aspen would rag on her for that. She dialed Aspen's number expecting to get an ear full.

"It's about time I hear from you!" Aspen said. "I'm waiting to hear all about this Hawaii trip Mom says you're off to and I don't even know when you were coming back!"

Even I didn't know when I'd make it back Moon thought. "I'm sorry but I was swamped today and I just did not have the time earlier."

"Where were you all weekend? Did you just get back?" Aspen asked. "I tried calling you at home yesterday but you didn't answer and I never got voicemail on your cell."

It struck Moon as strange that her cell wouldn't go to voicemail. It would have started to worry her a little but Aspen had launched into a long story about her husband Sam and something about Hawaii.

"We were both really concerned about your well-being so you can see how I'd be worried when I couldn't even get your voicemail," Aspen said.

Sam was an IT security expert who worked on cyber attacks and anti-virus. He was an intelligent computer nerd and this allowed him to work a lot from home. All he needed was a secure connection that the company provided and he was good to go. He did government work from time to time and sometimes he'd discover something he considered distressing. Moon thought this was just another of Sam's crazy conspiracy theories. She couldn't remember a single one of these troublesome tales of his that ever panned out.

Moon tried to brush off her sister's worries, "Look, it's just been hectic getting home and trying to get caught up. I'm perfectly fine, there's nothing for you to worry about."

Aspen reluctantly gave in and said to call her back soon.

Moon hung up the phone. *Yes I'll call you back but I have much more to think deal with than your husband's conspiracy theories.*

Moon left the office and did her usual after-work errands, boot camp, grocery shopping, and home. She had no idea that a tracking device was giving away her every move.

Moon arrived home, changed into comfortable clothes as she usually did and started dinner. She walked out to get her mail and instinctively glanced down the street and saw no strange cars. She wondered when she would stop looking.

Next morning at the office, Moon called her sister because she had some time and she knew Aspen would pester her if she didn't.

Aspen immediately started in on one of her long-drawn out stories, this one about cyber attacks from China and Iran. Moon generally tuned her out and let her ramble on until Aspen did pique Moon's attention.

"Sam's been working on some Homeland Security issues that came through Hawaii but this time he saw security breaches that were coming from inside the agency and he saw an internal email about a terrorist and a Hollywood connection!" Aspen seemed more excited about telling the news than showing concern for her sister. "Sam just wanted to know if you had heard of Arabs trying to get into Hollywood? He saw files on terrorist activity in Hawaii the same time you were there."

"Come on, Aspen, that's nothing new," Moon said. "People all over the world are interested in the movie and broadcasting business."

"Yeah, well Sam is looking at those internal security breaks. He said it could be like a rogue agent," Aspen replied.

Moon did find herself getting a little curious. "Has Sam told anyone about this?"

"No," Aspen replied. "He wasn't supposed to be looking where he was looking, but you know Sam, always the curious one."

"That's what killed the cat you know," Moon laughed.

"Well, there's probably nothing to it," Aspen said. We were just concerned about you."

Moon did appreciate that her sister was always thinking of her. When they were kids, she looked out for her baby sister but now that Aspen has a husband and kids, their roles seemed to have reversed.

Moon hung up the phone and wondered if there could be anything to this. *Could someone in Homeland Security be interested in Moe and they found out I was working with him? Everything started right when he contacted me.*

Moon was trying to remember when she first saw Richard down the street and when she first spoke to Moe. *This seems preposterous! I know Moe is genuinely interested in filmmaking. He already owns a theater company. But I think he was more worried than he let on about what happened in Hawaii.*

Moon's thoughts were disrupted by a buzz from Jennifer, "Hey Moonbeam, Frank on line one."

Moon hit the speaker button, "Frank! I was starting to think no news was good news. Are you calling to ruin my day?"

"Maybe a little," Frank confessed. "It's been tough to dig up but it seems you've been under surveillance by Homeland Security."

Moon wasn't surprised after all she's been through but still, the news was difficult to hear in so many words. Moon went into detail about what happened in Hawaii and even told him about Sam's discoveries.

"And that's not all," Moon continued. "I think somebody broke into my house while I was away. Nothing was taken so it would make sense they just wanted to look around. Although I have no idea for what!"

Frank tried to be reassuring, "I know it's gotta sound pretty fucked up somebody's been watching you but I really don't think they're going to be trying to hurt you."

"I could believe that," Moon said. "Especially since the Sheikh was so concerned about his own family. If I'm in danger from anyone it might be from one of his relatives."

"Yeah I think the real problem is with this Waseem fella and you just happened to get mixed up in it. I haven't turned anything up yet but I could keep lookin' into him," Frank said.

"Yeah, do that. See if you can find out if the Sheikh was ever connected to a violent crime," Moon said.

"Like if he ever had a girlfriend who turned up dead?" Frank asked.

"Damn it, Frank!" Moon said, raising her voice. "How is it you can make me feel safe and scare the crap out of me at the same time?"

"Aw hell, sweetie, I'm sorry!" Frank apologized. "But I'll get back to you with whatever I find, right quick. In the meantime, try not to worry about it too much. Who knows how many people the government does this to anymore and the dumbshits never even know. You just happen to be smart enough to figger' it out."

Moon spent the rest of her day wishing she could be as blissfully ignorant as those other dumbshits but they probably weren't the attorney for a Middle Eastern billionaire with crazy relatives.

It had been a week since Richard had attached the GPS to Moon's car and there were no new discoveries. She went to her office, her gym, and the same stores in her neighborhood. He thought it was funny she seemed to be on Franklin Avenue a lot. She was home most evenings but spent her Friday nights at the same Mexican restaurant. Definitely far from the Hollywood partying type. She went to the beach one weekend and to an address Richard determined was her parents' home. Nothing sinister in her travels or in what she was doing. During the week she would go to studios and the courthouse. His perverse side did miss peeking in the windows but that wasn't right and he knew it. He smiled to himself and thought this was safer and more thorough. He also knew it would build enough evidence to end the surveillance. He could move on to more interesting, but likely not better-looking, individuals.

Richard submitted a report to Cole with his evaluation, not that his opinion would matter. Cole didn't even respond. He seemed to have become involved in another project. Richard didn't care, he was paid for his time and this was easy money. He would just keep on this subject until told to stop.

Richard thought he could find a lot more of nothing if he checked on Moon's cell phone calls. He got the Geeks to send him a DVD with recent call transcriptions and audio. *This woman's on the phone a lot.* Richard looked over the list of calls and realized it would be a ton of work to go through it all and probably find nothing. But that was actually what he hoped to prove. He figured he could scan the transcriptions and look for anything that seemed like a red flag. Besides, some of the computer-generated transcriptions were pretty funny but Richard was still able to tell what the call had been about.

As Richard slogged through the calls, he found they were the usual attorney-client business conversations. Personal calls were the typical stuff. He thought it was nice Ms. Franklin talked to her parents a lot. And this Mohammed Waseem? He wanted to buy a movie production company and as far as Richard could see, there was nothing illegal about that. He spent the rest of the day reading call transcripts and listening to a few when it suddenly hit him that this hot woman did not have a man in her life.

chapter twelve

Cole

Cole had a crappy childhood and a failed marriage in his past but a lot of people have those issues too and they don't turn out like he did. He's entirely self-serving. He has a lust for power and a desire to put people in their place. Well, the places he thinks they should be.

One thing about Cole, though, he is very intelligent which makes him good at analysis. This is why he was so good at the CIA. When he worked there, Cole got to work alone a lot and this was when he was at his best. It got him a promotion but then he had to work with others. It seemed to work out because his subordinates all had to do what he wanted. He found he could micro-manage them as if they were parts of himself. He didn't notice or care if his staff was happy.

Cole had a bigger staff and more responsibility when he took the job as a division director with Homeland Security. He did well with this. His supervisors were in Washington so they had very little contact with him and he got the results they wanted so they left him alone. This was a fine situation for Cole. He is happy with the arrangement, though he really wanted to run the entire agency.

Cole is certain he is much smarter and more capable than anyone who's headed up the agency and he's definitely a better choice than any woman. He was determined to get attention from the higher-ups or even the President himself. Cole thought that if he could get the President's attention then he could eventually be appointed to his Cabinet.

He was very interested in what this Ms. Franklin and the Sheikh Waseem were doing and he knew it was going to be big. Cole believed that this Muslim Arab was going to use Hollywood to spread his hatred for America with Americans doing it for him.

Cole never really trusted these Hollywood types anyway. They were always making movies that subverted American values so it fit Cole's thinking that the stinking Arabs would use the cinema to ruin his country. He also thought making movies was a front for bringing more extremists into the United States so they could plan terrorist activity.

Cole just knew that he was going to find something big and he was determined to prove it one way or another. The trouble was the incompetents he had working for him could not find anything useful. He would make them dig until they found what he wanted.

Cole was sure capturing a major terrorist like this would mean a big promotion and a move back to Washington. He didn't like having to move to the west coast. He didn't like the weather, the beach, or the pretentious Beverly Hills and Hollywood types. He didn't like that all the regular people were into wheatgrass, yoga, running, and meditation. There was nothing he liked about the California lifestyle. So Cole was determined to pin this on those Hollywood people with whatever he could, this Moonbaby Franklin and her Arab lover. Of course, he didn't tell anyone his agenda or personal feelings on the subject. He kept quiet about all that as he usually did. Cole was the type of person who sat back and let others do the talking while he listened and looked for a weakness without revealing much about himself, his thinking, or his plans.

While Cole had Richard and the Geeks focusing on the Franklin case, he had other work to do. He had a meeting in Phoenix of the Directors, Executive Directors, and Under Secretaries. He was looking forward to the meeting so he could make himself known in person to key personnel and he could start laying the groundwork for his next great conquest. He wanted his name to be familiar to a lot of people so when he brought a bunch of terrorists to justice including a prominent American, they would recognize his importance to the agency.

There would be so many people at this meeting that Cole was concerned he would not get close to the right people. He was high ranking in his office but there would be many officials from FEMA, the Coast Guard, Immigration, Customs, even the Secret Service. It was going to be hard for Cole to get through all that interference. The highest-ranking person scheduled to give a presentation was the Chief of Staff and Cole wanted to be sure that the Chief knew exactly who he was.

Cole arrived in Phoenix and settled in to his hotel room before the initial meeting. He had to deal with the incompetents back at the office first. It seemed like they could not get up in the morning without his approval. Trouble was he caused this himself. His people had become so used to his micro-managing and his heavy hand that they were afraid to make decisions. He would never figure this out because he could never see a flaw in himself.

Cole made sure to position himself near the front at the first meeting. The man sitting next to him introduced himself as the Associate Deputy Under Secretary for Intergovernmental Affairs. Cole responded as he usually does, polite but indifferent. He didn't want the guy to bother him. *Loser! I'm not here to waste time with anybody in some useless office.* The man just smiled and looked back to the speaker's podium. Cole was thinking it will be better when they break out in the individual meetings for the different offices. *Then I will get a better chance to get noticed.*

Cole had no interest in socializing but after the meeting, he heard a few people were going to the hotel bar. It was quite nice and in the center of the hotel under a large atrium. He decided to go hang around to see who might be the highest-ranking person there and get an introduction.

It turned out all the people in the bar were low-level minions who never got out of town. It was obvious they didn't know what to do with an expense account so they all decided to get drunk on the agency's dime. Cole was disgusted with this behavior and decided to go back to his room. After all, he wasn't there to find new friends, especially people who were going nowhere and couldn't do anything for him.

Cole spent the first day bored with presentations about budgets and protocol. He could not get a front row seat at any of the presentations as they were reserved for particular people. This made him grumble about all the self-important people and instead he got a second row seat in the middle. This was not going the way he envisioned.

When the Chief of Staff stepped up to the podium, Cole wasn't interested in his presentation. He just wanted to make sure they made eye contact. He was excited by an announcement that the Chief would hold a meeting with all division Directors. This would be a great opportunity because his boss hadn't bothered to come. Cole would be able to speak for his office. He would be sure to highlight what he was doing personally and how his work was critical to the entire agency.

Cole made sure to show up at the meeting early in the hopes he could choose the best seat. He could hardly contain himself as he waited for it to start. He was sure after he got to speak directly with the Chief, he'd secure his next move up. The Chief was late but Cole tried not to mind so he could keep a positive attitude. After about ten minutes, a man Cole didn't recognize came in and introduced himself as some assistant; Cole wasn't even sure what the guy's position was. He apologized that the Chief was called away at the last minute and he would be conducting the meeting. Cole was so infuriated, he was afraid his anger would show. When it was Cole's time to speak, the no-name guy didn't notice anything and went on with the interview as if there was nothing wrong.

Cole didn't say what he had planned on saying to the Chief. He did say they were monitoring a situation that might involve Hollywood. The guy seemed somewhat interested but mentioned that there was significant support for the current administration among many of the highest profile people in Hollywood. Cole wasn't even sure what that was supposed to mean. He just hoped this low-level loser would report what Cole said to the Chief.

Cole left the meeting feeling dejected and pissed off at the same time. He felt like he'd been personally snubbed. He fumed. He vowed to make even the Secretary himself see how important he was and how this terrorist connection to Hollywood had implications for the entire nation. Then even the President would notice and appreciate him for his service.

When Cole got back to the office, he called a meeting of all his department heads and field personnel. Richard hated the meetings Cole would call after he had been away from the office as he always came back with some new bullshit guidelines and rules.

Cole wanted progress reports on all on-going cases. Richard had to talk about his findings in the Franklin case. He had to admit that there was nothing new and the subject was demonstrating the behavior of a person going about their normal, lawful routines.

Cole snapped at Richard, scolding him for reporting with an opinion. Richard insisted it was analysis and not opinion. Cole did not appreciate being corrected in front his subordinates and informed Richard he had better find something soon.

Cole told Michelangelo that he wanted all the Geeks on Ms. Elizabeth Franklin and the Sheikh Mohammed Abdallah Waseem. Cole told the group he wanted to know when the subjects took a shit, that's how detailed he wanted the intelligence to be. Richard just sat back and thought

Cole had lost his mind. He was ignoring all the evidence that they had.

Meeting adjourned and Cole asked Richard to stay. *Shit, it's never good when this maniac wants you in a room alone.* Richard didn't bother to sit closer to Cole, he just stayed in his seat.

Cole paced around the room, "Washington, do I need to put someone else on this case?"

Richard just shrugged, "No, I'm fine with it. I just don't see the situation the same as you."

"Alright then, you stay on it and you'll see I'm right as long as you haven't gotten personal about it," Cole warned.

Richard looked puzzled. "How could I get personal with it if I've never talked to the subject?"

Cole got directly in Richard's face. "I'm watching you, Washington, just remember that. Any more screw ups or I think you're sabotaging the investigation and you'll wish you never met me."

Richard stared at him. *I already do.*

Cole sent Richard a report from the CIA and a small FBI investigation from a number of years ago that had been conducted on the Sheikh and the Waseem family. He thought this might motivate Richard to come over to his way of thinking. Cole actually thought Richard was his best investigator and he'd find what Cole wanted if he'd do as he was told.

Richard left the meeting feeling drained. He didn't so much feel anger or fear for losing his job, just drained. This has been the pattern ever since Cole became his boss. At first, he felt fear and anger about the way Cole would treat him and others but as time went by he became apathetic. He just walked out of the office and went on with his job like a robot.

Moon hadn't gotten to see Moe in person again. She had briefly spoken to him on a few occasions but mostly she spoke to an assistant named Karif. Moe seemed to be in London a lot from what she could tell, busy with the theater company. The truth was she longed to see him and this was a little disconcerting as she should not feel this way about a client. She was not one to personally involve herself with people she worked with. She'd see clients occasionally at art openings or movie premieres but that was likely to happen, working in the entertainment business.

A couple of months passed and Moon was starting to forget about the trip to Hawaii and all the personal anxiety it had brought with it. As her business relationship continued with Moe, she became more neutral in her personal feelings and lost the distress she'd experienced over the trip.

Moon wondered if Moe had trouble with all his U.S. business dealings now. She imagined it could be like being German in the years following World War II. Germans who had not been Nazi sympathizers probably went through what the innocent people of Islam are going through now. She was convinced that Moe was just as he appeared to be, a business-person who loved the arts and maybe had some trouble with crazy family members. Who doesn't have a crazy uncle somewhere? The thought made Moon chuckle.

Richard also went on with his job, working more closely with the Geeks. He did not see the need to personally follow Ms. Franklin any-more and he hadn't been very good at hiding from her anyway. He did not want a repeat of the time she confronted him.

Richard was put on some other cases that kept him busy so for the Franklin case mostly he just reviewed the information that was still be-ing downloaded weekly by the tracking bug on her car. He never did see anything that could convince him that she was a danger to society.

Cole went on badgering the staff about the Franklin case even though they presented him with extensive data that showed nothing. They stopped giving him their personal assessments and let him draw his own conclusions. He was going to do that anyway.

chapter thirteen

Are They Ever Going to Meet Again?

It was Monday and Moon was looking forward to going to work as she always did. She thought back to that first call from Moe. It had been months ago and now the closing on the production company was coming up and Moe would have to come to LA.

Jennifer buzzed Moon for a call, "Oh Moonglow! The prize patrol's looking for you. Line three."

Moon crinkled up her face, "What? Who is it and why would you say that?" Moon heard Jennifer giggling over the intercom. She punched the flashing red light.

It had been awhile since she'd heard that smooth British accent. "Good morning Ms. Moon," The sound of Moe's voice could still make Moon melt. She gathered her composure and focused on business.

"Good morning! I was just speaking to the seller's attorney yesterday. I'm waiting on some final papers and then we can schedule the closing."

"Excellent, things are moving right along," Moe said.

"You are going to have to come here you know!" Moon reminded him.

Moe chuckled a bit, "Yes I understand, do you think I've been avoiding you?"

Moon played it cool, "I don't know, are you? Or are you avoiding something else?"

"Where are you going with this Moon?" Moe replied, a bit annoyed.

Moon decided to let it all out, "Our initial meeting was very interesting but then the Hawaii visit turned into quite, um, well let's say it was an adventure. And there were some unusual incidents here at home that were rather distressing and frankly it all seemed to start happening when I started doing business with you."

"You must believe me when I say I was profoundly sorry for what happened in Hawaii. I was only being cautious, to protect you from anything that might have happened. But please tell me, what sort of incidents did you experience there in Los Angeles?" Moe asked.

"Well, I had reason to believe someone was following me for awhile. Someone from the government. I believe my home was broken into but not to rob me. I think someone wanted to look around, search my home." Moon said. "And it all started literally the first day I talked to you!"

Moe let out a deep sigh, "I can only apologize again. I mentioned to you have I have some troublesome family members. I have a cousin who has become something of a radical. His activities and those of his fanatical associates have plagued me. My cousin does not believe I should have anything to do with American business or frankly anything that has to do with the West. He has been quite the problem for me and he has caused a target to be painted on the backs of my entire family. I have had to endure interrogations by England's MI6 and Interpol but I was cleared completely. They determined that my cousin and his associates have nothing to do with me."

"I'm sorry you've had to deal with all that but I do not appreciate having to be a victim of the fallout," Moon replied.

"I agree with you completely," Moe said. "My problems should not have to affect anyone else. Unfortunately it has become a fact of life today that people from the Middle East may be viewed with suspicion and radicals like my cousin make it justifiable. I've had to accept it as part of doing business internationally."

"Tell me honestly. Are there going to be any surprises when you're here for the closing?" Moon asked.

"My cousin has remained in Qatar for the last few months now and things have been quiet," Moe said. "But there is one precaution I can take. I have not been interviewed recently by the U.S. government and frankly that has been my fault, I have avoided doing it."

Moon was relieved there was something Moe could do to avoid possible issues. She urged him to get the interview out of the way before the property was due to close. He assured her he'd schedule it right away.

Moon hung up the phone and stared blankly out the window. She realized she was more concerned, not for the business deal, but for Moe and their non-relationship relationship. She tried to convince herself she was being silly and she should be more of an adult.

Moon decided that since she did not have a lunch appointment, she would go to the gym and work off the stress. She was hitting the spin bike hard when she noticed a tall man come into the gym and stand at the front for awhile before walking to the locker room. *I know that guy. Miramax party? No. Covenant House Gala? He does kinda look like Denzel.* It was going to bug her until she could remember.

Moon got Danny to spot her on the bench press. The tall man was doing squats on the Smith Machine.

"Hey Danny, do you know that guy doing squats?" Moon asked as she set the barbell back into the stand.

"Some new guy." Danny said. "Rick something. Why, you want to meet him?"

"No, he just looked familiar is all. Hey throw another ten pounds on the bar. I think I can lift it," Moon said.

Moon gave the barbell an explosive push when she suddenly lost hold of it. Danny quickly grabbed it and got it back into the stand. Moon seemed flustered and was breathing heavily.

Danny tried to calm her down, "Hey I think we got a little ambitious there, are you okay?"

"Yeah, yeah I'm fine. You're right, it's a little heavy for me, sorry." Moon looked across the gym and tried to catch her breath. *Stalker Guy!*

Moon felt more angry than scared. She was not going to let this go on any longer. She went back to the locker room. She was seething. *This means war.* She never abused the powerful connections she'd made through the years but it was time to call in some favors.

Moon called Jennifer and told her she'd be out for the afternoon. She felt like she had to do something right away. She went over to the DA's office to see Stan Davis.

"Moon! My day just got better!" Stan got up from his desk.

"I'm sorry to just drop in, I know it's been a long time," Moon knew Stan would do anything for her and she didn't want to take advantage of him but this was too important.

"It's okay, it's always okay! What's going on?" Stan asked.

"I need your expertise with an area of law that's way out of my specialty." Moon decided to choose her words carefully. "I have this client from the Middle East. Corporate executive. Oil money, of course. Muslim, of course. What do you know about government surveillance?"

Stan looked concerned. "Wow, that's a gray area," he said. "The U.S. Foreign Intelligence Surveillance Court operates in secret so it's rather controversial. Have you been ordered to turn over files on this client?"

"No, nothing like that," Moon said. "I think it's a matter of actually following a subject. Monitoring their whereabouts."

"I don't know if it's procedure for your area of business to screen a client for a watchlist. There's almost a million people on one of those lists now. There's one database that the profile criteria are so minimal I think they'd put your client on it if they thought he ate baba ghanoush too often."

Moon's lip started to tremble, "No, he's not on a watchlist. But that's not it."

Stan got up from his desk and moved a chair next to Moon. He squeezed her shoulder. "Moon, what is it? You can tell me. What's wrong?"

"It's me, Stan. This is about me. I think I've been under surveillance by Homeland Security!" Moon poured it all out in detail. She told him about the man lurking on her street who turned up in her gym, the strange device in the parking garage, the man who threatened her in the parking lot, and the break in. "I've had a PI looking into it and it appears to be related to this client. We had a meeting in Hawaii that turned into this bizarre ordeal. He admitted to me that he has a cousin who may have become radicalized but he's got nothing to do with that side of his family, Stan! He's a businessman, an oil company executive! Hell, he runs a theater company for chrissakes and all I've done is arrange a studio acquisition for him! I just don't get this! I don't get what's going on!"

Stan leaned back in the chair. "If I had not heard it coming from your mouth I would think this was the ranting of some delusional conspiracy nut."

"I'm not sure I'd believe me either," Moon sighed.

Stan looked deep in thought. "There were charges of illegal surveillance of U.S. citizens conducted by the previous administration and the use of erroneous information for illegal search warrants and wiretaps."

"I would never have thought just doing a fairly routine acquisition deal for a Middle Eastern client could put me on the government's radar like I'm...dangerous or something!" Moon was still trying not to cry. "Can you look into this for me?" she asked. "Whatever you might be able to find. I swear Stan, I thought it was over and I was even starting to feel like maybe I'd dreamt it but when I saw that man at the gym today I just about lost it!"

"You know I would do whatever I could for you," Stan said as he took Moon's hand. "Please don't cry about it. I'll look into it."

"I'm sorry to involve you in this but I just didn't know where to turn. You're the only person I know who might be able to get any real answers," Moon said, sniffling.

"I want to help if I can. You know how important you have always been to me," Stan said.

Moon pulled herself together and wrote Stan out some notes before she left. For the rest of the day, he couldn't focus on any of his other work.

Stan sat back in his chair and swiveled around to look out over the city. *What the hell is going on here? How could a government agency target somebody like Moon for terrorism?*

Moon knew calling on Stan to help could be a double-edged sword. She wouldn't want to find out that Moe had been part of some terrorist cell all along. The very thought seemed ridiculous but so did the idea that he could have a cousin who chose to be a radical fundamentalist when he could have lead the life of an oil heir.

Moon called Frank to tell him about Stan and the return of Stalker Guy.

"You sure you want to involve the DA?" Frank asked.

"I'm not really involving the DA, I asked a friend for help. I've known Stan since law school. He's good people. If he can help me, he will."

"Well I don't know what your buddy is gonna turn up that I couldn't," Frank seemed a little annoyed.

"I'm not criticizing you or your capability. I just think this is so covert that we can't punch through it with normal channels," Moon said.

"Awright," Frank said. "You know I just want to see this thing get straightened out and you back to your usual happy self."

Moon noticed a blank envelope in a delivery of documents from the courier service. It contained a handwritten letter that looked like it had been faxed.

My Dear Moon,

I am forced to send this by courier. I believe our phones are tapped, probably by Homeland Security. I believe your firm's phones are also tapped. I am forced to apologize again. I am the cause of these problems.

I would ask you to terminate the acquisition but that would be almost impossible at this point and I want this to work. It has become even more important to me because my family wants to stop me. I believe it will help all our causes for me to make films in America. I know I can change hearts and minds for the better.

I think it would be best for you to distance yourself from me. I am asking you to arrange for another lawyer to complete the work. I trust you to find representation for me that will be adequate and of course you will be well compensated.

On a personal note, I find you a very attractive woman. You are fascinating and brilliant and I was captivated by you when we met. I hope I am not being too forward in making this personal admission. I regret that we cannot pursue what might have been.

It is very difficult for me to say that I know you will be better off if we terminate our business relationship. I have scheduled a meeting with the State Department in two weeks so I hope that might improve things for me for the immediate future but I worry this may never end.

With deepest regrets,

Sincerely, Moe

At first Moon wanted to burst into sobs but she started to shake and a wave of anger came over her. *First of all buddy, you're not getting rid of me and second, whoever is interfering with my life is going to be sorry.*

Moon went out to Jennifer's desk, "I need your phone for a minute." She grabbed it and dodged back into her office.

Jennifer found herself talking to a slammed door, "That's not me in those naked pictures!"

Moon got Stan on the phone. "I just got some weird letter that appears to be from my client. It came by courier in a blank envelope. It looks handwritten but I don't know if it's his handwriting. He says our phones are tapped and he wants me to turn his business over to another lawyer."

"Wow. Well, first of all, find a bag or something and put the letter and the envelope in it. Don't fold it or anything. Who's the courier?" Stan asked.

"A1 Courier. We get deliveries from them every day," Moon said.

"Okay, get the letter over to me," Stan instructed. "Your phones. Just the typical business conversations these days? No unusual business or clients? Well, besides yours."

"No, just more of the usual. Jennifer Aniston wants eight million for her next picture. Do you care?" Moon said.

"Can't say that I do," Stan replied. "Hey wait, what phone are you on right now?"

"My secretary's cell," Moon replied.

"Okay, good," Stan said. "Just conduct business as usual, I know that's gonna feel weird but maybe it's a good thing if your calls are being monitored because whoever's listening is going to end up with a huge steaming pile of absolutely nothing."

Moon thanked him and hung up the phone. Jennifer peeked into her office. "Are you still reading all my sexting?" she asked.

"Yeah, you're a total perv," Moon said as she handed Jennifer back her phone. "Hey did we get any other deliveries today besides A1?"

"Nope, just Cameron and his hot legs. He shaves 'em. I kinda like it," Jennifer said.

"I said you were a perv," Moon teased.

Moon found a plastic bag for the letter and envelope. She realized she suddenly felt like she was handling evidence and she picked them up by her fingernails. She decided she would write Moe a response and send it to the office address they've been using for all the legal correspondence. *He has not heard the last of me, not by a long shot.*

The next few days Moon tried to carry on like everything was normal. She had this great weight hanging over her head and she could do no more about it then wait. Wait for others to help her. She was not used to waiting for anyone much less for help. She was used to waiting for reports and for court dates but this was different. This was her life.

Stan called and said they should talk. Moon was nervous because this could be all bad news but also there could be new information that might finally end it. She told Jennifer to hold down the fort and left the office for the day.

Stan's secretary was not at her desk when Moon arrived. "I gave her the afternoon off," Stan said as he closed his office door.

"So," Moon said. "Have I been aiding and abetting an enemy of the state?"

"Do you think you know everything about this Sheikh Waseem?"

"I know he runs a division of a multi-billion dollar oil concern and sits on the board," Moon replied. "I know he personally has operated a theater in London for over a decade. He contacted me to buy a studio and he can afford it. The man wants to make movies."

"Do you know much about his personal or religious life?" Stan asked.

"Well, no, not really. We had a rather personal conversation when we met in Hawaii and he talked about finding certain traditions to be oppressive but he was sent to school in the U.S. and England," Moon said.

"Personal conversation?" Stan's voice had an accusatory tone. "Did he talk about Islam?"

Moon was taken aback by the focus on religion, "We talked a little about religion, mostly about how we'd both drifted away from it. I said I wasn't very good at going to church anymore. He said he was about the same though he did say he'd explored Christianity but his family would not be happy about that so he just kept things the way they were to keep the peace."

Stan paused, thinking about what Moon had just said. "So you don't believe that he is a practicing Muslim?"

Moon started to get a little frustrated with Stan, "Look, I can clear this up. I watched him drink alcohol and I think maybe I saw bacon at his house. Oh and no long nasty beard. Are you happy?"

Stan acquiesced, "Yes, yes, fine! He's not very Muslim. We know that. And what else we know. We really can't be sure but as far as I can tell neither your name nor Mr. Waseem appear anywhere in any filings in the Foreign Intelligence Surveillance Court, at least not in the last several months."

"So there have been no court orders to gather records on me or Mr. Waseem and no surveillance ordered for either of us?" Moon asked.

"That's the way it would look but keep in mind it's not impossible that unauthorized surveillance was carried out," Stan said.

"You're right, that's not necessarily conclusive," Moon observed.

"Well there is one thing. A name did turn up in our research. A Kadyn Waseem of Doha, Qatar, great grandson of Sheikh Mohammed Waseem Sayyid, founder of Waseem Petroleum, and the first cousin of your client." Stan took out a photo of a swarthy Arab man who looked like so many others with a rough expression and long beard. "This guy has been a bad boy. He's suspected in a number of possible terrorist plots including the financing of a terrorist cell that had compiled a so-called assassination list of politicians who were instrumental in passing the burqa ban in France."

"So this Kadyn has been a person of interest?" Moon asked.

"Absolutely," Stan replied. "With his access to financial resources, he'll be near the top of the FBI's watchlist."

"He's got to be the family member that the Sheikh told me about." Moon sighed heavily. "Does this mean that contact with the Sheikh would be sufficient for me to be investigated?"

Stan took a deep breath. "Well. Hang on. I'm just about to blow your mind. Kadyn Waseem? He was in school with us."

"WHAT?!" Moon leapt from the chair and practically threw herself across Stan's desk. "I don't remember any Kadyn Waseem! Do you remember this guy?" Moon fell back into the chair.

"No, I don't remember him at all!" Stan said. "I remember there was a study group of Arab guys but I didn't know any of them and they all had names like Crown Prince Mohammed Ali bin Waddy Aladdin or something."

"Yeah I think I remember them vaguely. Corvettes and porn moustaches," Moon recalled. "We didn't really notice Arabs back then."

"Here's what I think and don't be scared," Stan said. "Your name comes up alongside the Waseem name and somebody discovers the direct connection you have to this Kadyn. Of all the lawyers his cousin could work with in LA, he goes to you? Boom! You're a bad lady."

Moon started to laugh. "You know what? This is like a great relief to find this out!" She smacked the arms of the chair and leaned it way back. "Seriously, I am feeling a strange sense of relief!"

"Okay then maybe you're ready for the rest of what I have to tell you," Stan warned.

"Please don't tell me you saved the worst for last though I think I'm a little numb right now," Moon sighed.

"My hacker, well let's just call him my investigator, found that you were pretty thoroughly researched. You didn't know it was happening, thank god, but you got the electronic equivalent of a strip search and an anal probe," Stan said.

"They wouldn't find anything illegal!" Moon insisted.

"You're right! They certainly didn't!" Stan replied. "But the nature of the search without cause and without a warrant was definitely illegal."

Moon was slumped in the chair. She felt drained.

"There's one other oddball thing," Stan said.

Moon closed her eyes. "Please, no, make it stop."

"Have you been setting the burglar alarm in your house for the last few months?" Stan asked.

Moon furrowed her brow, "Yeah?"

"The security company thinks you haven't been. I'd have that looked into," Stan advised.

Moon stared at the floor. "So what can I do?"

"I hate to say I think the Sheikh gave you some pretty good advice himself," Stan said. "Hurry up and get your business concluded with him and cut off all contact. I know it's a lot of money to walk away from and Bamberger will want to give you up for adoption but I don't see any other way. And don't even think about trying to file any charges for illegal search or surveillance. I don't think Edward Snowden needs a roommate, you know what I'm sayin'?"

Moon sat back up straight, "I don't want to cut off the client. The closing is soon, we're just waiting for some paperwork from the sellers..."

"Damn it, Moon!" Stan nearly yelled. "What the fuck does it matter at this point? You've got two choices, keep trying to help this billionaire play movie star or get your life back. Pick one!"

Stan slumped forward on the desk. "I'm sorry. I'm sorry. I just... You know I care about you...I just think this is in your best interest."

"I better go," Moon said quietly. They both stood up slowly. She didn't want to look Stan in the face. "I can't tell you how much I appreciate how much you've done and I know you care, Stan. I appreciate that, too."

Moon drove home feeling like she'd been beaten up. The only thing she could think of for the moment was that she wanted her Daddy. A girl is never too old to want her Dad's strong arms to hold her tight and for him to tell her he would never let anyone hurt her.

Moon called her parents and her mother picked up, "Hey, Mom."

"Yes dear, what's the trouble?" Anita said.

"Good grief, Mom. How do you do that?" Moon asked.

"A mother knows. What's going on, honey?"

"I just need someone to talk to, no that's wrong," Moon said.

"I need you and Dad to talk to."

"Oh, now you have me worried," Anita said.

"I just want to come over. How about I pick up some dinner?"

"You don't need to bring anything to come over anytime," her mother said. "You know us old people, we don't get out much so come over whenever."

Moon swung by Franco on Melrose for a pan of lasagna and the bruschetta her Dad loved. The stress of the day was weighing on her as she drove to her parents' house. As soon as Charles opened the door, Moon felt immediately cheered up and maybe also a little weepy.

"What's the matter my little Moon?" Charles said as he wrapped his daughter up in his arms.

"I just want to be here with you and Mom," Moon said as she buried her face in her father's neck.

"Come in, honey, come sit down," Moon's mom took her by the arm and the three of them walked into the kitchen. Moon climbed up on a tall stool as Anita unpacked the dinner and laid out utensils. As delicious as it all smelled, Moon didn't have much of an appetite and felt more like just having a glass of wine or three.

"Is there a new man in your life? He didn't break your heart already, did he?" Charles asked as he took a big bite of crispy bruschetta.

"No, Dad, nothing like that. Actually I wish it was something that simple," Moon said.

Moon started from the beginning and told them everything. She didn't leave out a detail, not even how she had been attracted to Moe when they met in Hawaii. These were her parents, after all, and she knew they'd see her through anything.

"Honey, maybe you should stay with us for awhile," Anita said. "We put some of your old bedroom furniture in the guest room. It would feel familiar and safe."

"Stay as long as you want," Charles said. "Could you telecommute for awhile? I could drive downtown and pick up paperwork at your office any time."

Moon's eyes filled with tears again. "You're the best, I love you both so much!"

"Well I've got a bone to pick with you, young lady!" Charles teased. "You didn't bring any dessert!"

"Oh I'm sorry, Dad. I should have ordered some cannoli," Moon said.

"But wait! What's this?" Charles opened the freezer door and made a flourish of producing a pint container. "Gelato!" They all ended up eating right out of the container.

"Why don't I come home with you and help you pack a few things," Charles said.

"No, I'll be okay. I feel so much better already being here with you," Moon hung on her father's arm. "I'm going to take care of this thing. I honestly don't think I'm in any physical danger and there's nothing they'd ever be able to accuse me of. Nothing!"

"We know that about you, honey," Anita said. "You've always made us so proud."

Anita piled Moon up with leftovers from dinner and a loaf of her famous seven-grain bread. Moon smiled, hugged her mother one more time, and headed out to the car.

Anita always felt a twinge of sadness anytime she watched one of her children go, no matter how old they got. A tear fell down her face and she turned and walked back in the house drying her cheeks.

Moon always looked in the rearview mirror when she left her parents' house. It's funny how she still could feel like a child when she was back at home with Mom and Dad.

Moon pulled the car into the garage and tried to balance the leftovers, the loaf of bread, her attaché case, and a jacket while getting the door open. She heard running feet and a door slam from inside the house. She dropped everything she was holding. Red sauce went splattering across the floor. Moon hit the garage door button and practically sailed underneath the rising door. She realized she'd dropped her attaché and ran next door to her neighbors to call 911.

Moon and her neighbors stood in the street in front of her house. They couldn't see anyone inside. Mike from next door said he looked from his backyard and couldn't see anyone behind her house.

Two LAPD officers arrived and they went into the house. It was an agonizing ten minutes before they came out, "You the owner of the house, ma'am?"

Moon shook her head.

"I'm Officer Malloy, this is Officer Reed. So do I understand you came home and discovered a burglary in progress?"

Moon was a little too dazed to speak and shook her head again.

"Nothing's too messed up, there are some drawers open and it looks like they rummaged around the place. We'd like you to come inside and see if anything's missing. We've called a technician to come take fingerprints off that back door so don't touch it."

Moon went in and looked around. She checked the bedside table for the Glock and it was still there. She knew they must have seen it but for some reason did not take it.

"Do you have a jewelry box or a safe, ma'am? Artwork, other valuables?" Officer Reed asked.

"The safe is still locked and my jewelry box looks untouched. See for yourself, my TAG Hauer watch is still here and my diamond earrings," Moon said as she held the box open. "I don't think they even opened it."

The technician arrived and dusted the backdoor and the handles of various open drawers. He took Moon's prints so they'd know which could be the burglar's.

Officer Reed watched the technician take prints off the alarm keypad housing. "Ma'am, the alarm system. Did you forget to set it before you went out today?"

"Oh no, I set it," Moon insisted.

"But the call came in from you, not the security company, is that right?" Officer Malloy asked.

Moon remembered what Stan had said earlier about the security company claiming she hadn't used the alarm in the last few months. Moon didn't want to get into it. "Um, I think there's been something wrong with it. I'll have the company come out and check."

"You should definitely do that, ma'am," Officer Reed said. "No point in having a system like this if it's not working. This could have been avoided if your alarm had been working correctly."

"Wait a minute," Malloy interjected. "Do you think the person who broke in here might have known it wasn't working?" The cops looked at each other and looked back at her in unison. "Have you had any work done in the house recently, ma'am?"

Moon shook her head.

"I have to ask you this question, ma'am," Officer Malloy said. "A break in with nothing taken? Are you maybe having any kind of boyfriend troubles at the moment? Girlfriend troubles? Uh, anyone treating you in a stalking-like manner?"

Moon gulped. She couldn't say anything. *If only they knew.* "No, no troubles like that," she replied quietly.

"You're sure there's nothing you want to tell us, ma'am? The police can provide protection to you if someone has threatened you or has been treating you in a stalker-like manner," Officer Malloy said.

"I'm okay, really. I'll call the security company tomorrow and get that looked into. I've just been so busy it slipped my mind," Moon said.

Moon had a pretty good idea who had been in her house. She didn't think she needed to leave. She needed a plan. She walked around the house, looking for what might be the best window to climb out of. The guest room had the least amount of shrubbery outside the window so she thought she could climb out and jump down the easiest from there. She opened the window and popped out the screen. She was able to climb out with ease. Once outside she saw some thick brush at the edge of her yard that led to a path up around the neighbors, in between and behind homes, and then out to Marmont Avenue. It was probably how the intruder had gotten away. She decided she would run that route in the morning and see where she could go once she got downhill.

It had gotten very late. Moon took the Glock into the guest room. She curled up in the single bed. She felt safer in a smaller room, in a smaller bed. She looked at the moon through the window and wondered what it might feel like to actually have to climb out and escape from an intruder in her home.

chapter fourteen

Preparation Meets Opportunity

Moon got up the next morning and flung herself out of bed. It was not a long sleep but it had been deep. She could not wait to go run and scope out her escape route.

Moon stared into the mirror. *I'm going to be ready for anything. Those assholes violated my home and privacy and they will pay if they do it again.* She sneered at her reflection.

She opened the guestroom window and climbed out. She got a little scratched up this time but she was up and running out her backyard and down the path.

The path ran up hill for about 150 yards and then leveled off for about 25. It ran down, winding around houses and fences, up and down the hills. Some of the declines were rather steep and she had to be careful not to fall but Moon could handle them. She was able to get to Marmont Avenue which she often ran anyway. She usually did not run toward Sunset Boulevard because of the traffic but she kept going down Marmont.

Moon ran around the grounds of Chateau Marmont which was kind of fun. She stood at the intersection of Sunset and looked around. Tacos. Liquor store. A bank. She walked across the street to check out a martial arts studio in a center behind the bank. That's when she saw it. Self-storage units.

Claire Danes' character on Homeland kept a whole go kit in a storage unit. Moon thought how she could store a backpack with supplies, a change of clothes, even cash. *And a motorcycle?* She rode a scooter when she was younger but that was a long time ago. She could take a riding course, buy a bike, and park it in the storage unit. *Yes, that is what I'll do!*

She ran home happy and feeling free from the paranoia of last night. Moon laughed to herself and thought of how easily she could escape from anyone coming after her. She knew the winding streets of the Hills so well, there were a few ways she could get down to Sunset and lose anyone who tried to tail her.

Moon put her plan into motion that morning. On the way into work, she stopped off at the self-storage units and paid for a year's rent in cash. She used her mother's maiden name; the manager didn't even ask her first name and just called her "Miss." She went by her bank and said her purse had been stolen with her checkbook in it. Her money was moved to new accounts and she got all new credit and debit cards. She felt weird doing it but she withdrew $30,000 in cash to be part of her go kit and to keep all her transactions in cash for awhile. She decided to pretend she was walking around with a wad like a wise guy.

She popped into a dollar store and picked up a few preloaded phones. Later, she called the security company and arranged for a technician to come out. She had her offshore account transferred to a different bank. She signed up for a motorcycle riding class. She'd have to get a motor-cycle license and the Feds would catch that pretty quick but what if they couldn't find the motorcycle? *That should confuse 'em.* She was pulling everything together and doing it quickly. She felt better about her prospects and her home, she wasn't going to let anyone scare her and win.

Richard heard about the bungled break in. He stormed into Cole's office and slammed the door. Cole didn't even look up, "I'm busy."

Richard had to work to keep his temper under control, "Why did you send someone else to search Ms. Franklin's home? I'm still on that case and I have a lot of time and effort invested in it."

Cole taunted Richard, "Oh, 'Ms. Franklin' is it? You don't like knowing someone else went into Ms. Franklin's house? Have you been visiting Ms. Franklin's house, Washington? Did you want to get another look in her panty drawer? Maybe take a souvenir?"

Richard rolled his eyes and huffed in disgust, "You know perfectly well I have been providing steady intel on the sub..."

Cole cut him off. "You're a complete incompetent, Washington. Anybody else would know exactly what the subject is planning with that Arab boyfriend of hers by now."

"Then why haven't you taken me off the case?" Richard demanded.

"Because you need to learn from your fuck ups which are MANY!

Now get out of here and bring me something I can USE." Cole ordered.

Richard walked out of Cole's office, realizing he made a big mistake with that confrontation. Complaining to Cole about anything will always be a no-win and probably make things worse. Still, Richard couldn't figure out what Cole's motives might be. Every detail of the subject's life had been scoured and turned inside out. She's been watched at her home and her office. Her phone calls have all been recorded. Every mile she's driven in her car has been logged for the past few months. She couldn't possibly have been able to keep anything hidden. So why does Cole want such a microscope on her? Richard decided maybe the subject he should be investigating is his boss.

Richard wanted to find out who did the Franklin job. Maybe Cole had given them some specific instructions for what he wanted them to find. Cole had a reason for not letting go of this case and he was determined to find it. He thought he'd start with Marty. He was a seasoned agent like Richard and not easy to rattle. He didn't have the best personality but he would tell you what he thought, whether you wanted to hear it or not.

Marty Post was a big man, strong and tall. He was a good six three and 240 pounds of muscle. He wasn't a body builder type, but he did work out like one and he was very strong. Marty followed the MMA fights and fancied himself a good fighter. This was more for show as Richard never thought Marty ever got into fights but Richard wouldn't want to test him.

Richard went by Marty's desk. "Hey man, what's going on?"

"Nothing. Just sittin' here with my thumb up my ass. What do you want?" Marty spit out his words with an attitude of contempt.

Richard was taken aback, "Whoa. Got something else up your ass besides your thumb?"

"Eh, sorry. Just thinking about what a prick Hargrove is," Marty said.

"He already ruined my day. What did he do to you?" Richard asked.

"Get this. Sends me off on a search I know he's got no warrant for. Claims he does, bullshit. Claims the subject is away from the premises. She's not, bullshit." Marty growls loudly, "Then when the assignment goes south, it's all my fault. BULLSHIT! Fuckin' prick."

"Let me guess," Richard says. "Lady lawyer's house in the Hills?"

Marty grimaces and grunts.

"I hate to tell you, number one," Richard said, "I'm sure Hargrove had no warrant. He sent you out on an illegal search."

Marty grunts again.

"And number two, you're really going to hate this," Richard warns, "Hargrove's got tracking on her car. He knew exactly where she was."

Marty could do nothing but grumble, "Fucking' prick."

"So what did he send you to find?" Richard tried to steer the conversation.

"That's just it, I don't know! Said she'd been conspiring with Muslim fundamentalists for years and was involved in planning terrorist activities. So what the fuck was I lookin' for? Some Muslim fuckin' prayer rug in the living room? A stockpile of C4 in the garage? I don't fuckin' know!" Marty was disgusted. "So what do you know about this case?"

"The subject's had surveillance on her for a few months now, turned up nothing," Richard said. "She's got an Arab client, he's a dead end. He's in theater, movies, wants to be a Hollywood player. He's got some relative who's on a watchlist but those damn people have families so fuckin' big you don't even know who your own goddamn brother of another mother is! Hell, forget about the cousins, every uncle's got ten aunts, whatever."

"So why isn't Hargrove letting go of this fucker?" Marty asked.

"Buddy, when you find that out you let me know! Richard slapped Marty's hand.

Richard walked back to his desk. Post has come to the same conclusion about this case. *Either Hargrove has lost his mind or he's not telling us something he knows.*

He called up the tracking on Ms. Franklin. Her car's parked at her office. *Nothing new.* He could just about follow her and get to where she was going before she did. If this woman is guilty of espionage, she hides it so well catching her will be next to impossible, finding her is simple. She has such a predictable schedule that she has no time for espionage or any other illegal enterprise.

Richard rubs his eyes, sits back in his chair, and ponders the problem. *Okay what do I do next? What if I look to prove she is innocent? Maybe a better tactic, maybe then Hargrove will let it go.*

Richard was quite happy about his new revelation; he had never approached a case in this way before.

Moon was working on a contract to sell some property in Beverly Hills when Frank called to see how she was doing.

"Hey Frank!" Moon said, cheerfully. "I'm about to go into a meeting, can I call you back?"

"Sure! I was just calling to find out..." Frank heard the phone disconnect. "Hello?"

A minute later, Frank's phone rang. It was Moon.

"I'm sorry about that," Moon explained. "There's a wiretap on my phone so I got one of those throwaway cells."

"Aw, hell, so you're still enjoyin' the shenanigans?" Frank asked.

"Just trying to make it through at this point," Moon said.

"I called to see how you're doing. Find out if you seen any of that workout buddy o'yours lately," Frank asked.

"No, but I haven't been going to the gym as much," Moon said. "I thought I might see that guy around downtown but I haven't."

"How do you mean?" Frank asked.

"Well, I don't go to the gym at lunchtime very often but he knew I was there so he must have been following me, right?" Moon asked.

"Not necessarily," Frank observed. "Maybe they got a bug on your car."

"Notice I'm not all that shocked by the suggestion," Moon deadpanned.

"Those things are just small devices, attach 'em with a magnet. Go out to your car and reach around up over the tires. Lemme know if you find something," Frank said.

"And what do I do if I find something?" Moon asked.

"Get the hell rid of it!" Frank yelled.

Moon was eager to run out to her car and look right away. She went to the parking garage and ran her hand up inside the body over the tires just as Frank said to do. She felt something over the rear passenger side. The magnet was so powerful she had to try to reach up with both hands to pry it off. When she pulled it out, the thing was just a small black box with one green light. She tried pressing what looked like a button but the light stayed on.

Moon was walking back to the elevator when an A1 Courier van swung around the corner. She saw the driver pull into the deliveries parking space. She walked around the van and reached up behind the rear wheel to the same spot where the device had been placed on her car. *You want to follow somebody around? Have fun.*

On her way home that afternoon, Moon had an odd realization that no one was watching where she was going anymore. She could drive any weird place she wanted and there'd be no one to wonder why she went there. *I'm going to Disneyland!* For now, she needed to get home in time to meet the technician from the security company.

Jorge arrived with a well-stocked truck and more tools strapped to his body than Moon had ever seen on one person. "You just had a break in, ma'am? I see ya got some fingerprint dust all over this keypad housing," he said as he scrutinized the main keypad by the front door.

"Yes, it was just the other night," Moon replied. "I think the system hasn't been working correctly and I didn't even know it."

"Well here's your problem right here." Jorge had pried the cover off the unit. "See this wire right here? See how it's bent and got like a crimp in it? See the cover's stripped off it and there's that thinner wire that's broke?"

Jorge pointed his Maglite at a tangle of small wires. "Your burglar must have put something with a clamp in there to do that kind of damage to the wires. Must have been something pretty sophisticated. At our end it just looked like you disarmed the system in the normal way and then never turned it back on. But to you it kept beepin' and you didn't know it was off."

"Well I want to upgrade my system. Is there a higher-end model that's tamper resistant?" Moon asked.

"Yes ma'am we can combine a more sophisticated code entry with a tamper-resistant unit housing." Jorge made notes on a clipboard.

"And I want to install cameras everywhere in the house. I want to see every corner of this place," Moon waved her arms toward the open expanse of her living room.

Jorge started walking through the house. "Okay so you want cameras positioned for full property coverage?" He waved his pen toward the living room windows. "Complete perimeter of the yard as well?"

Moon enthusiastically agreed. "Do you install the cameras so you don't really notice that they're there? I think it would be kind of intimidating to my guests, know what I mean?"

"That's routine, ma'am," Jorge replied. "Commercial settings they want the cameras visible but in a residence you want them to be unobtrusive."

"Sounds great," Moon said.

"So how do you want to view the video feeds?" Jorge asked. "We can wire the system to be viewed from a central monitor we install or you can log in from any remote computer, tablet, your phone, whatnot. You want the remote surveillance?"

Moon felt a chill up her spine at the sound of the word 'surveillance.' "I want the best, most high-end super gold platinum king's ransom system you have. Give me everything."

Jorge put down his clipboard. "Uh, ma'am. I know a lot of people can feel a little traumatized after a break in, especially after a home invasion like yours. Now you're getting up into five figures here. You want to take a few days to think about this? Get over the shock a little maybe?"

Moon couldn't help but laugh. "You know what? You're a good man, Jorge! I appreciate it, I really do! But I want the whole package and I can afford it. Sign me up!"

"Yes ma'am!" Jorge went through the whole house, drawing up a floor plan and pointing out to Moon where they'd install the cameras.

"Hey Jorge, can I ask you a question?" Moon leaned toward him and lowered her voice as if someone else was listening. Jorge politely played along.

"When you guys are doing the install, can you sweep the place to look for any kind of...little...thingy..."

"Bugs?" Jorge interrupted. "You think maybe your home's been bugged ma'am? We do provide that service, yes ma'am."

"We actually get called in by the studios to sweep for bugs quite often." Jorge seemed unfazed by Moon's request. "Closed sets, contract negotiations, that kind of thing."

"Add it to the list," Moon said.

Moon felt like she was setting a great big booby trap for anyone who tried to get into her home. Jorge and his crew would have the whole job done by early next week.

The motorcycle riding course was more fun than Moon expected. The people in her group were interesting and cool and she got some phone numbers to get together and ride. The instructor was a Harley man who taught cornering and braking skills with that old school rebel biker attitude. Moon had signed up by phone and the bug was out of her car so she figured no one could know she was at the course. She even paid in cash when she got there. She wanted to feel like she was taking her life back and the thought of riding a motorcycle in the wind was exhilarating. Even the short ride around the track brought back memories of being with her father on trail rides with a Honda 50.

The day Moon got her motorcycle license she couldn't resist wanting to buy her own bike right away. She always loved her car so she decided to research BMW bikes. The 800gs seemed to have everything she thought she'd need. It was off-road capable and it looked totally bad ass!

Moon went to the dealership where she'd bought her car and had it

serviced. She'd never been over to the motorcycle showroom. A salesman immediately hit her with a hard-sell pitch but she shut him down.

"I'm looking for an 800gs. Do you have one in stock? Preferably black
or silver," she asked.

The salesman knew enough to realize he was about to make the easiest sale of the day, "You're in luck! Right over here."

He started to talk about their financing plans but Moon already had
an answer, "I'll pay cash."

The salesman lead Moon over to the black model they had on the
showroom floor. "You could ride it home today if you like. Want to take
it out for a test drive?"

"No, I already know this is the model I want. I'd like to pick it up tomorrow," Moon said.

"Alright then," the salesman clapped his hands together. "Let's go sign
a few papers and you'll be all set!"

Moon left the dealership beaming! She spent the evening shopping
for a helmet and a rugged, roomy backpack. She picked out an organizer
and bought a complete set of items she thought she might need in an
emergency. A few of those pre-loaded cell phones would always come
in handy and it also occurred to her she should buy a pair of shoes that
would be good for wearing every day, all day. There's no telling what she
might have on her feet at the moment she has to make a run for it. She
drove home confident that she was thinking of every possible detail.

Richard got to the office and logged in to check the whereabouts of
Ms. Franklin. *Home, work, gym, home. Anything new today?* The map
seemed to take longer than usual to load.

"WHAT THE?" Richard leaped from his chair, sending it rolling into
the partition behind him.

The map looked like a squiggly cluster of tracks all around the downtown Los Angeles financial district but there were also trips out to Bur-
bank and two trips to LAX. The longest stop was at a Santa Monica
address off Pico Boulevard.

*A1 Courier Service. Aren't you clever? Well you know what? Good for
you, lady. Good for you.*

Richard slumped down in his chair. He couldn't help but feel a little
happy for Ms. Franklin. Still, if Cole didn't get his intel, there'd be hell
to pay. Richard would tell Cole the battery ran out on the device and he
would have to go swap it out.

He went by Ms. Franklin's office but he couldn't find her car in the parking garage. He drove out to the Hills and flew a small drone around her house. All quiet. He'd lost her for today. He would have to check her office again tomorrow.

What he didn't know was Moon was now parking her car in a pay garage across the street.

Moon got a cab ride to the BMW dealership from the storage unit. She'd stocked up the backpack and wore it as she ran to see how heavy it was. She was sure she could carry it for days if she had to but of course she hoped she didn't have to.

The bike was waiting and after signing more paperwork, it was hers.

Moon rode up into the mountains and got lost in her thoughts with the thrill and freedom she was feeling. She had not planned to take off and spend so much time riding but she was having too much fun and it was the most free she'd felt in months.

Moon ended up coming back through Sierra Madre and stopping at the Wistaria to have a beer. It looked to be one of those great little places she loved to find. A sophisticated menu and beautiful décor but with a laid-back, friendly atmosphere. The bartender immediately started chatting her up.

"How long ya been ridin'?" the bartender asked, as she set down a bowl of the restaurant's own freshly-made tortilla chips.

"About two and a half hours," Moon replied. "Oh wait!" She caught herself. "You mean how long have I been riding a motorcycle, not like how long today! Actually two and a half hours! I just got it!"

They both laughed. "My husband and I ride Harleys," the bartender said. "I don't see what the big deal is, seems like there's a lot of good bikes but don't say that to a Harley man!"

Moon took her beer to one of the tables outside. She watched people walking between the little tourists shops that lined the street. She realized she was feeling the most relaxed she'd been in a while. This was the first time in as long as she could remember that she had no plans or anything to rush to. She was amazed that a motorcycle could take so much of the stress out of life that she seemed to feel no worries.

The ride home went fast. She pulled the bike into the storage unit and locked it up thinking it looked lonely in there. She felt a pang of regret leaving it. And even though she'd spent nearly $14,000 on it, she felt really weird knowing she was leaving behind $25,000 in cash in a backpack.

With all the changes she'd made, Moon's life had reached a level of a new normal. She knew the phones at her office and her cell might still be tapped but she never discussed anything but business and she bought a new pre-paid phone every few weeks for any calls she wanted to keep from prying ears. She had gotten in the habit of crawling around on her garage floor every Sunday with a flashlight, looking for anything that might be stuck to the inside body of her car. She was rotating her parking spaces downtown and it was costing her a little money but it was well-spent in her mind and a small expense relative to other things she's paid for in the past few months. She had a small fortune locked up in a storage unit but she tried to think about eventually enjoying the motorcycle for fun. Blowing the $25,000 emergency stash on a luxury vacation would be a nice way to purge any lingering bad memories. It wouldn't be much longer that the studio deal would finally close and maybe this chapter of her life would be closed as well.

The day of Moe's interview with the State Department was coming up and the studio closing was next week so Moon was surprised she hadn't heard from him. But the bigger surprise was the day Moe's office left a message with a new number for his attorney: A direct line to reach Sheikh Waseem as the need may arise.

Moon could hardly believe it. *It's about damn time!* She did not hesitate to call the number and the voice was her friend Moe. Her heart sank a moment and she stammered to say hello.

"Are you alright, young lady?" Moe asked.

"Yes!" Moon laughed a bit. "I'm just relieved to hear from you. When I don't hear from you I worry you may be dealing with some difficulty."

"I am alright, I assure you I am simply very busy," Moe replied.

"Why would you wait to give me the interview details that you know I can't get to in time?" Moon asked.

"I said you are to distance yourself from me," Moe said. "Besides it looks as if it will be routine."

"I'm very insulted," Moon complained. "The business transaction is not concluded and I do not abandon my clients."

"Well I will be in Los Angeles next week and our business will be concluded then. I am grateful for your concern and your willingness to uphold your commitments as an attorney. You're quite a woman, Moonbaby Elizabeth Franklin." Moe said.

"You just get through your meeting tomorrow and be in LA next week for the closing so we can end this transaction and you can begin your new adventure. Maybe then we can put this behind us," Moon said.

"That would be nice but this type of thing will never be over for people like me. We will just have to keep fighting back from within to stop the crazy people from taking over," Moe said.

Moe understood the problems with Islamic extremists and he also understood why the U.S. would take extreme measures to protect its people. He just hoped the turmoil would end for Moon after this business concluded next week.

They talked for a few minutes and Moon found herself longing to see Moe again. She was excited that it would just be another week. Still, she really did not know what the future would hold after the studio deal was done. When they hung up, Moon felt inspired to say a quiet prayer. She had not said a prayer or talked to God in a long time, in fact, she had pretty much forgotten about Him. Today she opened the dialog again.

Moon gave up on God when she was a teenager. She still believed in Him but thought He was ineffectual. She didn't know why. Maybe it was because He chose not to help or maybe He really couldn't.

Moon had a best friend in middle school. Her name was Rose and she was a very sweet girl. Rose had stood up for Moon when she got picked on for being the new kid. They continued to be best friends through their high school years, as brief as those years were to become.

The two were inseparable except when Rose would spend time in the hospital. Each time Rose would be sick, Moon would pray that her friend would get better and she always did. When they were younger, Moon didn't understand. She didn't ask many questions back then though it upset her when their parents would keep the girls apart if Moon caught a cold. Over the years, Moon took responsibility to help her best friend. She'd make sure never to walk too fast so Rose wouldn't become winded and anyone who dared to call Rose "skinny" would not soon forget the verbal beat down they'd get from Moon.

The last time Rose was in the hospital, Moon prayed and prayed to God that her friend would recover. Moon had never prayed so much or so hard in her entire life as she did then. She had never wanted anything so badly, but God let her down.

Rose died and left Moon with a hole in her heart that would never be filled. Moon still aches when she thinks of Rose. Moon was angry with God for so long that she forgot Him. Until now.

Richard was working at his desk when he was ordered to Cole's office. A regular reaming was now routine. Richard prepared to get yelled at.

"Sit your sorry ass down," Cole ordered.

Richard took a seat. He felt oddly calm. He was prepared.

Cole had a look of disgust on his face. "So tell me, Washington, how could one of our GPS devices end up on a van belonging to A1 Courier Service?" he asked.

"I don't know," Richard observed, quietly.

"No clue, huh? Interesting. Well then tell me, Washington. How does a video of one of our drones end up on YouTube, posted there by an employee of the aforementioned A1 Courier Service?" Cole yelled, "You want to clue me in how that could happen, Washington?"

"I really don't know. Sir." Richard said. His continued calm was infuriating Cole further.

"OH! So you really don't know, SIR! There's a lot of shit you don't know, Washington! Why is it you don't know? It all seems too convenient to me!" Cole pounded his fist on his desk. "Get your ass outta my sight! You're suspended until I figure out what to do with you!"

Richard walked out of the office without a word. He decided to go get drunk.

"Anger is not a mixer," the bartender said as he poured Richard his second scotch.

Richard threw it back and slammed the glass on the bar.

"My boss is a cancer. He's a TUMOR! He's fuckin' dangerous, man." Richard's words were not quite slurred yet. "Gimme another one."

The bartender complied.

"He is a fucking danger to innocent people. He's gonna ruin lives. You just watch him! He's gonna ruin lives." Richard gulped down his drink.

"Gimme another one."

chapter fifteen

Shattered Dreams

Moon woke up the next day and went running as she usually did, this time was different though, she was talking to God. She was asking him to intervene and make the meeting today go well for Moe. She was painfully aware that she couldn't be there but desperately wished she could.

Moon realized that this was the second time in two days that she spoke to God and she hoped He would listen because so much at this point was out of her hands. Before the last few months, Moon remembered having control of every situation in her life, or so she thought, *well maybe the only time was when Butthead cheated on me,* she thought, *but I had control after that.* This was different, she had only God to help her now and she was asking for His help.

Cole had enough of Richard's stalling and making excuses about the bullshit innocence of Ms. Franklin. He found out through a source that the State Department was meeting with her Arab terrorist boyfriend in Paris and he would be coming to Los Angeles after he gets the Department's blessing. Well, Cole thought, they may cave on this bullshit towel head but he vowed to take care of business when that terrorist arrives in LA *That you could count on!* Cole thought.

Cole called Marty and the other operatives into his office for a meeting. He was taking control and he was going to get results, even if that incompetent Richard couldn't.

After the meeting, Cole made a call to Washington and he had a conversation about this assistant D.A. Stan Davis and how he was getting in the way of national security. The conversation ended with the agreement that Stan Davis would discontinue his investigation severing all contact with Ms. Franklin or else his personal and professional life would change dramatically.

Cole hung up the phone and leaned back in his chair with the assurance that Stan Davis would no longer bother him or his investigation.

Stan called Moon after his conversation with Mr. Hargrove.

"Hi, what's up?" Moon said cheerfully.

"I just got a strange call from a Mr. Hargrove from Homeland Security warning me about involvement with you and their case. I thought you were going to sever ties with that client from the Middle East."

"I can't do that Stan and you know it."

Stan raised his eyebrows, "Well they seem pretty interested in you and this client."

"He just had a meeting with the State Department and he is cleared for the transaction so I see no more problems."

"Hmm, are you sure because why would this guy call me now and basically threaten me and my job?"

"I don't know, Stan. I think this guy is crazy and he is imagining conspiracies where there are none."

Stan paused a moment and took a deep breath. "Well you know crazy people can be dangerous so I would watch your back, hon. I still don't like it and I have to stay out for now."

"I'm fine and I have my back watched and there is no need for you to be involved anymore. Thanks for all your help and your concern. I really appreciate it."

"Yes, I know you do and I appreciate you too and want the best for you, Moon. I hope you know that."

Moon smiled, "Yes I do. I have to go. I'm way too busy. Thanks."

Moon went on with her afternoon work schedule without thinking about Stan and what that all meant. She did, however, think about how the meeting in Paris went and why she had not heard from Moe.

Paris is nine hours ahead and she thought she should have heard from him already, but when did Moe ever do what she thought he should? Moe was always full of surprises and she could do without any more surprises, especially with this transaction.

By the end of the day, she couldn't contain herself and called Moe. He was immediately apologetic, "I was going to call you and I just got busy, please forgive me."

"Fine, if you tell me all went well with your meeting then I will."

Moe laughed, "Yes, yes it went very well, just as I knew it would. We have clearance from the State Department."

Moon let out a big sigh, "See? That was easy, why do you torture me this way?"

Moe laughed, "Really I'm not trying to torture anyone. Wasn't that outlawed by your president?"

They talked for a while. "I'm sorry Moon I have to get moving and you have to get to bed. We have some big days ahead of us," Moe said.

Moon would have talked all night, "Yes we do. I'll go but try not to keep me in the dark anymore."

"I'm sorry about that. It was not intentional," Moe apologized again. "I can hardly wait until the day we are reunited in America and we can move forward in a proper fashion."

Moon went on for a few more minutes describing how the process would proceed but she knew Moe must be very experienced in this type of business transaction.

Richard woke up the next morning with his head splitting. He looked in the bathroom mirror and saw dried blood all over his forehead down to his cheek. *Geez, it's not bad enough that my head hurts this much but what the hell is the blood all about?* Even the act of thinking was painful but he couldn't stop it. His inclination was to go back to bed and sleep off the headache but he couldn't take the time. He had to get back to making a plan to protect himself from whatever Cole was plotting because whatever that was, it wouldn't be good.

Richard took a few painkillers and made some coffee. A shower got him clean but it didn't bring back his memory or make his head feel better. He got dressed and went out the door, forgetting he'd made coffee until he ordered a cup at Starbucks.

Richard sat down at Starbucks, logged in to the agency's network with a backdoor password that one of the geeks gave him a while back. He needed it on a job that he didn't want traced and he just kept it quiet until he might need it again. This was that time. He wanted to check on what might be new with the Franklin case and if Cole or Michael was holding anything back. They did not seem to be; there wasn't much except some expanded reports on Waseem family members. The principals in the investigation were still Ms. Franklin's client and his terrorist cousin.

Richard couldn't find a thing illegal about Ms. Franklin's association with the Sheikh and this business they wanted to transact. He found a report from the State Department that had been sent just a few days before. It cleared the Sheikh for entry into the U.S. and for the purchase of an American movie and television production company.

Richard thought about what it all meant. *Cole had to have seen this even before he cut me loose. This may be why he was so damn mad. It was less about me and more about the State Department spoiling his plans. He also had to know I'd see this was a complete sham of an investigation. Now he thinks I'm out of the way but am I really?*

Richard realized he'd have to prepare for the worst, just in case he was wrong about something and Cole was that out of control. He found this very troubling. He had encountered power-hungry control freaks before but never someone he suspected would screw up so many lives just for his personal gain or was there more people involved. *Could someone else be pushing Cole's buttons and driving him this way and why would they do that?* Richard thought.

Richard saved all the files to a flash drive. The report essentially cleared this Sheikh Waseem which in turn cleared Ms. Franklin. He would have to be very careful from here on out. He could not have Cole suspect that he was even interested in this case anymore or it could be his life.

Cole was on track to pick up the Sheikh when he arrived at LAX. He expected this would draw very little attention from anyone except maybe for Ms. Franklin. He wasn't ready to pick her up just yet as she was an American citizen and he needed to have his bases covered.

Marty saw Cole's extension on his phone, "Yes what is it now?"

"I think you should rephrase that question, Post."

Marty didn't hold back the sarcasm, "Yes, yes, what may I help you with today, your honor?"

Cole groaned. *If only he wasn't so good at what he did I would send him off the planet. The people I have to put up with, well I won't have to, soon enough.* "Look I just want to know that you are on top of this. We can't have any more screw ups like your buddy Washington."

"He's not my buddy, got it?" Marty barked. He held the phone away from his face. "Fucking dumbass."

"What was that I heard?" Cole asked.

"Nothing...."

"Yeah I thought not," Cole responded.

"It's all under control. You need not worry your petty little head over it. Oh, I meant pretty head," Marty laughed.

"Do you have a contingency plan to handle Ms. Franklin if she gets to be a problem?" Cole asked.

"What? No, that's your call," Marty insisted. "I'm not fucking with that. I don't mind breaking in to her house or following her but I'm not taking a fall for anything more than that. That's for your pay grade."

"Just be ready to pick her up if necessary," Cole replied. "That's all I'm asking from you. You just need to be ready. Do you have the detention center ready?"

"Yes, it's all ready." Marty was eager to get off the phone. "Is there anything else?"

Cole left Marty with a warning, "Just don't give me any excuses if you didn't anticipate something. You better have planned for every detail."

Marty hung up and stared at the phone. *Fucking idiot.*

Moonbaby worked through the next week with nervous anticipation of her upcoming meeting and business closing with Moe. She was completely ready; it was her personal feelings that were making her nervous. She thought she was silly and behaving like a schoolgirl, but she worried that after such a long time there might be no future for her and Moe. She also thought about what she was going to do when the reality of Moe living and working here hit both of them. Was he going to be interested in her or maybe he would not be such an interesting guy after all. *No that is impossible! He is the most interesting man I have ever met.*

Cole was filled with nervous anticipation too but his was about the possibility of something going wrong and his prize slipping from his fingers. He felt like he had his whole life wrapped up in this and he was not about to lose now. He followed up with Marty so much it seemed that the agent's attitude had developed an almost murderous intent. Cole could handle Marty and, frankly, he needed him focused. If hatred for Cole was going to help, then so be it.

Moe was home again checking and re-checking on the contracts and terms for his upcoming acquisition in America. This would be the culmination of his life's work. He sat back in his office chair and looked out the window at Doha. *How different my view of the world will be in a very short time.*

The day arrived and Moe looked out the airplane window. He smiled as he saw the sprawl of Southern California far below. Usef sat across the aisle but he did not have such a relaxed look on his face. "Smile Usef, don't be so gloomy. We are coming to our new life in America."

Usef remained sullen. "Sorry, boss. I just do not have the same excitement you have for this country. I do not think they will like us as much as you think they will."

Moe smiled and thought about the future. *You will feel different, my friend, after a couple of months here. I promise you that.*

Cole was being a big pain in Marty's ass. He was asking the same questions repeatedly about their preparations and Marty was tired of it the first time. They were having ground control divert the jet to another hangar so they could control the area and there would be no witnesses. Marty assured Cole that this was not the first time he had done this and it would go off without a hitch but Cole was less then convinced.

Moonbaby was at her office making final preparations for the closing. She was expecting a call from Moe as soon as he landed and they would meet at her office shortly after. She felt all giggly inside but tried to shake that off. She just stared out her office window at the sky, thinking every jet that flew by could be Moe's.

Moe always liked to sit back and close his eyes upon landing. Ever since his days as a fighter pilot, he could never get used to someone else at the controls of the plane. The wheels touched down and Moe looked out the window at LAX and the city in the distance. He thought about all it took to get to this moment and how much he was going to have to put out to stay. It was a good feeling, better than he had in years. He remembered when he bought the theater in London. It was the same feeling only now it was ten times better.

The plane taxied past the private jet center that was usually used. Hatsu came back and told Moe they'd been diverted to another hangar because the main center was full. Usef seemed to be even more anxious than before. "I have a bad feeling about this," he grumbled.

Moe felt mildly annoyed. "Okay, stop! Usef, your paranoia is getting to me. They are full at the jet center. Probably backed up in customs. Nothing to worry about." He looked out the window as they were pulling into the hangar. A small group of men in suits stood in front of three black Suburbans. A uniformed SWAT team was at attention. *That's not customs.* Moe could see Usef had become very agitated. He asserted that he'd take charge. "Do not react provocative, my friend. I'll take care of this. We will be fine."

Usef had always trusted Moe since their days in the military, "Yes, boss, but this looks bad. I will do as you instructed."

Moe walked up to the cockpit and assured the flight crew he'd handle the situation. They would stay inside until he worked it out.

Usef opened the airplane door. Two uniformed men rolled the airstairs into place. Moe stepped out on to the platform and took a stance of confidence and authority. He looked out over the group below to see if he could tell who was in charge.

As he stepped off the stairs, Moe approached the group. "I am here on business. What is the meaning of this?"

Marty stepped forward and landed a powerful punch across Moe's jaw. Moe was stunned but managed to withstand the blow. The whole group rushed him and dragged him to the ground. Moe fought against the many arms holding him down. "I have full clearance to be in this country! You have no authority to do this!" he shouted.

Cole looked down at Moe with disgust. "Shut up! I'll tell you from now on when to speak." Moe mustered a mighty burst of strength and threw an agent off his right arm. Cole slammed a kick into Moe's side. He laughed as Moe struggled to regain his breath. He barked orders at the agents. "Get him out of here! We'll take care of the rest."

Usef watched from inside the plane and decided he had to take action despite the orders of the man who had once been his commanding officer. He retrieved his gun and told the flight crew to stay in the back of the plane. The pilot tried to hold him back but Usef felt his military training taking over. "You see what they've done to the Sheikh? I will not allow them to take him or us!"

Usef stepped into the doorway and leveled his weapon at the group below. Before he could speak, a shout of "GUN!" rang out across the hangar. A barrage of gunfire threw Usef's body backward into the plane.

"Goddamn it!" screamed Cole. "Now we've got big fucking problems!" He yelled up to the plane. "Everyone out with your hands in the air! Get out here now!"

Moe was hooded and handcuffed in the back of a vehicle. He was hysterical, pleading with anyone who could hear him. "Please do not hurt these innocent people, please, you have me, don't...." Marty opened the car door and slammed a punch to the other side of Moe's jaw. "Shut the fuck up!" he yelled.

The pilot practically had to carry Hatsu as he stepped over Usef's body. The crew walked out of the plane and down the steps with their hands in the air. Hatsu was sobbing so hard, she tripped and fell to the ground as she took her last step off the stairs. As she tried to get up, Cole pushed her back down. "All of you! Get on the ground and stay there! Keep your hands where we can see them!" The flight crew laid down on the ground. The pilot tried to reach out to Hatsu's hand; Cole crushed his fingers with his heel. He turned to the SWAT team commander, "Search them. They might be armed." Cole started up the airstairs and shouted orders at Marty. "Get in here and help me search this plane."

Cole kicked Usef's body aside as he and Marty searched the plane over and under to no avail. He was infuriated. Cole ordered Marty to retrieve a case he had in the trunk of his car.

Marty brought back a black case. "What are you going to do?"

Cole jerked the case from Marty's hand. "I'm getting us out of this mess and making you and me heroes, is that a problem?"

"Nope, I'll just be outside." Marty didn't really want to know what Cole was doing and headed out of the plane.

A few minutes later Cole came out and ordered the pilot to get up. He stood and looked defiantly into Cole's eyes. This pissed Cole off and he got right up in the pilot's face. "I want you to fly out of here now and go back to where you came from."

The pilot refused to show any fear. "We don't have enough fuel."

Cole waved to Marty and Marty was on the phone instantly. "I'll have you fueled and then you can go."

The pilot held his ground. "We don't have a flight plan. The control tower won't let us take off."

Cole looked disgusted. "You'll do what I tell you! You'll fly this plane out of this airport or you'll be in a detention center! Now get your ass back in that cockpit and take that fucker's body with you!"

The co-pilot put his arm around Hatsu and helped her back up the stairs as they all climbed back into the plane. The crew was relieved to get the door closed behind them.

As the jet started to taxi out to the runway, Cole got a Navy commander on the radio. "They are carrying a biological weapon on board. We stopped them from transferring it off the plane. They are attempting to escape and are heading due west over the ocean. The plane should be taken down over water so the pathogen will not spread and will be contained or diluted in the ocean."

The Navy Commander was hesitant but Cole wouldn't have it. "You cannot give them warning. If you do, they will release the biological agent into the air. They must think they are getting away. It is crucial that you shoot them down once over water and they do not see you coming."

The pilot and crew knew they didn't have a choice. The pilot instructed the co-pilot to go ahead and taxi out to the runway.

The co-pilot was nervous, "We will encounter other planes in line to take off."

The pilot stared straight ahead, "Just get us into a taxi lane and let's get the hell out of here."

As they maneuvered the jet out toward a runway, the crew realized other planes were clearing out of the way. They looked at each other nervously and confused as an air traffic controller's voice over the radio announced they were cleared for takeoff.

Cole had spoken to the security chief of the airport and the director of flight and ground control and explained the situation as he had with the Naval Commander. They were all very helpful as they would be helping to prevent another even bigger disaster than 9/11.

As Moe was driven out of the hangar, he could hear the jet engines of the plane. "What are you doing with those people?"

A voice came back, "We are letting them go. Now shut the fuck up or you'll get shut up."

Moon had hoped lunch would calm her down and she did feel better but Jennifer noticed she was not her usual self. "You're way too stressed about this, Moonlight. You handle this type of transaction all the time."

"You're right, it's standard," Moon replied. "This just feels different."

"It's because you're in love," Jennifer teased. "Moonlight in love. It sounds like a song."

"Ok, that's enough! Let's get ready." Moon gathered the contracts and they headed to the conference room. She asked the receptionist to let her know when the Sheikh arrived so she could come greet him personally.

The sellers arrived with their lawyers. Moon looked at the clock and they were ten minutes past the scheduled time. She assured everyone her client was likely stuck in traffic. But ten minutes turned into thirty and the sellers were losing patience. Moon excused herself and called Moe but it went instantly to voice mail. She started to feel very anxious and upset. She took a deep breath and decided to call the Jet Center. Without details of the specific plane, they couldn't help her at all. She could feel it in her bones that something was wrong.

Moon returned to the conference room and found the sellers on their way out. She tried to stop them at the door, "Please wait just a few more minutes. I know my client is coming and will be here soon, please."

"Have you spoken to your client?" the lawyer asked.

Moon looked down and sighed, "No. I tried to contact him but he was flying in from overseas today and may have been delayed."

The attorneys looked at their clients, "Give him ten more minutes? Might save us a reschedule." The sellers agreed to sit back down.

An hour later, Moon sat alone in the conference room, trying not to cry. Harold Bamberger appeared in the doorway. "Turn on the TV."

Moon found the remote and flipped it on. A reporter stood outside an LAX terminal, "We have a report from the Department of the Navy that the jet was shot down by the time it was about five miles off the coast."

Moon gasped, "Oh my God! This couldn't be...Oh my god!"

Possible Terrorist Attack Averted crawled across the screen below the reporter. "A representative from Homeland Security informs us this may have been a potential terrorist attack involving a biological weapon being carried on the plane. That report is unconfirmed at this time but a press conference is being scheduled and we'll be breaking into programming to bring you that live."

 Moon was stunned. "Does this mean the government shot down this plane? What does this...? He's not a terrorist! I...I have to go to the airport! Right now!"

Bamberger tried to be reassuring, "Keep trying his phone. He's probably just caught in the chaos and you will be, too, if you try to go out there."

"I can't just sit here with the phone. I have to go." Moon ran out of the building to her car. She tore out of downtown as quickly as she could. She tried every alternate street she could think of to avoid the jammed highway. The news reports were all over the radio.

"Breaking news, alleged terrorist plot foiled by Homeland Security. Plane shot down over the ocean. Details to come." Moon switched off the radio, she just could not listen any longer.

Moon called Frank to meet her at the airport. It would make her feel better to have him there. She got close to LAX but the police had all the roads closed off. Finally, she just pulled into a McDonald's parking lot to try to calm down and call Frank again. She hoped he might have been able to talk his way through one of the roadblocks.

"Nah, they won't let me through," Frank said. "You can't get in and you can't do anything about it anyway."

"So what the hell do you expect me to do?" Moon cried.

"Calm down! I'm going to head to one of the command centers. There's a captain I can speak to and I'm sure he can give me some answers. He's a friend, that's the best I can do at the moment."

"You've got to find out who was on that plane!" Moon begged. "Ask them where it flew in from! Frank, it can't be him! You've got to find out it wasn't him!"

"Go home, sweetie, just go home. Now let me go, I'll call you as soon as I have something."

Moon hung up the phone. She didn't want to go home but she didn't know what to do or where to go at this point. She'd just keep her phone clear until Frank called her back.

Moe was cuffed to a chair. He wasn't sure if anyone was in the room with him. He had been hooded and in pain for so long, time seemed to stand still.

All at once, there seemed to be activity in the room. He heard a door open and close then footsteps coming toward him. Moe could feel the anxiety rise inside him. He felt the pit of his stomach tighten up and his heart start to race. The hood was ripped off and he was blinded by the intensity of the light.

Cole dragged a chair over but Moe could only see a silhouette in front of the light. "I demand to know..." Moe is stopped by a hard blow to the side of his face.

"You demand nothing! I am the Man. You speak when I tell you to. Nod if you understand."

Moe nodded up and down. He tasted blood in his mouth.

"I'm going to ask you some questions and when I say 'answer' you will speak only to answer the question. Do you understand? Answer."

Moe responds, "Yes," half expecting another hit. When it did not come, Moe sighed in relief.

"Are you Mohammed Abdallah Waseem? Answer."

"Yes."

"Alright, you get it. You answer the questions like this and we'll be done and you can go. Do you understand? Answer."

"Yes." Moe's eyes were starting to focus on his captor. *But before I go I'll rip your tongue out, you fucker.*

149

"Why did you come to the United States? Answer."

"I came here to buy a movie production company."

"Wrong answer!" Cole yelled.

Another blow to the side of Moe's face was so hard, only the restraints kept him in the chair. He felt momentarily stunned and confused. *There's somebody behind me?* Marty had been standing behind Moe the whole time.

"Don't give me the bullshit cover story. Tell me the real reason you're here."

"That is the real reason!" exclaimed Moe just as he realized he hadn't heard "Answer." He took another blow to the same side of his face. He had to spit out the blood that was starting to fill his mouth.

"We're going to try this again and this time, I get the truth. Why are you here and who else is involved with your plans? Answer."

"My plan was to make movies. There isn't any..." This time, the blow to his face knocked him unconscious.

Cole got up and instructed Marty to put Moe in a room and leave him there. They would try again later.

Moe woke up in a concrete room about six by eight. It was like a small, unfinished closet. A screeching sound was so loud, Moe wondered how he'd stayed unconscious through even a few minutes of the noise.

Richard arrived at the office and was greeted by one of the clerical assistants. "I thought you would be at the airport or the alternate detention center."

"Oh, yes, I was but I had to come back and check on something for Hargrove. You know him, always sending me here and there." Richard laughed as he walked past her. *Good, she isn't going to stop me. Where is everyone?* He looked around a room filled with empty cubicles.

Richard headed off to find Michelangelo. He was a little taken aback when the kid seemed surprised to see him. "Why are you back so early?" Michael asked. "Everybody is still out at the detention center."

Richard stammered for a moment but quickly regained his composure, "Yeah, I just came back for some documents Hargrove needs. What a pain in the ass that guy is."

"Yeah, don't I know it. What an asshole." Michael turned back to his computer.

Richard got out of the office and thought about how he was going to intervene in this without becoming a target himself. *Does this mean*

Hargrove intercepted the Sheikh sooner than I thought? This could get ugly if it hasn't already. I have to get to the detention center but I should check on Ms. Franklin first. If Cole had the Sheikh already then picking up Ms. Franklin would not be far behind and Richard could not let that happen.

Moon arrived at home, confused and wondering what to do. She had never felt this lost before. She called her Mom but she couldn't even speak. She just started to cry.

"What is it, Moon dear? Honey?" Anita tried to get an answer but all she could hear were sobs.

Moon tried to speak through the tears, "My world is crashing down all around me and I can't seem to stop it. I don't know where someone is, someone who is really important to me. I think something really bad has happened but I don't know what and I don't know what to do."

"Sweetheart, start from the beginning. I'm here, I'm listening."

Moon's work cell rang. She didn't recognize the number but she was desperate to take any call. "Mom, I'll have to call you back, there might be news."

She picked up the other call. It was a male voice she didn't recognize.

"Hi. Um. You don't know me. But we talked once. I was parked in front of your neighbor's. I said I was working on the house."

Moon jotted down the number the man was calling from. "Yes I think I remember. How the hell could you have my number? Why are you calling me?"

"Ms. Franklin, I know I told you I was a construction guy but I'm not. I can't get into it right now but you have to trust me even if you don't want to. You need to get out of your house as soon as you can. Someone is going to come for you. They're probably on their way right now."

Moon couldn't process what she was hearing. "What, who? Who's coming for me? Who the fuck are you?"

"Please, Ms. Franklin!" Richard pleaded. "I'm only trying to help you! Please get out of your house! Take what you can and go somewhere safe!"

"How do you know my name? I want you to tell me who..." Moon heard car doors slamming out front. She could see two men coming up her driveway, one with a pistol drawn. She ran for her safe and opened it, stuffing all the cash in her pockets. She ran to the bedroom for her gun and secured it in her waistband.

Moon knew she'd have to put her escape plan into action. She ran to the guest bedroom and climbed out the window, just as she had practiced. It looked all clear so she made a dash for the path. She ran harder than she thought she ever had in her life. As she rounded the first turn of the hill, she tried to see if anyone was following her. It made her lose her balance and fall. Scrambling to her feet, she looked behind her and could not see anyone. She was running downhill so fast she thought she'd lose her footing but she managed to keep going.

Moon ran down to Sunset and across the street to the storage units when suddenly she felt gripped with a different fear. *Holy shit did I forgot the keys? No, no, they're in my pocket. Thank you, Jesus!*

Moon could barely get the keys out. She was so full of adrenalin and fear that she had to stop and take a breath. *I can do this, just relax and slow down. They are not behind you and they have no idea where you are.* She got the unit unlocked. The motorcycle was ready and all her supplies were packed. She put the helmet on and wheeled the bike out of the unit. *Wow, I really never expected to have to do this.*

Moon rode down the street. At the first traffic light, she looked around. Everything seemed normal. *This helmet is like a disguise.* The light turned green. *Wait. Which way do I go?* There was one glitch in the plan. For all her preparations, she hadn't thought about where she would go if she had to run.

She thought about her mother and how that conversation had been cut short. She knew whoever was after her would eventually get to her parents. Going to their house was probably a mistake but she couldn't leave them to worry. She'd go see her parents and then ride up into the mountains.

As Moon headed for Charles and Anita's, she started to worry about Moe. She wondered if he might be dead already, killed when the plane was shot down. Tears started to flow at the thought. *No! I'm not going to believe that! But what's happening? Who is that man who called? How did he find me? What could he know?*

She realized she might be in the news herself by now. She needed her parents to be ready for the string of lies that the media might report. Before she could leave town, she had to make sure they heard the truth directly from her.

Moon stopped at the corner of her parents' street and looked for signs that anyone might be lurking around. The street was quiet. Moon realized that she owed the little head start she had to whoever the man was who'd called her. She thought back to the brief conversation they'd had and how she'd suspected he was on her street because of her. She had been right all along.

Moon walked the bike around the side of the house and knocked on the back door. Her parents both rushed to the door, frantic.

"Thank god, honey, you've got us worried sick!" Anita and Charles pulled her into the house. "What's happening?" Anita sobbed. "You scared me with that phone call!"

"I have very little time but I'll tell you as much as I can." The three of them huddled in the kitchen. Moon struggled to get the words out, "That client I told you about. The Arab who was buying the studio. The plane that was shot down today. It may have been his plane."

Moon's parents gasped. Anita gripped her husband's arm. Charles felt immediately protective. "They can't connect you to any of that. If he was some kind of terrorist, you had nothing to do with it!"

Anita was fearful, "Is that what they are going to say on TV? That you're part of this somehow? No! No!"

"Mom, there's a madman...a whole government agency out of control! You know they've been watching me for months!" Moon sobbed.

Anita broke down into hysterical sobs; Charles held her and tried to hold back his own tears. "What can we do? What are you going to do?"

"With everything that was going on, I put together a plan. I just didn't think I was going to have to use it." Moon reached out to squeeze her mother's hand. "I have to go. I'm sure someone is going to show up here. Tell them you haven't even spoken to me in the last week. Use the acting lessons the both of you took years ago and act shocked at anything they tell you. None of it will be true."

"Where are you going to be? How will we reach you?" Anita sobbed. Moon took out the cell she had been using for personal calls. "Take this phone. I'll call you on it. Keep it hidden. I'll keep in touch, I promise."

She took out her work cell and ripped off the back cover. "I don't know why I still have this." She pulled out the battery and handed the pieces to Charles. "Smash this thing. Destroy it completely."

Moon hugged her parents and headed out the back door. She had tears running down her face as she thought this might be the last time she ever saw them.

Richard hung up the phone and hoped he got to her in time. *Damn it girl, I hope you saw some of this coming and had some kind of plan.*

Cole was hollering into the phone. "Tell me you have her in custody!"

"No sir. We've searched her residence and the surrounding grounds. She's not here."

Cole wasn't willing to accept this was happening. "So her car is gone?"

"No, it's in the garage."

"So she's still there somewhere!" Cole was getting more angry and annoyed. "Do I have to come find that woman myself?"

"No sir, we'll get out into the neighborhood."

"You fucking find her or it's your ass!" Cole hung up and dialed Marty.

"Your idiots lost her. I want this girl found! I better be able to count on you."

"I'll take care of it." Marty said, dryly.

Richard arrived in Ms. Franklin's neighborhood and set his little friend a flying. He saw Cole's men in Moon's backyard but no sign of her. It didn't mean they hadn't already transported her out. *Damn, I hope she got away.*

Frank had not heard from Moon in a while and he could not raise her on the phone, either at home or her cell. He decided to take a ride up to her house.

Richard watched the agents give up their search of Moon's home and drive off. He headed over to the house to look around for himself. He found the front door unlocked. He walked around from room to room; closet doors were open and they'd left the back door wide open to anyone who could have come in. *I'll close your house up for you, Ms. Franklin, it's the least I can do.* He wandered around the side of the house and saw some shrubs that were broken and stomped down in the middle. He followed a general direction out and noticed the path. Footprints in the dirt looked small, like a woman's. A few larger prints had to be the agents. Richard followed the path until he reached the street. *Maybe she took off this way.*

Richard walked back to the house but suddenly he wasn't alone. He reached for his weapon but found himself facing the barrel of a gun.

"Drop your weapon now!"

"No, you drop your weapon!"

"Drop it! Drop it now!"

"I'm Special Agent Richard Washington of Homeland Security and I'm ordering you to drop your weapon!"

"Well Special Agent Richard Washington, I'm Frank Cahill, a licensed private investigator, and I manage security for the owner of this home.

As far as I can see, you're trespassing. You want to tell me what you're doing here?"

"I'm going to reach for my ID and I want to see yours."

"No funny stuff." Frank held his gun steady as he reached into his jacket.

They held out their IDs and slowly lowered their guns.

"Alright, so what are you doing here?" Frank asked.

"I came to check on Ms. Franklin," Richard replied. "I couldn't get her on the phone. She may have been arrested and taken into custody."

"Arrested? By who? For what?" Frank asked.

"Let's not stand out here. If you want to talk, we can go do that. There is a McDonald's down on West Sunset. Meet me there."

They headed off to their cars but they kept suspicious eyes on one another as they walked. Richard had no idea why he was doing this but in the back of his mind, he knew he needed help and this guy might just be who he was looking for.

The next day Cole wasn't in a real hurry to get back to interrogating his captive. He knew the Sheikh would not be able to sleep through the noise they kept going in his cell all night long.

Moe couldn't even think by the time the noise was finally shut off. He had no idea how much time had gone by or even if it was day or night. He worried the silence meant he'd be questioned again.

The cell door opened and the bright light was pointed in Moe's face again. He could see only a silhouette coming toward him. He was pushed into a chair where his hands and feet were restrained. His interrogator was back.

"Good morning!" Cole said in a cheerful voice. "I hope you got plenty of sleep because we have a big day ahead of us, you and me. We are going to get to know one another very well or so I hope."

Moe squinted against the light and struggled to get his eyes focused. He wanted to see his captor. This asshole just wants me to confess to something I didn't do.

"So. I know you were educated here in the U.S. Why would you do that? Live among all us infidels? Answer!"

"I do not believe Americans are infidels."

Cole struck Moe across the face. "Don't lie! You came here to study us! To see if you could find weaknesses you thought you could use to eliminate us, isn't that true?"

"What the fuck is your problem?" Moe blurted out.

Cole smacked Moe harder. "I didn't say answer! You wanna know what the fuck is my problem, I'll tell you!" Cole got into Moe's face. "I don't like people like you coming to our country using our freedom, our education opportunities, and then trying to kill us. I don't like that you can fly around in your fancy jet airplanes bought with oil money that we pay for and use it to kill my people. Do you understand what the FUCK MY PROBLEM IS NOW?"

Moe sat in silence. *When I get loose, I'm going to rain hell down on you like you have never known, that's for damn sure.*

"Now you are going to tell me. Why did you come here and who else is involved? Answer!"

Moe took a deep breath, "I am here to buy a film studio and that is all." He waited for the hit but it didn't come. "I love America. I wanted to live here permanently and work among all of you."

"That's enough," Cole said. "I was hoping to do this the easy way but I guess it will have to get harder." Cole walked out. Moe could hear him giving orders. "I want the noise back on and keep it on."

Moe was released from the restraints and thrown against the wall of the cell. That infernal noise was back on even louder and the lights flashed on and off like a strobe.

Moe had no way to reference time; maybe it was hours later he found himself shoved into the chair again, the blinding light bringing tears to his burning eyes and the figure in silhouette looming over him.

"You're a smart guy," Cole said. "If you ever hope to see the outside world again, you'll wise up and start to cooperate."

Moe saw another person come in the room. He felt a sharp pain.

"What was that?" Moe said in a panic.

Cole gritted his teeth and slapped Moe's face. "You need to remember the rules! Now we've given you just a little something that will help the truth come out, it's not as much fun as the methods I've been using but it can be effective. The downside is we never know the exact dosage and even though we do our best to estimate, we have been wrong before."

Moe tried to pull against his restraints as he felt the injection taking effect. "Oh perhaps you're concerned what the side effects could be. Permanent hallucinations, insanity, or even death." Cole continued in a louder tone, "You brought this on yourself. I tried to talk to you nicely but you wouldn't have it, so now we do it this way."

The technician checked Moe's pupils, "He's ready to tell all."

Moe blinked his eyes but the bright light that had been blinding him now seemed to be in colors. The silhouettes in the room were blending together and he realized the arm restraints were all that were holding him upright. His head started bobbing and he tried to look up.

"All the rules are suspended," Cole announced. "But you'll tell me everything I want to know. Let's start. What is your relationship with the attorney Elizabeth Franklin and how is she working with you?"

"She's beautiful, isn't she?" Moe said, smiling. "I think I love her but I shouldn't say that. She's my lawyer but she's so pretty."

Cole knew he'd have to make the questions simpler. "What was she planning for you here in Los Angeles?"

"I'm gonna be a big movie producer and she was helping me! Maybe she'll help me out of my pants," Moe giggles.

Cole was annoyed; he looked up at the technician. "Did you give him too much?"

"His behavior is what I'd expect," the tech replied.

"So, he'll tell all and it's going to be the truth?"

"It's the truth as he believes it," the technician explained. "It makes people silly sometimes. You can get all types of emotions out of them. He could have some intensive psychological training that will mask the truth with all sorts of other responses like he is giving us."

Moe's head slumped forward. "Are you two talking about me? 'Cos I can hear you. That's not nice."

Cole thought he could get Moe upset, "You know we have Ms. Franklin in custody." Moe suddenly looked concerned and worried. "I see that bothers you, well it should, because she told us everything, everything you were planning to do."

Moe tried to hold his head up, "You better leave her alone! She's gonna help me be a big movie producer!" Moe laughs. "I'm going to be a big producer and you can't come to my movies!"

Cole huffs in disgust. "This is getting me nowhere." He turned to the technician, "You must have overdosed him. This is just babbling bullshit."

"No," the technician replied. "He is telling you what he thinks he knows."

Cole tries one more time. "What is Kadyn planning? Where is he?"

Moe seemed to perk up a little. "He's a bad boy! Bad boy, I hate America! Bad boy. He's home. I sent him home. Go home! He's bad!" Moe slumped back down and started to cry. "Why are you bad? Why? Why? You make Dad mad. Why?" Moe went into a slurred mumble. "Don't hurt people...don't hurt. No hurt...No bad. Hurt...No."

Cole looked up, exasperated. "That's it, this is over. We go back to my methods when this shit wears off. When we have his girlfriend, then he'll start talking."

Richard and Frank met to discuss their parts in Ms. Franklin's life as of late. Frank was fairly forthcoming about how Moon had asked him to check out this mysterious stranger watching her. Richard sensed that Frank had a fatherly concern for Ms. Franklin. He admitted to being that mysterious stranger but explained everything that he'd been ordered to do. They talked for a couple of hours over coffee. They agreed they both had an interest in pursuing this as allies.

chapter sixteen

Running Alone

Tears streamed down Moon's face as she rode away from her parents' house. *I need to stop crying or I'm not going to be able to see.* She had to start thinking about where she would go. *I need to go far enough away where they wouldn't look but close enough to get back when I need to.*

Moon decided she would run up 14 and over the hills, then down to Littlerock. She had an old family friend who still lived there or so she remembered. Uncle Harry was an old hippy who had a little farm that grew vegetables and she thought maybe a little pot, for medical use of course. He would be happy to put her up a day or two. She thought about the last time she saw him and that must have been fifteen years ago or longer. She thought about another alternative but Uncle Harry would be pretty much off the radar.

Riding gave Moon a lot of time to think. She thought about how she could help Moe, if that were even possible, and how she was going to get proof of her innocence. That should be easy seeing as she was guilty of nothing.

It had gotten late by the time Moon pulled into Littlerock and she found her uncle Harry just as she might have expected—passed out on his couch. He was in a cheerful mood as he woke and saw an unexpected visitor.

"Hey Moonbaby my girl it's been a long time. What brings you out here to Nowheresville?" Harry reached out to give Moon a hug.

"I was just traveling through the area and thought of you and supposed you might have a couch I could crash on for the night."

The old man furrowed his already grizzled brow, "Oh honey I have better than that for ya but I'm not really buying the story. Still you don't have to explain to me, you know that. Come on in, take a load off my dear."

Harry opened the door on an ancient Frigidaire, "Want a beer? I'm gonna have one myself. You didn't bring any did ya?"

"No, but I can go out and get some if you like." Moon offered.

"Nah, maybe later." Harry said as he popped the tab on a can of Bud.

Later? Moon thought. *It's already late enough but I bet you were out for a while and now you're ready to party.* Moon chuckled at the old hippy. *Uncle Harry hasn't changed a bit except to get much older.*

"Tell me all about what you been up to in the big city," Harry asked as he settled back down on the threadbare couch.

Moon caught him up on her parents and Aspen and told him about her work. Harry used to be one of her parents' counter-culture friends and for awhile he was pretty big in the art scene. But he loved to drink too much and smoke pot so he moved out to the sticks and has been using up all the money he made as an artist.

Moon could see Harry dozing off repeatedly as she spoke, until he was sawing logs as loud as a mill. She took the beer out of his hand and covered him with one of the Indian blankets that appeared to be part of the decor. She went ahead and started looking around the little home. Harry seemed to have a room ready for a visitor. It was not very clean but Moon was tired and it was a bed. It was not long until she was fast asleep.

Moon awoke early even though she was still tired. She couldn't lie there any longer, all she could think was what was she going to do about her situation. Harry was already up and cooking in the kitchen.

"Hey girl! I thought you were a dream I had. You have a seat and I'll fix ya something to eat!"

Even though Harry abused his body with pot and alcohol, he ate good. He scrambled up egg whites with turkey bacon, and some kind of flat bread. Moon ate while Harry rambled on about life out here and old times with her parents.

After breakfast Harry said he needed to go out for a few hours but he would be back around lunch time and she could come or go as she pleased.

"All I need is a place to make some calls and check on the world behind me," Moon replied.

Harry laughed. "I'm down with that honey but don't get stuck back there, man that's a bad trip." Moon wasn't completely sure what he meant but it seemed like good advice, especially right now.

Moon called Moe's business number. The assistant she'd spoken to before said they also had not heard from him but he'd keep in touch. This had her seriously worried. Moon wondered what they could know or how they would know anything more than she did. As she stared at her phone, it rang an unidentified caller. Should I answer it or not. *Very few people have this number but nothing should surprise me at this point.*

"Is this Ms. Franklin of Los Angeles?" the man asked in a strong Arab accent but with good English diction.

"Who is this?" Moon asked, cautiously.

"This is Kadyn Waseem, I am Mohammed's cousin."

"The same cousin who caused him so much trouble in Hawaii?" Moon asked.

"Well, I'd call it something entirely different but I suppose from your point of view it was trouble."

Moon could just hear the smile behind the voice. "Alright. Just so I know who I'm dealing with. So where is Moe?" Moon asked.

"Moe? Is that what you call him? Well I suppose he started that in college." Kadyn said. "Mohammed is not here and I was going to ask you the same thing. What have you done to my cousin?"

Moon's heart sank. She'd held out a little hope that he was back in Qatar. "I don't know what happened to him but I suspect, if he's alive, that he's being held by the US government."

"Well, what are you doing about it? You're supposed to be his attorney, are you not?" Kadyn demanded.

"Yes, I am or I was his attorney but authorities showed up at my home and I don't even know why. I can only assume they came after me for the same reason they may be holding Moe...uh, Mohammed."

Kadyn was getting confused and angry. "What? What is that you are saying?"

"I'm saying that my own government wants to arrest me or worse. Someone in the government has a hard on for me!" Moon shouted. "Is that clear enough for you? Now I need your help if you would choose to do so."

Kadyn calmed himself down. "I have to think about this and what can be done. Also I will have to report this to Mohammed's father."

"Don't take too long. I'm afraid for Moe's life and I'm not sure what I can do about it," Moon's emotions were coming out in her voice. Kadyn could tell she had fallen in love with Moe.

"You don't remember me, do you?" Kadyn asked.

"Um...no. Why should I?" Moon really didn't remember him so she felt she wasn't lying.

"It was a long ago," Kadyn insisted. "We were in law school together."

"Well. I've been told we were in school at the same time but I do not have any memory of you being there," Moon replied. "I think you are part of the reason I am under the shadow of suspicion."

Kadyn got defensive, "I am not your troubles, Missy. You are, by seducing my cousin and perverting him with your ways."

"I'm not going to argue with you about any of this, now or ever," Moon replied. "I want to know what you are going to do to help and that is all. If you aren't helping then I see no reason to speak to you any longer!"

"No! Do not hang up!" Kadyn pleaded. "We have a mutual goal and that is to bring my cousin home. I will get back with you soon."

Moon set the phone down and thought about what she could do next. She thought about calling the man who'd warned her. He got me out safe. *Without his call, I would not be free now.* It was worth a chance.

Richard and Frank had been going over a plan of action. Frank felt they had enough evidence to send to the Justice Department or the FBI but Richard cautioned against it. Richard believed there was someone above Cole who'd been giving him orders from the beginning.

Richard answered a call from an unknown number. A low, timid voice was on the other end.

"This is Moon Franklin. Is...is this the man who called me?"

Richard's heart lifted. "Thank God you got out! I'm glad to hear from you!"

"Who are you? Why did you call me?" Moon asked.

"Yes, of course. My name is Richard Washington. I'm an agent with Homeland Security. I was assigned to conduct surveillance on you but I never saw that you were involved in anything illegal."

"You're right, I'm not," Moon replied. "So, do you know anything about Moe? Is he alive?"

Richard was momentarily confused by Moon's question. "Oh, you mean your client? The Arab? He's in custody."

Moon was relieved to know Moe was alive but distressed to find out for sure that he was being held. "So isn't there something you can do?

He's just as innocent as I am. It sounds like you should know that."

"It's not that simple. Ms. Franklin," Richard explained. "I have been suspended and my boss would not expect to see me at the detention center. But I crossed paths with your private investigator, Frank Cahill. We were both at your house, trying to figure out what had happened to you."

"Frank? Oh thank God! Frank will know what to do and he will help." Moon was silent a moment. "But why should I trust you now? How do I know this isn't a trick to pick me up? Maybe you want to bag me to make yourself look good."

"Really?" Richard asked, incredulous. "Why would I call and warn you? I'm on your side, believe it or not. It would be easier on both of us if you believed it but that really won't stop me because I have to stop a maniac."

Moon took a minute to think, "Okay, I just need to be comfortable with you and I guess that will take time."

Richard was apologetic, "Look, I've put myself out there. I confessed my sins to Frank here and I'm not sure what he is going to do after this is all over. But I am not going to let Hargrove get away with this!"

"Who's Hargrove?" Moon asked.

"Cole Hargrove, my boss, the maniac I have to stop. He's been giving the orders to pursue you and Mr. Waseem."

Moon sighed. "So where do we go from here?"

"Do you have a safe place to stay another day?" Richard asked.

"Yes, but..."

"Stay there." Richard said. "I know you want to do something but just staying safe until I know more is the best you can do. We need to see what Hargrove is going to do now that you have slipped through his fingers. If I know him and I do, he will be beside himself with anger."

"I can stay here a little while but I can't guarantee how long," Moon replied.

"Okay I'll call you back soon. Sit tight, Ms. Franklin."

Moon hung up and looked out the window at the wind kicking up dust. She closed her eyes and tried to imagine how she was going to be able to just wait and not do anything. She wished she could make it all go away.

Richard turned to Frank, "She is going to do something stupid. I just know it."

Frank disagreed, "Nah, I don't think so. What I know of her, she never does anything stupid. Though she may do something we don't like."

"Well, she won't sit still long and Hargrove won't either so I'd better insert myself into that situation. She and her Sheikh are in danger if we wait."

Cole demanded a status report and he wanted good news. Marty couldn't give it to him, "We don't have Ms. Franklin in custody."

Cole was obviously irritated.

"We believe she left in a hurry, maybe just as the team was surrounding the house." Cole stayed silent as Marty continued. "There was a glass of water on the counter and an open bedroom window. Her safe was open suggesting that she was in a hurry."

"That means she has cash. We don't know how much, but how did she know we were coming? Did someone warn her?" Cole pondered.

"She installed a mess of cameras since the last time we got a report on the house," Marty said. "She could have seen us coming and then got out the window. There was evidence of that in the bushes."

Cole said, "Ok, so she's a planner. She prepared for us and I assume she executed her plan in whole or some part." Cole paused thinking to himself.

"Tell me about the cameras." Cole asked.

"She got the inside and outside pretty well covered. She spent some serious money," Marty explained.

"Where do you think she went?" Cole asked.

"We found a path that goes between houses and out to the street. From there she could have gone any direction." Marty thought for a moment. "She doesn't live too far from Sunset."

"Fucking people everywhere," Cole observed. "She probably went in a convenience store, called a cab. She could be with family or friends right now."

"Get someone over to her parents' house and get a tap on their phone," Cole ordered. "Go over her profile and put surveillance teams on her friends and family in the general LA area. Get on it now, I want this woman found."

Cole wondered in the back of his mind if he was underestimating Ms. Franklin and how capable she might be. But he's more concerned about how to handle his prisoner. *How am I going to get him to talk without killing him first?*

Richard pulled up to the detention center gate. He still had no real plan what he was going to do besides just get inside. His key card still worked but he was keenly aware of all the cameras zooming in on him. So far, he was getting past all the card readers into the more secure areas of the center. *If Hargrove was going to get rid of me, he would have had my security clearance revoked. Interesting, I wonder what he has planned.*

The building was oddly deserted. The first person he ran into was the security guard at the office corridor.

The guard frowned at Richard as he buzzed him in. "Mr. Hargrove won't be happy to see you."

"He never is," Richard laughed.

Richard walked slowly down the hall so he could try to peer into the security center. Several agents would be monitoring a bank of screens that covered the entire center.

Just as Richard had taken a few steps down the hall, Cole emerged from his office and caught his eye. "I thought I sent you home."

"You did," Richard replied, "But I didn't know it was house arrest."

"Why are you here, Washington?"

"You know I can't keep my nose out of this business for long," Richard said. "I thought I'd see if you were still mad at me and if I could get back to work?"

Cole waved Richard into his office. "Sit down; we'll discuss it."

"So, you want to come back to work? Have you worked out all the problems you had with the Franklin case?"

"I believe so. I reviewed more evidence that made me see your point of view." Richard said.

"More evidence? Who gave it to you?" Cole asked.

"It was in a file on Ms. Franklin's history that for some reason I didn't see earlier," Richard explained. "There was a connection to the principal that I did not know about. It would have been beneficial for me to have had that info before I started watching her."

Cole got defensive. "I didn't think so at the time and some of it was need-to-know but I see where that could've been a mistake." Cole leaned back in his chair. "I'll grant you that but explain your incompetence."

"I don't think I've been incompetent," Richard asserted. "It was more underestimation of the subject's capabilities and I think we have both done that."

"Don't try to get me involved in your problems, Washington."

"Do you have her?" Richard blurted out.

"The fact that you ask that tells me you know the answer," Cole conceded. "Let's just say we both have underestimated this woman."

Cole leaned forward. "Alright you can come back to work. Report to Agent Post. Help him apprehend the subject then we'll talk about your complete reinstatement."

Richard reached out his hand to Cole, "Thanks! I won't let you down."

Cole frowned. "Better not, now get out."

Richard felt excited and nervous as he walked out. He was eager to call Frank with an update, "I'm back in. First order of business, we plan a way out for the Sheikh."

"I'm going to assume you handled that boss of yours pretty well," Frank said.

"He thinks he is a step ahead of me," Richard laughed. "I've got to go make an appearance with the agent managing the search for Ms. Franklin. Let's meet at the usual place. Give me two hours."

Cole called Marty to give him instructions. "Washington's back on duty. I've got him reporting to you now. He is supposed to help you apprehend Ms. Franklin but I want you to watch him carefully. I think he is up to something and I want to know what."

"Really, now I have to babysit? What do you want me to do with him?" Marty grumbled.

"Get as much information out of him as you can about Ms. Franklin and watch him closely." Cole ordered. "See if you can figure out what he is after."

Richard caught up with Marty at the main office. He was his usual grumpy, bored self.

"So Hargrove has you reporting to me now. He doesn't trust you but you know that already. That's why he sent you to me."

Richard didn't expect Marty to be so forthcoming but he is unpredictable. "Yes, but don't get used to it. I won't be under your thumb long."

"All I need from you is info that can help me find the Franklin girl."

"I don't know what I have to offer more then what is already in my report," Richard replied.

"What do you know that I may not that could help us find her?" Marty asked.

Richard thought a moment, "Well, she has few friends, mostly work associates, some casual friends she met through her gym. She has a sister here in town and her parents are here also, but you know that already."

"Yeah, yeah, I know that already but what about the casual friends? Marty asked. "You think she would seek out any of them in a time of trouble?"

Richard thought for a moment, "The only person I would think she might gravitate to would be an old college friend. She's a reporter at KTTV."

"Okay that is easy to find out," Marty replied. "We have surveillance on her parents and sister already and nothing is coming up with them yet, so she's not there now. The friend could be something new."

This was working out better than Richard thought it might. "Yes I would do that. She might be at her friend's but I wouldn't rush in. I would watch a while and pick my moment. She is a smart one and might see you coming." *Good, he'll focus on this a while and he'll tell Hargrove I gave him a lead, both will be good for me.*

"Yeah, I would see it that way if I were you! Seeing as how she saw you coming a fucking mile away!" Marty laughed.

Richard got up and left. He could hear Marty laughing from down the hall. *You can think I'm a doofus if you want, as long as I can count on you not to change.*

Richard left the office, watching for anyone following him. He went by a Starbucks and sat out front with his coffee, scanning the area for anyone sitting in a car or even an eye in the sky. Fifteen minutes went by and Richard was sure Marty did not have him followed so he headed out to meet Frank.

Moon was not good at sitting on her hands but that is exactly what she had to do until she heard back from Richard or even Kadyn. She thought Kadyn could be unpredictable so she needed to be ready. It was a good thing she had her nutty Uncle to keep her company for awhile, at least in between his alcohol and pot-induced naps.

Moon was bored and decided she could use a few things so she went in search of whatever passes for shopping in this small town. She took her Uncle's old truck; she knew no one was looking for it or a person of her description driving it. She was happy to find a little general store with some shorts and t-shirts she could wear to go for a run.

The whole area was rural, blighted, and littered with old singlewide trailers. There were some old homes like Uncle Harry's but nothing very nice. The ground was dry like a desert and the wind kicked up dust. Moon was a little uncomfortable with the dryness but she was running and that was glorious. Little did she know that this was the last time she would run for fun for a very long time.

Richard walked in the diner and saw Frank sitting reading the paper and doing sudoku.

"Alright, game over. Let's get down to business," Frank said as he folded up his paper.

Richard filled him in on the conversations with Cole and Marty and the detention center where Moe was being held.

"Okay how do we get in?" Frank asked.

"We will get to that later but now we need to be careful," Richard replied. "I'm back in but I'm not completely trusted yet. Hargrove never trusts anyone completely."

"How long will they keep the Sheikh there?"

Richard took a deep breath. "I don't know. It isn't a long-term holding facility. When they think they have all he knows he will be either shipped to Guantanamo Bay or shipped out in a casket."

"Do you think Hargrove is so screwed up he would kill him?" Frank asked.

"I don't know," Richard replied. "But we can't take the chance so we need to act soon. Besides, I don't think Ms. Franklin is the type of person to sit still for long and that could complicate things."

"I agree," Frank said. "She is going to want to be part of this and I don't see us stopping her. She can be very headstrong and impatient."

Richard hadn't considered all the angles. *I don't know what I was going to do with her except try to keep Ms. Franklin safely away from Hargrove.*

Moon had breakfast with her Uncle that morning and again he went off to do whatever it was he did in the mornings. He didn't ask questions of her so she wasn't asking any of him. She liked having the place to herself so she could ponder how to fix this mess and not have to answer any questions. So far, she was not doing well at it. She was going to depend on getting information out of Richard if she could.

Moon looked at her watch and decided it was time to call her Mom.

Anita was relieved to hear from her daughter. "I'm so relieved to hear from you! Where are you dear?"

"I don't think I can tell you that at the moment but I'm good and safe and somewhere no one would expect."

"As long as you are safe." Anita sighed, "I just don't know how to respond to all this, no one ever imagines being in a situation like this."

"I know Mom, but I still believe right will win out. Too much is on the line and lives could be lost. People have died already."

"The story of that plane has been all over the news. They are saying it was the greatest threat to Americans since 9/11."

"They killed innocent people on that plane, Mom! There were no terrorists. It's all bullshit!"

Moon got it back together. "Have you noticed anyone outside or a strange car around the neighborhood?"

"No dear but I haven't been out much. I'll ask your father."

"Can I talk to Dad a minute?"

"I don't know where he is, dear. Probably the garage. You know your father; when he's stressed out he polishes his car."

"Okay, well, I need you to talk to Aspen and tell her to stay clear of anyone wanting to talk about me. Don't call her; her line is probably bugged. Tell her to insist she doesn't know anything and hasn't spoken to me in a few weeks. Okay Mom? Can you do that?"

"Yes dear, I'll do it," Anita started to cry. "When are you coming home?"

"I don't know, Mom. I hope soon but we need to be prepared if this goes on a while. I love you, I have to go."

"I love you too, Moon."

Cole went to the detention center to check on his prize. Agent Link Meyer was on duty.

"How's my favorite inmate today?"

"He's sleeping comfortably at the moment," Link reported.

"What! Did you turn off the noise?" Cole yelled.

"No, jeez you think I'm an idiot? You told me to continue until you said stop." Link said.

Cole ordered Link to open the cell and turn off the noise.

"Good morning, sunshine." Cole said with a smile.

Moe's face was swollen and covered with bruises.

Cole shouted into the cell, "We have another big day ahead! I want you to get ready."

Moe did not look up.

Cole slammed the cell door. "Feed him and get him cleaned up." He stared in through the small window. "He looks like his brain is fried."

"No doubt," Link replied. "That noise has been blaring non-stop. Anyone would be more than fried by now."

Moe remained motionless in the corner. *Don't give him anything. Don't react. Don't move. I'm going to get you one day, you fucker.* He had gotten very little sleep but he was actually starting to get used to the noise.

He dreamed of Hawaii and home. He imagined Moon was there. He saw her with hair of gold, flowing all the way down her back, and she moved as if she floated. He saw her on the beach, walking in and out of the surf; she seemed to be covered in diamonds but at the same time, he felt she was naked.

Moe felt strong emotions of protectiveness, love, and lust all at the same time. It felt very primal. Then suddenly the dream was over. *Well at least I could dream, that was a sign of some deeper sleep.*

Moe was planning his escape. He was thinking where his opportunity could be to find a weakness in his captors. He was fashioning a type of lock pick out of the aglet of his shoelace. Moe wore very high end shoes with metal aglets. He had been working on it for some time. He did not know if it would work but he had the time and the need.

He's always handcuffed during the interrogation sessions. He was hoping to hide the pick in between two fingers and use it as he was escorted to and from the interrogation room. He was slowly pinching the end trying to keep it stiff and at the same time pulling it out away from the shaft of the shoelace. It was a long shot but the only one he could think to do.

Moe felt he was just about ready but he thought he should get some sleep while the noise was not blaring away.

Richard and Frank were formulating their plan to get Moe away from Cole when his phone rang.

"Well, there's our girl now."

Moon was eager for news. "Do you know where he is and how are we going to get him out?"

"That's exactly what Frank and I have been working on, and I think we have a plan."

Richard laid it all out. The plan was very risky and if it went wrong, they would all be Cole's captives or worse. If they were going to attempt it, they'd have to move in the next twenty-four hours.

Moon was nervous and excited at the same time. She was anxious to get going and starting to pack up her motorcycle. She looked around the shabby little house. *Uncle Harry sure was a help when I needed it.*

Richard rose from the table, "I'm going to miss this place I think."

"We can come back after this is over and have pancakes," Frank said as he tucked a dollar under the coffee cup.

Richard and Frank stood beside their cars.

"Okay, I'll meet you outside the center where we discussed."

"I've got it," Frank said as he climbed in behind the steering wheel. "See you there."

Richard got in his car. *God I hope this goes as planned.* He looked up to the sky, made the sign of the cross, and turned the ignition key.

chapter seventeen

Escape or Die

Moon was ready for her drive back to civilization. She left a note on the table thanking Harry and saying she will come back for another visit soon, she promised.

Moon made the long ride back to the LA area and was getting nervous she would be late or she wouldn't be able to find the meeting place Richard had chosen. She was very anxious by the time she turned a corner and saw the two men and their cars parked on a dusty lot.

Moe blinked his eyes, surprised that he woke on his own. Usually he awoke to someone unlocking and opening the cell door. It was such a simple thing he took for granted in the free world but never would again. *Not one day,* he thought.

Moe turned his attention to his pick work. He was careful to make it look as if he was trying to sleep and was fidgety so they wouldn't think he was doing anything. So far, it seemed to work. He was happy with his prize now and so he just stuck it between two fingers and practiced holding it. He felt he could do this without anyone noticing he was handling anything, but more practice couldn't hurt.

Moe heard footsteps coming down the hall. He froze a minute, suddenly feeling very anxious about what he was going to do. His plan would either work or it wouldn't. *What if it works and then I can't get out of here?* The dread was building inside his heart and he was starting to feel nauseous.

The window in the door opened and Link told Moe to turn around and put his hands out for the cuffs. Moe concealed the pick between his fingers and complied.

Moe let out a deep breath as Link cuffed him. *Okay, he did not see the pick. Now I'm one step closer to freedom. All I have to do is pick these cuffs while not being detected and step two is done.*

Link placed the hood on Moe's head. Moe was turned around then lead out of the room and down the hall. Moe was more nervous than any time in his life because his very life depended on success.

Moe was stopped and he heard Link opening a door. *It's now or never.*

Moon pulled up to the lot.

"Hello gentlemen, are we having a good night?"

Frank laughed. "Yes it had better be a good night or we all will be in a world of pain."

"Alright lets be a little more positive about this shall we?" Richard said. "I know how these people work and we can do this as long as we all play our parts properly."

"Okay let's do this!" Moon shouted.

Richard told Moonbaby to turn around.

"Hmm, I hope your intentions are honorable," she said.

He placed handcuffs on her that he had filed down so they wouldn't lock. He lifted up the back of her shirt to place a small nine-millimeter gun in her waistband but she already had one.

"Looks like you've come prepared!" he said, surprised. "I hope you can shoot as well as you say but I'm hoping it won't be necessary."

Moon nodded, "Me too and I do alright."

Moon got in the backseat of Richard's car. Getting Frank into the building was going to be tricky.

"You must time it so they don't see you on camera," Richard warned.

"I think I can pull it off as long as they behave as you said they would," Frank replied.

Richard assured him. "Oh, they will, it is a built-in response, they can't help it. As soon as they see I have a prisoner, not to mention the one they are after, at least one of the security guards will start for the front door. That is when there will be only one looking at the cameras and he will be watching me. As long as you stay just one step behind and out of camera view, I can get you in, unnoticed."

Moe just about had the cuffs undone as he was being escorted into a room. He heard his captor closing the door when the cuff popped open. He pulled off the hood to see Link turning around. He slammed Link with an uppercut hard enough to knock him out.

Moe was so proud of himself he didn't notice Marty in the corner. Marty started clapping.

"You are a feisty fucker, aren't you?" Moe's heart sank but Marty did something unexpected. He pulled out his gun and set it on a table.

"Let's see what you can do with a real man, shall we?" Marty taunted.

Marty advanced towards Moe quickly. Moe got into a defensive position with his hands up. He realized that he still had the cuffs hanging from his wrist. Marty was a quick man, much faster than Moe anticipated. He was in Moe's face almost immediately. Moe went to block a punch but Marty kicked him hard in the side of the knee. Moe almost went down but regained his footing and jumped back up. Moe felt the pain in his knee intensify and he wondered if he could even stand after that.

Marty came at him again with a flurry of punches but Moe surprisingly stepped out of his way, blocking each attack and stepping to the side so Marty missed with a big right hand.

"Okay you can still move after that kick. Good, I hoped you had some fight in you," Marty laughed.

Moe just followed Marty with his eyes.

"Not talkative huh? No problem. I'm not really either." Marty said.

"Then why are you running at the mouth so much?" Moe replied.

Marty came at Moe in a frontal assault, throwing punches left and right. Moe blocked each one. This seemed to frustrate Marty to no end.

Marty then jumped like a cat to the other side of Moe and slammed a fist into his side. Moe felt a pain he had not felt before and the pain was excruciating; he almost passed out. *Get it together man or this guy is going to kill you one piece at a time.*

"Now that one had to hurt! I hit a home run there," Marty laughed.

Moe just silently moved across to the other side of Marty. Marty made another move like the first one but Moe was ready. He stepped sideways, dipped, then came up and slammed Marty with a hard right hook to the face. He struck out a side kick so hard to Marty's kneecap that he went down in a heap, screaming in pain. Moe could see blood soaking through his pants. Marty was not getting up from that one.

Moe quickly kicked Marty hard in the head and knocked him unconscious. He dragged him to the middle of the room and strapped the unconscious agent to the chair.

Link was regaining consciousness. Moe jumped on Link, pinning him down, and started searching his pockets for the key to the cuffs.

Richard pulled up to front gate. Frank was tucked in the back of the car. Richard pushed the intercom button and identified himself and his prisoner. The gate opened and the voice on the other side said he would notify Hargrove that he had Ms. Franklin in custody. Richard was surprised Cole was there; he'd hoped he wouldn't be.

Richard got to the door with Ms. Franklin in tow. He pushed her in with one hand and palmed a sticky piece of tape in the other. As he walked in, he stuck the tape to the lock so it would stay open for Frank to sneak through once he was at the other door.

Richard got into the hallway and let the door shut behind him.

"Hey where am I taking her?" Richard shouted.

The security guard's voice echoed out of the speaker. "Take her to the holding facility and Cole will meet you there."

Damn, Richard thought, *I did not expect Cole to be here at this hour.*

Frank slipped in through the doorway and stood behind Richard.

"We are going to the cellblock. You go take out those two guards," Richard whispered.

Frank winked, "I'm on it."

Frank headed down the hall. As he rounded a corner, he almost ran right into the guard coming to meet them.

"Hey, who the hell are you?" the guard shouted.

Frank shot a taser into the guard's chest. He went down shaking. Frank cuffed and gagged him faster than either of the men thought a person could. *I did that pretty well. I guess I'm not all washed up after all.* He took the guard's keys off his belt.

Frank headed off to the guardroom and used the passkey on the door. The guard inside turned in his chair.

"You're supposed to be meet...Hey, you're not Jones."

Frank raised his pistol at the guard. "Why no I'm not, what was your clue? Now let me see your hands and no sudden movements. I'm not going to hurt you unless you make me, so no hero shit. Okay?"

"Yes sir, no hero shit," the guard replied as he held up his hands.

Frank restrained guard and went back to retrieve the one he left in the hall. He placed both of them cuffed together back to back on the floor and gagged. He used tie straps to secure their feet.

"Look, sit tight and you will live through this, got it?"

The guards nodded.

Frank sat down and began looking at the monitors. He saw two men fighting and one on the floor on the Interrogation Room screen. It looked to Frank to be the Sheikh and he looked as if he was losing the fight.

Frank buzzed Richard on his radio, "Hey stop, are you at the cellblock yet?"

"No, almost there," Richard responded.

"I've got an interrogation room on a monitor," Frank said. "A guy's getting the crap beat out of him. I think it's the Sheikh."

"I know where that is!" Richard turned to Moon. "Get out of those cuffs and follow me now!"

Moon felt a moment of panic and drew her weapon as they turned down the hall.

Moe found the key and was furiously trying to unlock the other side of the handcuffs. Link was regaining consciousness rapidly and when he was fully aware of his situation, he brought a leg up and around Moe and with great flexibility, swept Moe off him but not before the handcuffs clicked open.

Moe went toppling over. He looked at Link and rose to his feet as Link did the same. Link still looked a little out of sorts so Moe did not hesitate. He lunged at Link to throw a hook to his face but Link was faster than Moe anticipated. Link stepped to the side and swung a leg out and Moe went toppling head over heels. *Crap,* Moe thought. *That was fast.*

Link reached around behind him and pulled a gun from under his shirt. Moe saw the gun swinging around pointing at him. *Fuck I forgot to even check him for that.*

Marty was back in the chair and in between his groans in pain, he would shout to Link, "Get him, kill that fucker now!" Then he moaned.

Link leveled the gun at Moe.

Moe held up his hands. "Don't shoot."

Moon and Richard appeared at the door. Moe saw this and his heart lifted and he smiled.

"What are you smiling at asshole? I got you." Link growled.

"No, asshole, I got you!" Moon said, as she placed her gun squarely in Link's back. The blood drained from his face as he realized his victory lasted only seconds.

Link dropped the gun. Richard quickly wrapped tie straps around his wrists and shoved him toward the chair Marty was sitting on.

"You fucking traitor," Marty yelled. "Your life is null and void now, you piece of shit!"

"Just shut the fuck up!" Richard punched Marty hard in the jaw. "I've had enough of your mouth."

Richard tied Link to the back of the chair, "Keep quiet or you'll get the same."

While this was happening, Moon and Moe were just kind of standing there, staring at one another. They both had disbelief on their faces as if they never thought they would actually see each other again. They both said at the same time "Are you okay?" and laughed.

"Reunion's over," Richard interjected. "We don't have time for mushy shit now, let's get moving."

"I, for one, have had enough of this place." Moe exclaimed.

Richard got on the radio. "Frank, we got the Sheikh and it's secure here. Now get out and meet us in the front."

Cole was getting happier by the minute after hearing that Richard was bringing in Ms. Franklin. He had really thought Richard was playing for the other side.

Cole stood there with great anticipation. *Should I go and meet them in the front or stay here? I'll stay here, greet Ms. Franklin, and make a lasting impression. Then she will be on her way to spilling her guts. Yes, that will be good.* So he stood there waiting. It seemed like a long time. He kept nervously looking at his watch and then the door, wondering why it was taking so long for Richard to get her down there.

Cole called the security office but got no answer. He called Marty, then Link, and there was no answer there either. *What the fuck, why is no one answering me?* He decided something was very wrong and went to check the security office by way of the interrogation room.

Frank was rushing down the hall. He turned the corner to the last hallway and ran straight into Cole. They both were stunned and looked at each other before they could react. Frank was faster on the draw and swung out, pointing his gun at Cole but Cole was quicker and back-handed Frank's gun, slapping it to the floor.

Frank started to lunge for the gun on the floor but Cole leveled his weapon at Frank's head.

Cole smiled, "Where is your band of merry men?"

"I don't know what you're talking about," Frank said as he tried to reach for the gun.

Cole pistol whipped Frank in the face, "Never mind! They aren't going to get away. Get up!"

Cole was leading Frank down the hall when Richard's voice crackled over the radio. "Is that Washington?" he asked. He snatched the radio away.

Cole spoke calmly into the radio, "Hello traitor. I have one of your men with me now so you better stop what you are doing and give up."

Frank yelled, "Don't do it! Go now, leave me here!"

"Shut up!" Cole yelled and turned back to the radio. "If you care at all for this individual you will comply."

Richard looked at Moon and Moe, "Let's go." He held the front door open.

"You can't just leave him here!" Moon exclaimed.

"Yes I can," Richard replied. "What is Cole going to do with him now? He isn't going to hurt him with the three of us on the loose."

"How do you know that?" Moon questioned. "You can't know that."

"That man is a psychopath," Moe said. "I believe he is capable of anything."

"Get in the car now or it will be over for all of us!" Richard hollers. "Frank knew the risks."

Moon looked brokenhearted but she walked to the car.

"I hope you're right," Moe added.

Richard just looked back over his shoulder into the building. *I'm sorry Frank. I hope you can get out of this one.*

Cole and Frank reached the end of the hall. Cole saw the trio getting away and started to shoot but realized he wasn't going to get them; they were already too far away.

As Richard swung the car around to rush through the gate, he looked in the rearview mirror to see Cole yelling. He turned to Frank and shot him in the head.

Moon screamed as Cole pulled the trigger, "Shit, shit, shit, he just murdered Frank!" She turned to Richard. "You stupid ass! He did kill him and you're responsible!"

Moe reached out to Moon and wrapped his arm around her, pulling her close to him. She turned her head into his chest and cried. Moe felt pain in his ribs but the pain of seeing a man murdered was worse.

Richard drove on as fast as he could without drawing attention.

Cole got on the phone, "We have an incident at the center that needs cleaning. Get a crew here." He made another call to operations and ordered a drone up in the air immediately to track Richard's car. He walked back in the building to start assessing the damage. His first discovery was the two guards tied together.

"You fucking bozos are supposed to stop this shit from happening," he said as he cut them loose. "There is a body out front that I had to take out in the escape attempt. A crew will be here soon to clean it up so one of you get out there and wait and the other get to the two agents in the interrogation room."

Cole sat down and stared at the monitors. He had two agents tied up where his prize was supposed to be. He shook his head. *I work with morons, now I have to fix it, fuck.*

chapter eighteen

Freedom's Cost

Richard looked cautiously up to the sky. "We'll have to get out of this car soon."

Moon was still crying. Moe was shaking from the whole encounter. He never expected to see these people just at the right time because if they hadn't been there, he never would have made it out.

"You could take Frank's car," Richard proposed. "No wait, damn, Frank would have his keys, shit!"

"We could try to hotwire it," Moe suggested.

"No that shit only works in the movies." Richard started thinking aloud. "By now Cole has started to cover his ass and ordered a drone to start searching for my car." He looked at the couple in the rearview mirror, "Ms. Franklin do you think you can take the two of you on your motorcycle?"

Moon wiped her eyes, "I suppose so, but I thought you might have a plan to hide Moe."

"I did," Richard explained. But we don't have time any more. I want you to take the bike north and east through the back mountain roads. Find an out-of-the-way place to settle. I'll change cars, find a place of my own, and we can try to meet up later. We need new identities and we need to get across the border."

"Why don't we go to the authorities and explain what has happened? I assumed that was going to be the plan," Moon asked.

"We can't do that yet," Richard warned. "Cole is still riding high on the news that he stopped the biggest terrorist threat since 9/11. They are never going to believe our story. You are now wanted people and I'm a traitor." Richard parked the car and turned around to Moon and Moe. "Your life is over. They will tell all your family and friends that you were involved with a terrorist and a traitor."

Moe concurred. "He is right. We need to get out of this country now. Then I can make contact with my people and we can get to a safe place. We can work on our defense on our own time then."

Richard reached into his pocket and held out a flash drive. "This is everything. All correspondence and every electronic file. But remember Cole is smart, he will start covering his ass. This will be no use unless we find an honest person who can start running this story. I also don't know how far up the ladder this goes." He handed the drive to Moon. "Now take it and get out of here. I'll call you in two days."

Richard walked them over to the motorcycle. Moon reached up to give him a hug, "Thank you and I'm sorry I got you into this and ruined your life."

Richard started to tear up, "No honey, this was my fault and I ruined your life, but if I can, I'll try to get it back for you." Richard got back in his car. "Now get the hell out of here!"

Moon started up the bike and Moe got on the back. He was more weight than she expected.

Moe sensed her unsteadiness, "I would drive but I've never done that before. I can fly a jet but I never handled a motorcycle, sorry."

"We'll be fine," Moon put the bike into gear and left nothing but dirt behind her.

Marty thrashed against the restraints, jerking Link back and forth. He started to yell at Cole the minute in walked in to the interrogation room, "Get me fucking loose of this whiny little fucker. I'm going to rip those people limb from limb, now get me out of here!"

Cole cut off the restraints, "Calm yourself now! This is your own fault, both of you. I would expect it from Meyer, he's weak, but you, Post?"

Marty tried to complain but Cole cut him off, "Time to shut up Post. Looks like it's time for the doctor also. Did the big bad girl do that to you or the towel head?" Cole laughed. "Maybe it was Washington?"

Marty exploded, "That mother fucker, I'm going to make him wish he was dead before I get done with him. Traitor mother fucker!"

Cole looked down at Marty's blood-soaked pants leg. "Yeah, well first someone is going to have to shove your knee bones back together. But you might just bleed to death before they get to set it."

Marty looked up and snarled, "Thanks a lot for the concern."

Cole turned to walk out, "Meyer, get off your ass and come with me. Post stay put." Cole laughed all the way down the hall.

Cole got back to his office and called the NSA about the drone. He was given a direct line to the pilot. He reported that he wasn't receiving the GPS signal from Richard's car.

"God damn it!" Cole complained. "Why can't anyone around here do anything right! I'll get it to you."

Cole had a new GPS placed in Richard's car when he started to wonder about Richard's loyalties. He got a records officer on the phone and retrieved the GPS tracker. He relayed the info to the pilot, "Keep in touch. I'm heading out with my team shortly."

Cole called his team members into the briefing room. He explained that two terrorists and one traitor were on the loose and were bent on destruction so they had to be taken out with extreme prejudice.

As the team members headed out, Cole ran into Marty being loaded into medical transport.

"They are going to patch this leg and then I'm in a car with you on this one," Marty insisted.

Cole leveled a look at Marty, "We'll see."

Moon was frantically driving the motorcycle down this street and that with no apparent rhyme or reason. Moe was holding on tight but he was noticing that they didn't seem to be going in any particular direction.

"Where are we going?" Moe shouted.

"I don't know, just away from back there."

Moe took a deep breath, "Richard said to get north and east for a couple of days."

Moon looked out at the road ahead. "Yes, sorry, I was just not thinking. We'll go up and into the mountains and look for a place to spend the night. Then we'll see what tomorrow brings."

Moon took the next highway on-ramp going east. She was hoping they wouldn't think of her going this way.

Moon and Moe traveled what seemed to be an endless dark and twisting road. In reality, they had only traveled twenty-five to thirty miles but they were physically and emotionally exhausted. This was a fact Moon was trying to ignore. Moe looked badly beaten and might have some broken bones. That was the least of it, the psychological damage of his torture and captivity could not be measured yet.

He was very good at covering up, but she could feel his restlessness and exhaustion behind her. They were on a long, dark twisting stretch of Mt. Baldy Road and there seemed to be no sign of life past the tiny community of Mt. Baldy. Moon's panic that they would be on the road until Moe fell off the back or she crashed was increasing with every turn. She was coming around another twist in the road when she saw a small sign for cabin rentals.

She pulled the motorcycle in around a short dirt road and up to what looked as if it could be an office. As they got off, Moe needed all his strength to slide off the cycle and not fall in a heap on the ground.

Moon was watching Moe and it broke her heart to see such a strong, proud man in such condition. She quickly dismounted and tried to help him but he stood up with a forced dignity and said her help wasn't necessary. She knew it was his pride and his strength that was all that kept him standing.

Moon walked up to the door and rang the bell. A man came to the door with a pleasant smile and asked what he could do for them.

"Could we rent a room for the night please? We have been on the road for quite a long time."

The man smiled and opened the door and invited them in. "Why yes come in. What kind of person would send such tired people as you back out into the night?"

The man looked at the register, "Hmm, trouble is I only have the most expensive room available. I am sorry but it is all I have."

Moon looked at Moe. He was putting up a good front but looking worse every minute. "Yes, yes please we would love it."

They paid cash and Moon wrote fake names in the register. The man gave them a key and directed them up the hill and to the right. He offered to walk them to the room but Moon said they could find it and they would see him in the morning.

Moon helped Moe inside and settled him on the bed. He sat there a moment, staring off in the distance.

"I'll be right back. I'm just going to unpack the motorcycle," Moon said.

Moe blinked his eyes, "I'll help you." He started to try to get up.

Moon put a hand on his shoulder, "No, you sit, it's just a few things and I can get them myself."

Moe looked down at his knee. The swelling was getting significant.

Moon came back in with the essentials including a first aid kit. She looked at Moe in the eyes and face. There seemed to be some bruising and swelling on the side of his face as if he'd been hit repeatedly.

"My face is fine," Moe said. "Those are older wounds and they have started to heal. I'm having trouble with my knee and my side hurts every time I breathe."

"There's a cold pack in this kit," Moon said. "I think we need to put it on your knee first. I can make one for your side with ice and a towel."

Moon laid Moe down with a pack on his ribs. "I'm going to help you take your pants off so no funny stuff, yet." She smiled and evoked a small laugh out of Moe.

"I'm not sure I could manage anything funny at the moment," Moe said.

Moon carefully eased Moe's pants off, exposing his knee. It was turning purple but she didn't think anything was broken. Moon wrapped the cold pack around it.

Moon asked if she could remove Moe's shirt so she could get a look at his ribs.

Moe smiled, "So my pants, now my shirt. Are you sure your intentions are honorable?"

They both laughed but Moe caught himself. "We have to stop doing that. It hurts too much."

Moon wanted to cry and Moe wanted to hug her and never let her go but instead Moon just examined Moe's ribs. It did not feel like anything was broken.

"I think you have one or two cracked ribs but in my experience cracked ribs can be painful for a long time. Sorry."

Moe just shook his head. "You have nothing to be sorry about. You saved my life and I am forever in your debt."

"Thanks," Moon replied. "I'll hold you to it if and when we get somewhere safe and put an end to this madness."

Moon retrieved some pain medication from the kit and a glass of water for Moe. He drank it and laid back down on the bed. She covered him with the blanket then went about sorting through her survival gear.

After a while, she was going to change the cold pack on his knee but he was asleep already so she didn't disturb him. His knee and side both looked better already but probably still hurt.

Moon took a shower and tried to relax but it was a strained relaxation.

Are we ever going to be able to relax again? It seemed so hopeless but she would rest while she could.

She climbed into bed next to Moe. He did not awaken as she slipped under the covers. She turned off the light, put a hand to Moe just to feel him breathe, and closed her eyes.

Cole was not getting any sleep and neither was Richard. After leaving Ms. Franklin and the Sheikh, Richard drove to a storage lot for RVs and boats. Richard had a truck there that he did not want to part with but seldom used as he always had a government-issued car.

Richard was thinking about his poor planning for escape. He just didn't think it would go this way. His plan was to have Ms. Franklin get away with Frank's help and it would look as if Richard was just a victim in all of it. Didn't work out that way, Richard thought. *Sorry Frank. I truly am, I never wanted to see you hurt or anyone for that matter. That Hargrove is a psycho bastard.*

The drone pilot contacted Cole and said he was on the target.

"Relay the coordinates and I'll have my team on it," Cole said. "Where is he?"

"We picked the signal up in Vernon and he's driving south towards Huntington Park," the pilot reported.

Cole was puzzled a bit, "How long ago did you pick it up in Vernon?"

"A little while ago, he was northeast of there and as I was flying, he stopped and before I could get there, he was on the move again," the pilot explained. "We are flying through the city of Los Angeles air space and we do not have a flight plan or authorization. We have to use caution and I have to fly under the radar. It's not as easy as you think."

Cole was impatient, "I don't care how easy or hard it is. I just want to find that car and bring in the subject."

"I'm on it. He's not getting away." The pilot asserted.

In a few minutes, Cole got a call from the team that they were behind the subject's car. He called the pilot, "My agents are on the vehicle. Watch for people exiting. I'll need you to track them."

The agents forced the car to pull over. They were surprised because it was not the subject they thought they would find. It was two high school age kids. They got out of the car with their hands up. They said they were just riding around.

Richard knew Cole didn't know about the truck. When he got close to the lot, he left the government car on a street in what was not the nicest neighborhood. He left the keys in it hoping someone would steal it and drive it around, that way he could buy himself more time.

He left the car and started walking; it was only about a quarter of a mile to the storage lot. *Best scenario,* Richard thought, *the car would be stolen and driven far away from here.* This would work to Richard's advantage. *I need and deserve a break after everything about this night went so badly.*

Richard got to the lot, located the storage unit and found his truck inside, closed his eyes, and asked God for it to start. The starter slowed a moment then caught and the engine came to life. *Thank you, I needed that.*

Richard's truck was a 1978 C10 Chevy, it was his father's old truck and he could not bring himself to sell it. It was a constant bother, as it always seemed to have issues, so a couple of years ago he forked over $25,000 to have it restored. A local shop did a good job and it looked mostly new and ran well. Richard didn't drive it enough so it seemed to have battery problems every time he needed it.

The kid whined, "It was just sitting there with the keys in it. We didn't see any harm in driving it around. We were going to return it after we were done, really."

The lead agent was angry. "Shut up and get the hell out of here or I'll lock you up and throw away the key, now!"

The kids ran off feeling lucky and unsure of why cops let them go.

Cole was furious with the pilot. "If it didn't take you so long to track him, we would have him in custody, you stupid ass."

"I don't have to take that shit from you. Get someone else next time!" The pilot cut communications off with Cole.

Cole called the agents off and told them to get back to the base. He sat back in his chair and thought about the situation. *Richard has another car or something.* Cole buzzed Michael with the geeks.

"Nerd man, I need you to find some information. Richard Washington has another vehicle. Find it. I'm also thinking Ms. Franklin has some alternate form of transportation and I want to know what. Get on it."

"Okay, but what if they just borrowed something?" Michael asked.

"Don't worry about it." Cole hung up. Yes, *Ms. Franklin might have borrowed a car.*

Cole called Neal Baker. "I need you to start putting pressure on all of Ms. Franklin's family and friends. I need to know what they know about her disappearance and if they helped her in anyway. Tell them she is wanted for questioning in a drug-related matter and is on the run. Tell them if they don't cooperate, it will not go well for them and they might get Ms. Franklin hurt."

"Got it. I'm in the car now." Neal was already on his way to Charles and Anita's.

"We may have to release the same information to the media and the local police. That should make life difficult for Ms. Franklin and her friend. Now get me results!" Cole slammed the phone down. *I'll find all three of you and then you'll wish you were never born.*

Richard was on the road reviewing all his alternatives. He had some choices but he needed money now. He got off the highway and rented a room at a fleabag motel. He needed to get to his bank first thing in the morning and get all his cash, if he could. He hoped that would be enough to get him back with the Sheikh and Ms. Franklin.

Neal pounded on the door of Moon's parents. Charles came down downstairs. His first thought was that Moon was hurt or dead. *Get that out of your mind. This is what she said might happen.*

Charles opened the door.

"Are you Mr. Charles Franklin?" Neal demanded.

"Yes I am, what is this about?" Charles asked, already knowing the answer.

"It's about your daughter, Ms. Franklin. Do you know where she is tonight?"

"No, isn't she home?" Charles asked, innocently.

Neal laughed smugly. "You know she's not home. Stop playing games with me, Charles."

Anita came to the door, "What's this all about, Charles?"

"This man is asking about Moon and being very rude about it," Charles said.

Neal smirked and shook his head, "No Charles, I'm not, but you're being stupid and lying."

"This conversation is over!" Charles said as he tried to close the door.

Neal stuck his foot in the doorway and pushed his way into the house. "I'll tell you when this is over!"

Charles told Anita to call the police and turned back to Neal. "I'm telling you to get out of my house now!"

"Your daughter is involved in some very bad business and we want only to help and protect her," Neal insisted. "I'm here as a courtesy to you. If you don't want to help her then it's no skin off my nose."

Charles scowled at Neal, "She'll be fine and we don't want or need your help. Thank you and good night. The police are on their way."

Charles slammed the door shut in Neal's face.

Charles took a deep breath and looked at his wife. "I really hope Moonbaby knows what she is doing."

Anita looked deep into her husband's eyes, "She is our daughter and has always known what she was doing, I have to believe she is safe." *I hope I'm right because I'm not sure this time. Moon please be careful and get through this.*

Charles looked out the window. "That man is still out there, sitting in his car."

About that time, a patrol car pulled up. The man got out of his car and showed his ID to the cops. They all talked briefly. They gave back the man's ID and he walked to his car. The two police officers walked to the house as the man drove away.

Charles opened the door to the police officers. They told him the man was from the National Security Agency and he doesn't have to talk to him. As the officers were heading back to their car, one of them turned around. "You know he's coming back. He seems very motivated, so I would be ready if I were you."

Charles and Anita watched the police drive off.

"We need to call our lawyer in the morning. Oh damn, that would be Moon," Charles observed. "We need to find one soon."

Neal called Cole. "The Franklins clammed up and called the local police on me."

Cole frowned. *Another dumbass I have to contend with.*

"I'll get a court order then we will turn their house upside down. They will wish they had cooperated from the beginning," Cole laughed. "Now get to Ms. Franklin's sister and friends in the morning. I'll call you when I have a judge's order, then you can bring them in."

Richard unlocked the door of the little motel room. He was exhausted. He laid down on the bed, kicked his shoes off, and closed his eyes.

chapter nineteen

Love and Pain

Moon awoke the next morning with Moe's arm around her and thought *I wonder when that happened?* She smiled to herself and slid out of bed.

"Good morning and where are you going?"

Moon turned to see Moe sitting up, "Coffee, I need coffee, and I'm starving."

As Moon walked into the bathroom, Moe found her t-shirt surprisingly stimulating even with all his aches and pains. *She is beautiful even in the morning.*

Moon closed the bathroom door and thought, *Gosh, he is good looking even in the morning.*

Moe examined his knee; it did look a lot better. The swelling was down and he could move it with less pain. He stood and limped to the window; it was a sunny morning.

Moon exited the bathroom dressed and ready to go out, "I'm finding coffee and maybe something to eat." She could not help but steal a glance at Moe's incredible physique.

Moon was a little embarrassed when she noticed Moe gazing back at her. "That would be great I'll get cleaned up while you do that."

She walked out the door and on to a path. Signs pointed to various areas of the compound including community washrooms, meeting hall, and a Zen garden. A little store looked like the best option. Moon arrived back at the room with fruit, bread, and coffee.

Moon and Moe ate and drank their coffee in silence for a while.

"What are we going to do now?" Moon sighed.

"We are going to be fine," Moe assured her. "All I have to do is get a hold of some of my people and if we can make it to Canada they can get a plane to us."

"Canada is a long way from here and we have a motivated nut bag after us. What about Mexico?" Moon asked.

"They will assume we are going that way because it is closer and Richard told us to go that way. I'm assuming he wants us in Canada. I think I can get us transportation out of Canada easier than Mexico. You are correct on the nut bag portion and the distance, but we can do it. I don't know how yet but we will do it," Moe explained.

Moon smiled. *Why is it I believe you?*

Moon got up to examine Moe's wounds. She asked how his knee and side felt.

"They are still sore and bruised but I think they are better."

Moon smiled, "Can I take a look?"

His side did look better. His knee had been worse but looked better than last night.

Moe tried to stand but stumbled. Moon was right there holding him up and as they tumbled on the bed, they embraced.

Moe found himself on top of Moon. "There has to be a God because I do not deserve a person as you in my life, you are a treasure."

Moon smiled and kissed him full on the lips, not a simple kiss, of the morning or for a thank you kiss but a long sensual kiss.

Moon closed her eyes and after they stopped, they both looked at each other and said at the same time, "Oh, I'm sorry." They laughed and Moe rolled to the side.

Moe started to kiss her again and Moon responded. He started to work his way on her again and between her legs and she responded by letting him in. Their kissing got more passionate and heated. Moon started to remove her shirt while Moe was starting to remove his but all of a sudden the pain in his side was so great, he gasped in pain and froze.

"Oh no are you alright?" Moon asked.

"Give me a minute I'll be alright," Moe replied.

"No, I don't think so, not today." Moon said with disappointment. Moe stroked Moon's face, "I'm so sorry but I believe you are right. I'm just not physically up to this."

"No, don't be sorry there will be plenty of time later," She assured him.

Cole woke up in his office chair angry and uncomfortable. He went off in search of coffee and wandered into the break room. After wandering back to his office, he got a call from the local FBI chief.

Cole answered and the man identified himself, "This is Donald Williams of the FBI in Los Angeles."

"Yes, hello this is the Assistant Director of Homeland Security Cole Hargrove. What can I do for you?"

"My people have done a preliminary investigation of the murder site of Mr. Frank Cahill at your DHS facility," Williams explained.

"Okay and how can I help?" Cole asked.

Don went on to say, "I still have some questions about what you have reported and what we have found, or maybe what we haven't found that differs in what we have been told."

Cole was not comfortable with this line of questioning, "Look, this is all preliminary and we will just have to make an appointment to iron out all the evidence but right now I have fugitives on the run and that takes priority at the moment."

"I understand and I'll put my entire office at your disposal if you need."

"Thank you, Mr. Williams but I think we will try to keep this low key as we don't want the public to panic, thinking that terrorists are running around free in southern California." Cole wanted to get this guy off his back.

"I think you're making a mistake not utilizing all that I have to offer but it's your call at the moment so I'll hear from you soon and we can iron out the evidence as you say," Williams responded.

Cole did not like that last choice of words. He hung up the phone and thought, *This person is going to be a pain in the ass but I'll deal with him later.*

Cole called Michael into his office. He arrived nervous and hesitant but that was how he always appeared.

Richard was up bright and early. He had no time to waste; he knew Cole wouldn't be waiting around. Richard looked up one of his secret contacts that he knew from the Naval Intelligence. Remy Hurteau was an expert in documents and forgery. These have become more sophisticated and harder to forge over the last few years but Remy could do it. Richard knew he operated under the radar and Remy owed Richard for all the years he let him go on.

Remy would not work for terrorists. He mostly worked for rich people who needed to start over somewhere else to avoid prosecution either by government or by some other underground force. He worked mostly for the mob.

Remy wasn't very excited to hear from Richard but he listened. Richard told the whole story and Remy became very interested as he was never a fan of government. He operated in the US and not his home country of France because he'd gotten into a small altercation with the French government. This made him anti-government and much more on Richard's side now.

Remy agreed to make the necessary documents for all three of them but this would be the last job he'd do for Richard and he expected a lot of money. Richard assured him they could pay but he needed the documents in two days.

"Are you crazy? I can't get that done that fast! These are complicated pieces of work and can't be rushed or they won't be any good!" Remy complained. "I'll need at least a week."

"Nope that's no good," Richard insisted. "We might be dead in a week. I have to get out in three days tops."

"Three days, hmm, oui, but this is going to cost more."

Richard called Ms. Franklin. Moon answered, "Yes what is it?"

"Well I expected a better greeting than that," Richard balked.

"Look I didn't know who it was going to be and I didn't want to give myself away."

"Sorry, that's okay," Richard replied. "You are cautious and you should be. Are you in a safe place?"

"I think so," Moon replied.

"Good. Stay there for another day if you can. I'm working on new identities for all of us and a border crossing. Then we can plan our take down of Cole in a safer environment. How is our friend?"

"He is beat up but looking better," Moon said. "Nothing he won't recover from, given time."

"Okay, I'm going to have to move fast. I believe they will be able to find me easier so I need to move around more. How far north did you get?"

Moon sighed, "We're not very far but we are secluded and I don't believe anyone would think to look where we are."

"We can't get too far away from each other because we need to eventually meet so I can give you the documents and instructions," Richard said. "I need you to text me some photos that can be used for the documents so find a white background and take some close-up pictures."

"Moe is going to need makeup," Moon said, looking over at Moe.

"Do what you have to but get them done ASAP."

"Why are you doing this?" Moon asked. "I mean, why are you putting your life on the line for us?"

Richard was caught off guard, "Some of us try to do the right thing. Some of us are good people trying to protect America and its citizens. We are not all evil and misguided like Cole Hargrove I want you to understand, Ms. Franklin..."

Moon interrupted, "Call me Moon. Please, you have earned that."

"Thank you, Moon," Richard stammered. "I need you to understand that when we first met on your street way back when, it was just a routine investigation and nothing more. After the first week, I told Hargrove I believed you were not a threat to anyone, much less the government, but he wouldn't listen. I guess he had other information that kept him interested but as time went on, I realized that his interest was in making a case whether there was one or not, just to get personal recognition. I was not going to be part of that. I'm not much different from many government employees. I like to believe that most would act the way I have and try to stop a person such as Hargrove."

Moon took a deep breath, "Thank you, I'm sorry I pressed you but I'm just at my wit's end. I needed to know what you just told me, thank you."

Moon ended up the call and turned to Moe, "Did you hear that?"

"Your side, but I got an understanding of the conversation," Moe replied. "He is on our team and the past is the past. I never saw that man participate in any of the recent actions of his agency. He wasn't one of the people that I saw at the detention center."

"Yes I believe Richard has proven himself," Moon agreed. "Now I worry about him."

Moe reached out and touched Moon's hand, "I don't think you need to worry about Richard he seems to know what he has gotten himself into and he knows his way around. We are lucky to have such a man on our side."

Michael took a seat in Cole's office. "I have good news, sort of..."

"Better have good news or walk your ass back out and get me some," Cole grumbled.

"We found through the DMV that Agent Washington has had a 1978 Chevrolet truck for about ten years."

"That's pretty old. He won't get far in that," Cole observed. "That's sort of good news, what else?"

"Ms. Franklin bought a motorcycle recently, a BMW."

Cole rubbed his chin, "A BWM you say, that's interesting and it wasn't in her garage, so where was it?"

"That I don't know. Could be anywhere, at someone's house or in a storage unit."

"Storage unit, hmm." Cole leaned back in his chair. "Good now get out and find me more information like this, I need to know where these people are."

Cole turned around in his chair, *So she knew something was up for a while, but why buy a motorcycle? Hmm, I'm going to have to look for storage units near her house.*

Neal arrived at Moon's sister Aspen's address and knocked on the door. An attractive blonde woman answered the door.

Neal smiled, "I'm from the Department of National Security and have some questions about a Moonbaby Franklin."

"I have nothing to say, goodbye." Aspen tried to shut the door but Neal blocked it with his foot. "Get your foot out of my house now!" Aspen yelled.

"What is it with you Franklins always shutting the door in my face?"

"Well maybe we don't like you and we don't have to speak to you. Did you think of that?" Aspen snapped.

"Ms. Franklin is in a lot of trouble and you could help her but I need a minute of your time to explain." Neal said. "Are you Aspen, Ms. Franklin's sister?"

"Yes I am."

"Then wouldn't it be in your and your sister's best interest to give me a minute of your time?" Neal asked.

"That's a loaded question," Aspen replied. "Step back and I'll come outside for a minute."

Neal stepped back, "Did someone warn you about me, tell lies about me?"

"Oh, not lies," Aspen replied.

"So they did, look your parents and I just got off on the wrong foot, it was late and I was cranky and they just woke up. I should have put off the interview until today but this is an ongoing investigation involving national security," Neal said.

"Look you have a minute only so get talking." Aspen said forcibly.

Neal swallowed hard, *Man, this family is a pain in the ass.* "I believe your sister has been kidnapped by an Arab sheikh and a traitor we had working for us. Frankly, I shouldn't be telling you this but I figure the truth always works."

"Kidnapped you say?" Aspen asked. "By the Arab she met in Hawaii?"

Neal smiled to himself, *Good she's biting.* "Yes, as difficult as that sounds, I believe it is true. Others, including my boss, think she is voluntarily up to this neck deep. I just don't see it that way and I want to help."

Aspen started biting on her lip and looking indecisive. Neal saw this and thought, *Just a little more and I'll have her.* "Look, she is in real danger at this point from the people holding her and from her government and I'm the only one standing between them so if you're not going to help then I'll go and you can call me when you decide to."

Aspen looked panicked, "No, please don't go. Come in and sit down where we can talk. I'm sorry but our family knows she could not be guilty and all of you people seem hell bent on convicting her."

"Thank you," Neal replied. "I'm not one of those."

They went in and sat down. Neal questioned Aspen and she responded, even telling him about what her husband had thought. Neal was so proud of himself, he sat there smugly writing down everything she said.

After about a half an hour Aspen seemed done.

Neal smiled, "Thank you, you have been extremely helpful."

"Please help my sister. She is a good person," Aspen begged.

"I'll help her I just hope it's not too late." Neal walked out to his car. He was eager to get Cole on the phone, "I know where she is or has been, so we can get going."

Cole was excited, "Where is she?"

"She is probably with family friends in Littlerock."

Cole was puzzled, "Littlerock, Arkansas?"

Neal thought, *Jeez this guy is an idiot he doesn't even know his area's geography.* "No, Littlerock, California, about a two hour drive. The guy's name is Harold Morton and I have his address. He was apparently an old hippy artist friend who made a lot of money in the seventies and eighties but ditched regular life for this podunk town."

Cole was happy for once, "Get to the airbase and I'll meet you there, oh wait we might as well drive. Meet me at the office and we'll head over together."

Moon and Moe stepped outside. It was a beautiful day and they couldn't keep cooped up in the room. The grounds were serene and relaxing. The cabins were actually part of a retreat for Buddhist study and meditation. Moe was still not moving his normal energetic speed. As they walked, Moon would occasionally have to reach out and support him when he would start to stumble, so she walked very close.

They sat down together in a beautiful Zen garden.

Moe looked pensive. "You know this is not the way I had planned our time together. I am grateful that if I had to face this type of challenge in my life it was with a person such as you. It seems I have been looking for you all my life and when I find you, I'm in a position of losing the very life I have been waiting for. Do you understand?"

Moon put her arm under and through his holding his hand and said, "Completely." They looked into each other's eyes and smiled then looked back out into the garden and sat in silence.

One of the monks walked up and sat down on the ground next to them, "It is a peaceful place on earth."

Moon thought *Yes it is. Too bad we won't get to keep that peace for long.* Just as she thought that the monk said "We never get to keep our peace for long when something else disturbs the chain, all we can hope for is to be allowed to visit the peace once more and eventually forget the disturbances, only remembering the chain of peace." Moon sat there thinking about what the monk had to say so she turned to ask him a question but he was gone, as if he never sat down.

She turned to Moe, "You did see the monk, didn't you?"

"What monk?" Moe laughed, "Just kidding, I saw him sit down."

"I didn't see him rise and leave."

Moe smiled, "Monks are supposed to be quiet."

Moon turned to Moe, "Why don't we take the serenity and bring it back to the room." She smiled and winked.

Moe got the message, "I think I can capture that back in the room."

They made it back to the room with Moe leaning on Moon, but not as much now, his knee and ribs seemed to be getting better or maybe he was just getting better at ignoring the pain.

Moe sat on the bed and Moon stood in front of him smiling, she took off her shoes, then slowly she slipped off her pants revealing long beautifully tanned legs and as Moe's eyes moved up these flawless brown columns they rose to culminate in a beautiful v shape at her hips with black silk panties barely hiding the treasure beneath. Moe looked back into her eyes as she pulled her shirt over her head and removed her bra. Moe could not help but look at her chest and think what beautifully formed breasts she had. None of this round ball-like Hollywood shape but more like God would have made. Her shoulders and arms were muscular and lean, not large but defined as if a sculptor had chipped her out of marble with skin so soft and flawless that she looked photoshopped.

Moon leaned over and kissed him on the lips and Moe thought her lips and breath tasted like the golden honey they made in Eden. She helped him off with his shirt and as she did her eyes and hands, momentarily paused on his tight chiseled chest with his soft dark chest hair running through her fingers. She looked down as her hands lowered past abs that looked like a new washboard. She went further as she found the button to his pants and started to unfasten them.

As she pulled them off, she lost her balance and fell on top of him with his hands on both side of her face. He pulled her close to his lips again and they kissed deeply and passionately. When they came up for air, they both hurriedly removed their undergarments and Moon slid on top of him again.

She felt his washboard stomach rub on her thighs as if he was massaging her with warm soft knuckles. Each time she moved, she felt a warm wet feeling that made her want him inside of her.

They made love what seemed to be an eternity with no thoughts of pain or discomfort. Moe completely forgot all his pain, all he felt was himself inside her. Moon thought that she felt connected on not only a physical level but also she felt as if their souls touched. She had never felt this total release in her being before, it was as if they truly melded into one, spiritually, emotionally and physically.

They both collapsed in each other arms with the feeling of such ecstasy that they would find it hard to describe.

Moon lay there thinking that this man was the most giving lover she had ever had, she found it hard to imagine, as he seemed not to care about his pleasure but more for hers.

Moe was laying there feeling that this woman was the most understanding and intuitive lover he had ever had and he was never letting her go.

As they lay there catching their breath Moe turned to look at Moon, she had her eyes closed as he watched her. He thought *I have been in love with you even before I knew who you were but how do I tell you that.* Moon felt his presence and opened her eyes only to meet his gaze.

Moon said quietly, "I think I'm in love with you. Whoops, did I really say that?"

"Yes you did and that makes it easier to tell you how I feel." Moe looked deep into her eyes as his were welling up. "I was just lying here thinking how I have been looking for you all my life and would it be too soon to tell you, now you have told me." He leaned over, kissed her, and said, "You are never getting away from me again, where you are, I will be to the end of time."

Cole and Neal were on their boring long drive out to Littlerock, the only thing that kept them from complete boredom was the fact that they still anticipated finding Ms. Franklin and her cohort in crime. Cole was as excited about this as he was anything he could remember.

Michael called Cole and told him they got a hit on Richard's bank account. He cashed out and closed the account.

"What have you uncovered for Ms. Franklin's bank accounts?" Cole asked.

"There has been no activity as of late and I put a block on her accounts. The bank has to call a number for reporting before they can do any transactions," Michael reported.

"Good work, tell me when there is any activity, I don't care what time it is."

Cole hung up and look over at Neal, "Finally some of you are coming through. I have been waiting for eternity for this."

Neal looked back and smiled *Dumbass, you think that is a compliment, jeez.* Neal just kept driving and smiling.

Richard got all his money out just in time. He really didn't believe he was going to get away with it until he walked out into the parking lot. *It's my money, so why do I feel like a robber, damn government.* He laughed at that thought, after all, he spent most of his adult life working for the government and now he's a fugitive from the very same.

Richard got into his truck and proceeded to drive far away from the bank because he knew it would not be long before Cole and his band of misfits honed in on him. *Okay, where do I want to go and waste some time?* He determined that he would drive up the Pacific Coast Highway, find a place on the beach, and sip drinks on the beach before hell started breaking loose.

Aspen went in after talking to Neal and felt much better about the whole affair; little did she know she'd given him the most valuable information they had to date. It wasn't ten minutes later that Aspen got a call from her mother.

"Hi Mom. Any news on Moon?"

"No honey and there most likely will not be for some time. I'm calling because there is this unpleasant man who paid us a visit last night."

"Yes I heard. He came by here..."

"You didn't talk to him, did you?" Anita asked.

"Yes I did. He explained he'd been rude and tired but he was looking to help Moon and..."

"Oh no, Aspen you didn't tell him anything?"

"Mom, he said he wanted to help her. I didn't believe him at first and I threw him out but we sat down and he explained he was here to help."

"Aspen, he only wants to help himself and not Moon or any of us."

Aspen was quite upset with herself but Anita said she would fix it. She called Uncle Harry and warned him what was going on, that some government people may be coming to see him. Harry said in his usual way that it was no problem-o and he would crash with a friend in the hills for a couple of days. He was used to avoiding government people.

Anita hung up the phone and looked at it wondering when Moon would call next. She knew Moon wasn't staying with Harry anymore so there wasn't any risk to Moon, but still, she wanted her to call. She just sat there staring at the phone.

Aspen was so upset after talking to her mother, she called her husband. He was not happy with her either and she got more defensive with him than she did with her mother. He told her they would talk about it more after he got home. Aspen hung up the phone thinking maybe they are all wrong, maybe the agent will help. She knew this was probably a pipe dream but it helped her cope for the moment.

It was late afternoon and the sun was just setting behind the mountains. Moon and Moe had gone outside again after buying some groceries from the little store. They were sitting out on a deck looking down the hill towards other cabins and buildings all nuzzled into the landscape.

Moon asked Moe about his life growing up in the Arab world. "I have only experienced your culture and that part of the world through books and the media and you know how different media portrayals can be, how do I say, lacking."

Moe smiled and took a bite of an apple. He took a deep breath and looked up. "I always look to the sky and then imagine I am at home. The sky is not so different from any other place in the world. What I'm trying to say is I was not raised so differently than any other child. My parents love me and had the same concern for my success and well-being as any other parent around the world. I went to school studied math and science, religion, mine and others."

Moe could see Moon was surprised, "You didn't think we would study other religions?"

"No, I didn't actually."

"It was a Muslim school," Moe explained, "but it was more like your Catholic school. I understand they teach about other faiths around the world. It is just another way to understand people."

Moe continued, "I latched on to the studies of the arts and sciences at an early age. I loved the old *Star Trek* series, *Twilight Zone*, and others like them. We did not get much modern western movies and TV shows but we watched what we could get a hold of, my cousin and me."

"The same cousin who was so much trouble in Hawaii?" Moon asked.

"Yes that very one, but he was different back then," Moe replied. "We were rebellious young people who frankly did not have the faith in our religion that our parents wanted us to." Moe stopped for a moment and looked back up at the sky. "I was fascinated with space, airplanes, and movies. I was very much like any other child from the United States. That is why I wanted to come to America for my education. Once I was here, I really got my fill of movies, technology, and your customs. But I thought Americans, while free to pursue any dream they wanted, mostly sat and wasted their time. I did meet some very strongly motivated working people. This was where I met a woman, not a relationship that was sexual but very personal anyway. She held down two jobs, working day and night for years, eighty hours a week. She supported her kids and made sure they had a good home and an education but what was most impressive to me was how independent she was. She didn't need the government's help and never asked for it. Women in our world did not appear that way. My mother is a strong woman in her own way but for her to decide to go to work and choose to do that would be a foreign thought. She never would have thought that way. My father also had many wives and my mother was his first but she took the role that life gave her and she did well with it. American women are so different."

"After awhile, I started to live life as if I was raised here. This was a problem when I went home after college graduation. It was such a problem my family eventually gave in and allowed me to move to England and study there further at a military academy. I used my military service to my advantage to go and study more although my real motivation was just to get back to western civilization."

"So that is where you learned flying and military tactics?" Moon asked.

"Yes, but what I really found was the theater. It became my passion. I love the reality of it and the feedback you get and feel from a live audience. I was not into acting but I loved the writing, producing, and directing. I could not tear myself away from it so after a few years, I bought a company. I had to get control of more of the family business so I could branch out and that is exactly what I did. That eventually led me to you and my future. Remembering the influence of that strong independent American woman led me to want to be closer to you. There you have it in a nutshell."

Moon thought for a moment, "What happened to change your cousin? You mentioned your childhood and you seemed to be on the same path then he veered."

"Yes, we were, but when I went away to America, he went away also and we seemed to be on the same path but his changed. He got to law school later in life and met some radicals and they worked him over good. He also had some disappointments with the school and its administration and that cemented his point of view from that moment on. I love my cousin but we do not think alike at all, we are complete opposites."

"Now what about you?" Moe asked. "I have been talking far too long."

Moon looked thoughtful, "I have loving parents also. They tried as hard as they could to be good parents but they were always into 'their' thing at the time. My father worked hard in the entertainment business as an agent so he was busy all the time but he would take me with him. I would go to the backlots while movies were in production and watch the actors, directors, and all the other people that it took to make a film. I wasn't a big movie fan because I saw so much of how they were made but I was a fan of the process. That's probably why I got into the business I did."

"My father never got a boy so I became his de facto son and he took me fishing, hunting, and shooting. I used to ride motocross and that ended when I took a spill and broke my ankle. My mother was not going to stand for that anymore and frankly, I didn't mind quitting."

"My mom was also responsible for instilling me with my independence. She was always doing her own thing and dragging us girls to whatever protest or charity event she was volunteering. She loved to cook and I grew to love that also, I wasn't looking to learn so I could get a man, I was looking to learn because I loved to eat. I learned early that my love for food had to be counteracted by exercise so I started to run."

After years of running, I grew to love it just for the action, not the good it was doing or the eating it was counteracting but just the running. I can get into myself fully and work out all sorts of problems when I run or I can just run free with all my thoughts."

"It seems your cousin and I were at the same law school for a time and that might be what got me on this watch list. I don't remember him but he told me a few days ago when I called."

Moe looked a little disturbed. "You called and talked to my cousin?"

"I called your office when you didn't show up for the closing because I was concerned. I also went out to the airport but could not get very far. Your cousin called me back and asked me a bunch of questions." Moon noticed that Moe looked a little distressed. "I'm sorry but I didn't know what else to do. You were missing. I was hoping you were still home and were just delayed."

Moe spoke up, "No, I am truly grateful for all you have done for me. It's just that my cousin is so unpredictable and getting him involved could just complicate things."

"How much more complicated could it get?" Moon joked. "I don't want to think about any of this for a couple more hours. We will get plenty of it soon."

Moon stretched out in front of Moe and leaned back against his chest. He wrapped his arms around her and hugged her tight, kissing the back of her head.

"What a shit hole," Neal remarked as they drove into Littlerock. "I hope we don't have to spend much time here."

"Keep quiet, just drive and when we get close, find a spot where we can view the house without drawing attention," Cole said.

Neal found a spot that covered most of the front but had decent visibility of the back and side of the house. They settled in for a while, both hopeful that activity would show itself soon. Cole was not a patient man.

They sat in the car in silence for about an hour and a half until it was getting about time for most people to start coming home from work. Cole was looking at intelligence on this Morton person and he did not have a job so he could be unpredictable coming home. "Have you seen any movement in the curtains or anywhere around the house?"

Neal woke from his trance and said, "What me?"

Cole shook his head, "No, the steering wheel, what the fuck are you doing?"

"I've been paying attention and no I haven't even seen a curtain move. I don't think anyone's home."

Cole thought for a moment. "You go up there and act like you're selling something and knock on the door."

"What am I selling?" Neal asked.

"I don't give a shit. Make something up. Just go see if you get anyone to come to the door."

Neal groaned, "Okay but if I were them and I was in the house, I wouldn't be answering the door. If they are in the house, they'll see me walk back and get in the car. Won't that get them suspicious?"

Cole sat there shaking his head in disgust but realized Neal had a point. "Okay just sit tight and we will wait some more."

Neal looked at Cole, "You're not used to stakeouts are you?"

"Don't you mind about what I'm used to," Cole grumbled. "Just sit and watch silently, unless you see something."

Neal looked over at Cole. *This is going to be a blast sitting with him, I'm going to have to do this more often.* Cole then looked over at him and Neal just smiled back.

Aspen was upset with what she had done and was on the verge of hysterics. Sam was pissed about the whole thing but couldn't express his feelings because his wife was falling apart. Sam grabbed his work laptop and brief case and told his assistant he was going to work from home as he had a family emergency.

By the time Sam got home, Aspen was in full-blown panic, crying and mumbling. He asked where the kids were and she told him at the neighbors in between her gasps for air. Sam tried to hold her until she calmed down.

Sam suggested they contact Moon through a text.

Aspen tried to talk through the sobs, "Could we? Will that be safe?"

"Yes," Sam assured her. "I have a way through my laptop to text her and then get a secure Skype connection going."

Aspen's eyes cleared up and she got excited. "Yes, let's do that."

Moon was lying back in Moe's arms almost sleeping when her phone buzzed. "It's a text from my brother in law. He says he has a secure way to call him and others if I want."

Moe looked skeptical, "Are you sure?"

"Sam is a computer genius. If he says this is safe and secure than you can count on it."

Moon followed the Sam's instructions and there he was, looking at her on her phone.

"Hold on, someone here is dying to talk to you," Sam passed the phone.

Aspen's face appeared on the phone as she started to cry again, "I'm sorry, I messed up everything." She explained through the tears what had happened but Moon was worried about Uncle Harry. Aspen explained that they'd warned him and Moon felt better about that. She was also concerned that her parent's phone was tapped and now Cole knows she stayed at her Uncle's home.

"Okay, thanks I get it. I won't be traveling there again so you can relax. I am happy you could call and tell me. Now I know better than to go there again. Is Sam there?"

Sam popped his face in view.

"Can we send information back and forth this way?" Moon asked.

"Yes," Same replied. "I believe they may be monitoring our personal phones and maybe even my business line but they can't listen in to this nor can they track it and I wouldn't send any text or email any other way except through this process."

Moon said, "Good. We were given evidence about the investigation and proof of our innocence and the guilt of the man in charge of all this madness, but we don't want it public yet. We need to play out our hand a little longer."

Sam was surprised. "Why, why would you wait?"

"Because we don't know how far up this goes and we don't want it to come out until we are sure it is safe."

Sam pressed her, "We could get this out to the media and don't you have a friend in the D.A.'s office?"

Moon sighed, "Yes but they got to him and he is of no help now but if the winds change he could use this, but not yet. You have to trust me."

"Is there a person you know in the media that you would trust?"

"Yes," Moon said. "My old college roommate, Jan. She's a reporter. I would trust her with my life." *God knows what they have said to her or told her about me,* Moon thought.

Sam sent instructions on how to transmit data securely. Aspen looked on with tears, "Moon you take care of yourself and get home soon."

"I hope so sweetie, bye." Moon said as she started to choke up.

Moe wrapped his arms around her, "We will get through this and have our revenge."

Moon pulled away just a little. "No, not revenge. Justice, it is always about justice."

Cole and Neal were still watching Uncle Harry's house when a call came in from Michael.

"I have some intelligence you might be interested in."

"Yes, yes hurry up." Cole said in his usual impatient tone.

"We've been listening in on communications of Ms. Franklin's parents and they made a call to the Littlerock area."

Cole frowned, "When?"

"Umm, yesterday."

Cole was furious, "And you're just telling me now!"

"We just got the transcripts now and were reviewing them."

"Why don't we have someone assigned to listen in real time so they can report on these things as they are coming out! Get someone on that now! I have been sitting here, wasting my time, watching a house that no one is in and probably won't be in the foreseeable future!"

Cole ended the call and looked at Neal, "Let's get the fuck out of here," then mumbled something like fucking incompetents can't trust any of them to do anything right.

Richard was sitting on the beach with a margarita. *This may be my last good day on earth. I'm going to make it a good one.* A call came in from Moon. "You shouldn't be calling me now."

"Relax, Richard. We have a way to communicate without Cole or any of his minions hearing or tracking us."

"How do you manage that?" Richard asked.

"Long story, but my brother-in-law is a computer genius and he told us how."

"Cole has people like those also, so don't get so smug. We shouldn't be using this just haphazard," Richard warned.

Moon took a deep breath, "I'm not. I thought this was important and I'm calling to give you the information so we can communicate this way in the future.

Moon told him how to log in and then said she would text him the instructions. They agreed they would pick a meeting place tomorrow after Richard settled on one. He had to arrange to help get them out of the country and they needed their new documents.

Richard went back to his drink. *No way will I ever underestimate you again, Ms. Franklin. I believe you may get us all through this.*

Marty arrived at the office with the aid of crutches. His leg was fixed with one surgery but the doctors said he would require another. *I'm not going to sit in no hospital waiting for that shit!* Marty thought. Marty hobbled into the main offices and past Richard's empty space. *Fucking traitor, I'm back and I'm coming for you.*

Marty got all the way to his own desk before he realized the office was mostly empty. "Where the hell is everyone?" He picked up the phone and called Cole.

"What is it now?"

"What the fuck Hargrove, you should be happy to hear from me and where the fuck are you?"

"I'm driving back to the office now, where are you? You're supposed to be in the hospital."

"I'm not staying there. I told you I would be back and we would take care of the traitor and his bitch."

"You're in no condition to be part of any of this yet," Cole insisted.

"I'll be the judge of that. You worry about the others. I'll be just fine. When will you be back here so I can get an update? There's nobody here."

"Okay sit tight. Call down to Michael and he will bring you up to date." Cole hung up the phone and turned to Neal. "That's dedication for you. Broken leg and all and Agent Post is ready for action again."

"Post is insane and probably a robot, kind of like a terminator from that movie," Neal replied.

Marty got on the phone, "I need a driver. Get a driver in here." Marty stared at Richard's empty desk. *Where are you, Washington? Where would I be if I were you?*

Richard looked at the text he received from Ms. Franklin. The instructions looked straightforward. Call a secure number; it would route and re-route the text or call to multiple IP addresses so it can't be traced.

Cole got back to the office and called Marty and Michael into a conference.

"Any activity on any of the lines we are monitoring?"

"No," Michael reported. "There was some brief contact with Ms. Franklin's brother-in-law at his office and the parents received a Federal Express package."

Cole sat there thinking. Marty chimed in, "So what the fuck are we sitting around here for?"

Cole looked at Marty, "What would you have us do, drive all over LA stopping at every hotel and citizen looking for them?"

"No, but we could put out an APB with the local police saying we are looking for some persons of interest in the foiled attack."

"That could work, it might flush them out but we don't want to use their names because the media would have a feeding frenzy and they would run around looking up and interviewing all their families and friends," Cole said.

"So who gives a shit? Let them interview them. We can do what we want in the name of national security."

Cole looked over at Marty. *Dumbass. It's not really your fault you don't understand.* "We can't do just anything we want and we need to keep this quiet until we have them back. We could send out the descriptions and maybe even release a statement to the media. That would generate a lot of leads but they would be handled by local law enforcement. We could then pick and choose the ones we thought were worth investigating."

Michael and Marty agreed.

"I can get back to investigating how they are communicating. This might lead to where they are and where they are going. We do know where Washington made his final cash withdrawal but we don't know where he went after that," Michael explained.

Marty nodded, "That means they are sticking around here for a reason."

"Or are they?" Michael asked. "They could be out of the state by now."

Cole put his hand up to his chin. "They are either sticking around to get to me and publicly denounce our department gathering evidence but that seems farfetched. What could they be doing?"

"Fucking traitors," Marty growled. They are waiting for someone to give them a way out!"

"They very well may be in Mexico about now," Cole observed. "That's where I would go, but they might anticipate us to assume that and go another way. Canada maybe. Post, you start working on that."

Cole turned to Michael, "You get to work on looking at all the correspondence they may be having with others, cellular and online. I'll get the descriptions and APB out to the local authorities. We will flush them out and then flush them down the toilet like the pieces of shit they are."

Marty went back to his desk thinking he would rather be in a car chasing them than in an office chair making calls. *I'll get in the car soon enough. When I find you Washington, I'll pounce on you like a hungry tiger.*

Moon was getting a little antsy sitting around the Buddhist sanctuary. It was beautiful and quiet but she was not good at doing nothing. She asked Moe about their plans after they got out of the country.

"If we can get into Canada and close to the northern coast," Moe explained, "I can arrange a jet to meet us and take us to Hong Kong. From there we can find more discreet travel and get to a home my family has in Thailand."

"Won't the U.S. Government know about the house in Thailand?" Moon asked.

Moe shook his head, "No, they should not. It was purchased through another company and is listed as owned by a Spanish national. We should be safe there long enough to devise a plan to get our freedom and our reputations back and put Cole Hargrove and his people out of business."

"We have to find out who he answers to and who has knowledge of his actions or we will never be free and I will never get my life back," Moon said.

Moe squeezed her hands, "I will never leave you now and we will get your life back as long as I'm allowed to be in it."

Moon smiled, "Yes, it's enough that we will have each other. Our lives are already changed far better than I could have dreamed. We just have to get these people off our tails and put a few of them away forever. Frank's life deserves justice."

Cole got busy putting out the information law enforcement needed to get an APB in the works. He also got out press releases to the local media that they were looking for persons of interest in connection with the airport incident. It was not long before the local media was soaking up the story. Cole hung up the phone with his last interview, *Okay, your time relaxing and hiding is over, people. Soon I will have you all and then we will see who is smiling.*

Cole called Marty. "Have you found anything on a forger?"

"We have put most, if not all of them, out of business," Marty replied. "I suppose they could use one overseas. I'm checking on that now but I have to use other operatives and they are not as reliable as the people we control."

"Okay, we may not even need that if what I just put into place works out," Cole replied.

Cole's secretary buzzed him, "You have a call from Washington D.C. can you take it?"

Cole thought, *Great, this is what I need now. Washington bothering me.* "This is Hargrove."

"Your handling of this Waseem case is concerning me."

Cole frowned, "Why would it concern you? I have everything under control."

"That is not what I am hearing. You have five dead and you have put out information to the media that sounds to me as if you are desperate. You already have the whole country happy a terrorist plot was avoided. Why would you complicate it more with lies and innuendos?"

"I'm not," Cole insisted. "You can be assured of that. I just felt we could give the media something to do. They have no idea what is really going on and frankly they don't want to. We are just using them to flush out our prey faster then we can on our own. Los Angeles is a big city with many places to hide."

"I'm sending my right arm in on this so I can get regular updates."

Cole panicked, "No, you do not need to do that. I told you I have it. I don't need another person just getting in the way."

"It is done. They will meet with you soon as I can arrange it. I expect your complete corporation. Do we understand each other?"

Cole had reservations, "Yes I understand."

Cole hung up the phone and stared out the window. *This is not going to be good. I already have the local FBI on my ass. Now I have to deal with someone's lackey from Washington.*

Cole called Marty, "We need to get on this pronto..."

"What the fuck do you think I'm doing, playing with myself?"

"Dump the attitude, Post. Washington is sending some pain in the ass so we need to have this wrapped up before they get here."

"Okay, I'll work as fast as I can but you know how this works, it can take time," Marty insisted.

"We are out of time."

Cole called Neal and order him to meet him in the garage. Cole was thinking he needed to physically track Richard. He thought he knew Richard as well as anyone, if not more. He felt if he could experience what Richard had, he might get some insight on where Richard would go. *Might as well do this I'm getting nowhere here in the office.* He met Neal and they set off for the bank that was Richard's last known location.

Richard got a little tired, not of the beach, it was more that he just kept the margaritas coming and he was a little drunk. He got up and walked back to his room. He picked up another drink on the way, just so the buzz wouldn't wear off anytime soon. He turned on the television and started out for the balcony to sit and enjoy his last drink. He stopped dead in his tracks and turned up the volume on the TV. The news was reporting a breaking story about a terrorist plot and Hollywood. Richard got a hold of himself and thought, *okay Cole, game on, you must be getting desperate or you grew a pair of balls.*

Richard sat literally on the edge of his seat, watching the news report.

"Just in, we have a late breaking update in the story about an investigation of the terrorist plot that had the Navy shoot down a jet earlier this week. There seems to be some persons of interest involving a Hollywood connection. We go to our reporter outside the LA County Sheriff's office."

"Good evening, yes our sources say that the jet that is suspected to have had a bio-weapon on board has a Hollywood connection with three persons of interest. As we last reported, we were told there was a terrorist plot to set off a bio-weapon in Los Angeles and the Department of Homeland Security interrupted the terrorists at the airport. They tried to escape in their jet and maybe set the bomb off over LA but they were shot down over the Pacific. This resulted in three of the terrorists' deaths that we know of. Now it seems two maybe, three Americans with a Hollywood connection were involved."

"The suspects are described as a black male in his late forties or early fifties, a white woman in her middle thirties in the company of an Arab male thought to be from Iran. They are driving a 1960s truck and a BMW motorcycle. They are presumed armed and dangerous."

"In other news there was a major freeway crash involving..."

Richard turned it off and thought *okay, I can work with this. It seems Cole did not intend this to get to the media just yet but it also means he is getting desperate to find us. He has no idea where we are or he would have kept this all quiet and captured us on his own. I wonder if Ms. Franklin heard the story.*

Moon's parents were watching the news and became extremely agitated at the information reported. Anita wanted to try calling but Charles talked her out of it.

"How about that phone Moon gave us, can we use that?"

"No, she specifically said not to call her," Charles insisted. "She would use that to contact us if and when she thought it was safe."

"Do you think I could call Aspen and Sam to see if they know what to do?" Anita asked.

Charles shook his head no. "I believe they have our phone bugged and they are probably listening to Aspen's also."

"Damn it, Charles, I'm going over there then."

"Alright, I'll drive you."

Anita was relieved, "It will make me feel better and I just can't sit here after that news report."

Aspen was surprised to see her mom and dad at the door. "What is wrong? Have you heard from Moon?"

Anita looked at Aspen and Sam nervously, "Did you see the six o'clock news?"

Aspen shook her head no, "What was on the news? Is Moon okay? I don't like the look on your face."

"Moon is okay as far as we know but there was a newscast and we think they were describing Moonbaby and her friend from the Middle East," Anita said. "They also talked about a third person, a man in his late forties or fifties but we aren't sure who that is."

Aspen looked at Sam, "This looks bad. They are actually describing Moon. What if they announce her name? They must be getting desperate and are releasing information so they can find them."

Sam nodded, "I'll contact Moon and see if she has heard this yet."

Anita balked. "No! No don't do that, Charles and I think we are all bugged."

Sam took Anita's hand. "Don't worry. I have a way that they won't know a thing."

Anita turned to Aspen, "Have you been helping and not telling me?"

Aspen smiled, "Yes Mom, Sam has it under control, at least the communication part. We still don't know how to help Moon clear her name and get back to a normal life."

Sam brought in his laptop and showed them a half a dozen stories that essentially said the same thing as the news report.

"I don't think it is a story about Moon, or did she have a motorcycle that we didn't know about?" Sam asked. "The descriptions are a little vague."

"Mom, Moon never had a motorcycle has she?" Aspen asked.

"Yes but it was a dirt bike and she was very young. I don't know of any recent purchase," Anita replied. Charles shook his head as if he did not know either.

Sam chimed in, "Do you know a person with a sixties-era pickup truck?" They all shook their heads no.

"Well this is a problem for Moon and her friend," Charles said. "As whoever is at the bottom of this is now putting it out to the public and that can't be good."

Richard got up and looked in the mini-bar. He pulled out a little bottle of bourbon and downed it in one swig. He thought that was probably as expensive a quickie as he'd ever had. He got out his phone and dialed up Moon on the secure connection.

"You look awful," Moon said.

"Thanks a lot, I don't feel great either," Richard replied.

"You coming down with something or are you drunk?" Moon asked, knowing it was the latter.

"I was on a one day vacation so don't give me crap and what was it I called you for anyway? Oh yeah, have you watched any TV?"

"We don't have television here, so no."

"Well Hargrove is getting desperate," Richard said. "He's attempting to make our lives more difficult. He has put out a story to the media with our descriptions claiming that we are armed and dangerous terrorists with an Iranian connection."

Moon frowned, "Terrorists? Which must mean he is tying us the bullshit terrorist story about Moe's jet they shot down. This makes sense as he probably feels pretty good about himself with the media broadcasting the story all over."

"He put out a description of our vehicles and that's much better than our physical descriptions," Richard said, somewhat slurring his words.

"Okay so we will have to watch out when we start moving," Moon said. "Do you know what he told the local police? I'm assuming he talked to them before the media?"

"Yes, the media would have received the story through a police source so I assume he put out an all points bulletin on us," Richard said. "What I don't know is what he instructed them to do if they think they see us. I can't imagine he instructed them to apprehend. More than likely it was to communicate our position back to him but they could have been instructed to apprehend us and that would be bad."

"You stay safe. We are counting on you at this moment," Moon said with a tense smile.

"It will be your friend's turn soon enough and I'm counting on that," Richard replied.

Moe leaned in toward the phone, "Do not worry my friend, you get us out and I'll get us the rest of the way."

Moon sat back in her chair and went deep into thought. She thought about her house, her job, Jennifer and Harold. She tried not to think about those people but every now and then, she did. It caused her great pain most of the time, but not this time. Now all she felt was anger. Anger for the life some psychopath took from her, anger for her government that instead of protecting her, falsely accused her and forced her to run and defend her life.

She looked up at Moe, *I am so lucky to have you in this time of great peril.*

"It will be alright," Moe assured her. "We will prevail against all the wrongs done to us. I will not let anything happen to you."

"I know. We will protect each other. We will be each other's rock to build a new life on." Moon replied.

Moe looked out the window and thought *I need to get better God so I can protect her. If you are there at all, I need your help now.*

chapter twenty

Take the Long Road

Richard awoke the next morning with a wicked hangover. He sat on the side of the bed with his head in his hands and tried to massage the pain away. He set up the coffee maker and washed his face with cold water. He brushed his teeth as best he could with no toothbrush.

Richard poured his coffee and sat down with his phone. He looked up an old friend with the LA sheriff's office. Lt. Jarred Barrow already knew there were fugitives on the run.

"I understand you're looking for someone in your office who has turned."

"What have they told you?" Richard asked.

"We got three descriptions that aren't very specific. We also got descriptions of two vehicles that were interesting, but you know that already. I wish we could apprehend but your boss won't let us. They are supposed to be tied to the plane they shot down but frankly if they were I think they would have all of us on it so most of the officers aren't putting much stock in the request. Now don't you rat on me and tell your boss I said that because officially we always cooperate with other agencies."

Richard thought *okay this is good. He doesn't even know it's me they are looking for.*

"I was just checking to see if you had the info you were supposed to and I don't have any new news. Sorry you still just need to report and not apprehend." Richard said.

"So I guess these are either not really important targets or they are highly important and you and your boss want to keep it all quiet." Jarred was probing for more information.

"They are not that big a deal but my boss and some others are just incompetent and they needed help from the locals. You know bureaucrats don't know what the fuck they are doing." Richard laughed as he hung up the phone.

Great, Richard thought, *they aren't taking it very seriously so it's not as bad as it could be. But some dumbass beat cop still might get overzealous and want to make a name for himself. We need to be careful plus how many BMW motorcycles and '60s trucks are driving around LA?*

Richard went down to the lobby to find food and something for the pain in his head that wouldn't go away. He had breakfast and enough coffee to turn his hangover almost into a memory enough that he could function again. He phoned Remy for an update.

"Do you have my packages yet?" Richard asked.

"Not completely. Why are you bothering me?"

"Look, Remy, the situation has changed and I really need them bad and soon."

"I told you before, you cannot rush this type of work and I'm already rushing."

Richard signed deeply. "I know but I'm in a real bind and I needed this yesterday. If I could get them sooner, I would be forever in your debt."

There was silence for what seemed like eternity. "Alright, I will have them tonight."

"Thank you!" Richard arranged a meeting place and time later that day. He texted the news to Moon with instructions to bring lots of cash.

Moon looked at Moe, "I guess it's time to go today."

"Was that Richard?" Moe asked.

"Yes, he has an address where we need to meet him tonight."

Moon texted Richard back with how much cash she had. It was about half of what was needed. She also said they would need money after they got over the border.

Richard texted back that they'd be fine. He needed to know about how much Ms. Franklin might have on her and if she had enough for them to make it out. He just didn't want to tell her that.

Moon went to maps on the phone and looked up the address.

"It looks like it's about two to three hours travel time depending on traffic."

"Sounds like a long time in the saddle, partner," Moe joked. "Are you up to having my big butt behind you?"

"Yes, silly, and your butt is rather nice and definitely not big. I think we should leave early so if we want to stop and rest or find we have some problems we won't be late."

Cole and Neal were at the bank where Richard had stopped the day before.

"Why did he come all the way up here, unless this was his way out of town?" Cole wondered.

"This would be the way to go to get out," Neal suggested. "I would go northeast and out of California."

Cole frowned, "That would be what most people would do isn't it?"

"Maybe, but it seems that would be the best course of action," Neal replied.

Cole was looking around, "The most popular choice would be to go south into Mexico. That is what most people would do. That is why Washington would not do it, but why come this way unless he wanted us to think he was going north? He might have come this way leading us off so we would think he was going south."

Neal looked confused, "Where would he go then?"

Cole smiled. "I know where. Get in the car. I think he was leading us northeast towards Nevada and beyond but I think he is going up the coast into northern California. If for some reason he is still in the area, he might try to blend in with the tourists and beach bums."

Neal looked at Cole as if he was crazy and got in the car. "Okay, where to?"

"Let's start on the beach at Malibu and travel north."

"Isn't this really a shot in the dark?" Neal asked.

"You have something else to do?" Cole snapped.

"Nope, I'm with you the whole ride," Neal said as he put the car in gear.

Richard gathered what little things he had and left the motel room. He didn't relish hanging around but he didn't want to have his truck that was so easily identifiable on the road longer than necessary. He found a sports pub across the street where he could sit and waste time in relative anonymity.

Cole and Neal drove up the coast. Cole knew it was a long shot but he was tired of sitting around the office waiting on others to do their job.

Marty was scanning the coast also. He had a description of Richard's truck and he was looking in hotel parking lots. His driver was getting more and more impatient but he wouldn't dare let on to Marty. By the time they reached Carpinteria, he was ready to turn around, thinking his idea was not paying off.

Marty and his driver stopped for lunch at a bikini bar near the beach. They settled in for an hour or so to drink beer and eat warmed up frozen chicken wings.

As Marty was enjoying the show and the beer, he wondered what was going on back at the office and if there was any new information. He made a call back and found out Cole was out coming his way. *Interesting,* Marty thought, *Hargrove is actually out investigating a hunch. Not like him at all.*

Marty rang up Cole, "Hey, old man what are you doing out of the office. You're going to hurt yourself."

Cole did not think that was funny, "I didn't tell you we went out because you are in no condition to be out following up leads."

"Oh really?" Marty replied. "Is that why I'm sitting near the coast in Ventura after scouring most of the coast?"

"Ventura? Why would you go all the way there?" Cole inquired.

"I just felt that if I were Washington, I would have to stick around town somewhere waiting for a way out of the country I might as well stay near the beach and the tourists."

"That is what I thought," Cole said. "We are on our way in your direction so stay there until we arrive."

Marty gave Cole the directions and name of the bar and hung up.

"Interesting," Cole said, "Maybe there is something to this endeavor after all."

Neal nodded, "Maybe you and Post are more alike than you think."

"Yes, very funny Baker. Just concentrate on your driving."

Moonbaby and Moe were all packed up. Moon paid for another day even though they were leaving. She felt there was nowhere to hang out and the less they were on the road the better. Also, this way the monks would think they were still there if they happened to be questioned. That was highly unlikely but it was another reason to pay.

Moe was walking much better but Moon knew his ribs were still sore. He was not a complainer so it was hard for Moon to determine his pain level.

Moon was all packed. "Are we ready for this?"

Moe cocked one eyebrow, "We, or do you mean me? Yes I'm ready."

They got on and said goodbye to the tranquility of the Buddhist sanctuary. Moon thought, *It was nice while it lasted. Into the fire we go.* She put the bike in gear and headed down the road.

Moon took the road back the way they came two nights ago towards LA. It was risky but she knew the fastest way was back was on the freeway. The motorcycle was a great way to unwind most of the time, however, this moment it was working against her. Her doubt was turning inward and eating at her inside out.

Cole and Neal were on their way to meet Marty. They got a call a local police officer had spotted a truck that matched Richard's. Cole got on the phone and instructed the dispatch officer to relay the location and tell the officer to back off; they were on their way.

Neal started speeding up as he turned around in anticipation of catching Richard. Cole was catapulted into the window and his phone went flying onto the floorboard with a thud.

"What the fuck are you doing!" Cole yelled.

"I'm sorry I'm just excited that we have a lead and I want to get there fast."

"Well slow the fuck down you idiot and get us there in one piece." Cole screamed.

They traveled a while but it seemed to take longer with both men hopped up with adrenaline.

"There, look there!" Neal exclaimed.

"What, what am I looking at? Oh shit! Pull in there, yes!" Cole exclaimed.

"Do you think it is?" Neal asked with nervous anticipation.

"Just get into the parking lot," Cole ordered. "This is the address and there is the cop who called it in."

The parking lot was not very large and they didn't want Richard to see them if it was Richard's truck they saw. They wanted to follow him and find the other two. Really, Cole just wanted Waseem and Franklin; Richard was just a nuisance. They pulled up to the police officer and Cole flashed his badge and instructed they had it under control. The officer reluctantly agreed and off he went.

"This is too close, look across the street. Go there and pick a spot we can watch the front door and the truck." Cole directed.

Neal did as he was told but he was filled with nervous excitement and almost plowed into a parked car as he executed Cole's orders.

"Get a hold of yourself man or we may blow it," Cole scolded.

"Yes, sorry, I just can't believe our luck. To have him spotted just where you thought he might be."

"Blow your mind another time. We will just sit here calmly and wait," Cole instructed.

Richard looked at the clock. He called Remy and asked him to meet earlier.

"You're in luck," Remy said. "I just finished up. I want it all to cure a bit before turning it all over to you but I can get there a little earlier."

"Good I'm leaving now and will get to the meeting spot in about two hours."

"See you then," Remy answered.

Richard paid his check and walked through the kitchen to the back door.

The waitress called out, "Hey you can use the front door, sir."

"I'll go this way if you don't mind, thanks," Richard said. He walked out into the light and heat of the waning day.

Cole and Neal were so intently looking at the front door to see if it was their prey coming out that they missed Richard coming out the back. The truck crossed the parking lot and pulled out to the street.

Cole exclaimed, "Damn, is that Washington? He's on the move!"

Neal mumbled something as Cole was verbally pounding him to get moving and out of the parking lot.

About that time Marty called, "Where are you guys?"

Cole excitedly exclaimed, "We have found Washington and we are following him."

"Fuck yeah!" Marty exclaimed, "Tell me where you are headed and I'll take him down!"

Cole interrupted, "No! No, you're not, not yet. We are going to follow him to see if he meets up with Ms. Franklin and her friend! Don't you dare get close!"

"Okay, okay I got it," Marty. "You want me to call in a drone to help follow him?"

"Yes, do that. I'll text you our position and keep texting any change. You just stay off him, Post. I don't want him spooked."

Marty felt the air let out of him, "I know, I'll wait to have my turn."

"Exactly. When I have the other two I'll let you have Washington for a few minutes." Cole promised.

Richard was driving down the highway very aware of the people around him. He was glancing nervously around, looking for local police or highway patrol. He was not thinking someone could already have him in their sights.

Cole and Neal were far enough back that Cole was nervous about losing Richard but Neal said he wouldn't. They were waiting until the drone pilot called them with confirmation that he had the truck in his sights.

Richard wasn't concerned. *What am I worried about with all these people around? The cops have too many other people to worry about and even if they see me, they can't remember all the vehicles and people wanted for questioning.*

Richard started to relax, sit back, and concentrate on the long road he had in front of him.

Cole got the call that the drone pilot was cruising about 17,000 feet and was almost on target.

Marty was trying to catch up to Cole and Neal's position with far less calm and control than he should. It seemed his driver couldn't do anything right and while going fifteen miles an hour over the speed limit, he still wasn't driving fast enough for Marty. The driver just kept quiet and drove as fast as he could without stirring up the local authority. Marty, on the other hand, didn't care.

Moonbaby and Moe were back on the freeway, fearlessly riding the BMW through traffic. They couldn't comfortably exceed the speed limit so they were not going to attract the highway patrol with their driving.

Moon felt Moe trying to shift into a more comfortable position while at the same time not disrupting the motorcycle's path. It was a lot of weight on the bike and Moon's intention was for it to be a solo experience. That went out the window when they kidnapped Moe and Moon had to help him get away, so they were making do with what they had.

Richard had the feeling he was being watched about the time he pulled out of the restaurant. He dismissed it as paranoia but now he caught a glimpse of the same car hanging back about 200 yards. This was something they would do while waiting for drone surveillance. They would then drop back far enough that the subject would not see them and then they would rely on the drone pilot to give them directions. Richard decided to test this and pulled into a gas station. If he was being followed, he might catch a glimpse of them.

Richard didn't want to try a high-speed maneuver to lose them because he might get the local police involved and with a description of his truck out there, that would be a problem.

He pulled in as if he was going to pump gas and waited to see what the car behind him was going to do. He saw it pass by and sure enough, it looked like Cole with Neal driving. *Damn,* Richard thought, *This is going to fuck things up.*

Right after they passed by, Richard sped out of the station and traveled the opposite way. He turned down another street and kept turning right and left until he was two or three miles out of his original path. He pulled over into an alleyway and looked at his GPS. He calculated a new way around to his original destination and proceeded on his way again, constantly looking in the rearview for his tail.

Richard was thinking, *Does the drone already have me in its sights? Is it up there reporting my position even now?* Richard could not be sure that he was free from their spying eyes.

Richard kept driving and thinking about what to do now. If he kept on plan and they were following with a drone then he would not be able to lose them and he would lead them right to his contact. He could not do that to Remy, besides they might just pick him up and what would become of Ms. Franklin. Richard was in a pickle what to do.

Richard kept driving for about twenty minutes and finally came to a decision. He would have to call Ms. Franklin and have them meet Remy. That would be risky as Remy does not like to meet new people and he might just take off and then they would all be in trouble. He really wasn't relishing his choices at all, *How do I find out if the drone is following me? There's no way to know.*

He would just have to call Remy and Ms. Franklin and change plans. He would then lead the drone on a wild goose chase and try to meet up with Ms. Franklin later if that was possible. Maybe it would have to be across the border.

Moon was riding along making good time when she felt a vibration in her side. At first, she thought it was the BMW doing something it shouldn't and then she realized it was her phone.

"Ms. Franklin, I'm sorry I'm calling but we have to change plans," Richard explained.

Moon was nervous, "What do you want us to do?"

"I need you to make a stop that I was going to make before I was meeting you. I have a man who has made us all new identities and we need them to proceed further. He is a skittish man but I think I can get him to agree to meet with you instead of me."

Moon was concerned about the change, "What is happening to you? What is changing the plan?"

"I think I'm being followed," Richard admitted. "I saw Hargrove and an agent pass by me as I pulled off the road. I think I have lost them but I can't be sure that a drone pilot is not still following me so I can't risk it."

"What are you going to do?" Moon asked, very concerned.

"I'm going to lead them off in another direction, away from you and the meeting place," Richard said. "We will have to meet up later when I can be assured I am free from them. The pilot can't stay in the air forever so I believe I will have some moment of freedom. You just have to be there for those documents or this will be all for naught. We will never get out of the country."

"I understand," Moon replied.

"He will have a contact name that I have arranged for you to get across the border. You can't use the scooter and you can't walk across. He is very reliable and you two will be fine."

Moon looked at the phone then looked up at Moe, "I'm glad he is on our side."

"I'm glad you're on my side but yes, it is good to have someone like Richard with all his talents on our side," Moe said. "I will be of more use once we get into Canada."

Moon smiled and touched his cheek. "I'm happy I'm with you also and you are already a great help, now let's go."

They had their instructions and the new meeting place wasn't too far out of their way so they were getting close. Moon was not too sure about all this and she was getting more and more nervous as the miles clicked off.

Richard looked in the rearview and couldn't see a tail but he was ready to give them the slip. "Well boys let's go for a ride, shall we?" He laughed out loud feeling more in control.

Cole was furious with Neal as they passed Richard and he saw him looking at them. "Goddamn it, I told you to back off now look what you have done! Shit, I should be driving but then I would have no use for you!"

Neal just sat there, silently letting Cole blow his top. He knew it was better just to shut up and Cole would cool off over time. He looked for a place to turn around knowing Richard was probably out of there already going some other route trying to lose them.

Neal was unconcerned with Cole's rant and Richard's trick. He knew that the drone would be on target soon and it would spot Richard's truck. That truck was not exactly stealthy.

Cole was on the phone to the drone pilot ranting about how they lost or how Neal lost their subject but the pilot didn't care.

"I'm almost on target," the pilot reported.

Cole frowned. "How can he almost be on target when we have lost it?"

Neal knew that was rhetorical and kept driving and looking for Richard's truck. He realized that Richard was going on a road in the same direction for a while so Neal calculated the area he was most likely heading. He turned the car around and got back on the highway they were traveling and started back in the same direction they were going.

"What the hell are you doing now?" Cole asked.

"I'm going back in the same direction that we were when we were following the subject. I believe he will get back on this path again further up the road and we will establish a connection then. The drone may also pick him up," Neal explained.

Cole let out a deep breath, "Fine, you better hope that you're right."

Marty called to say he saw Richard pull out of the gas station and he was trying to keep up with all his turns. "I'll find him. Don't you two worry your empty little heads about it."

"Post is an ass but he does get the job done," Cole observed.

"Yeah if you like a bull in a china shop," Neal grumbled. "The guy has no class."

"I'll give you that." Cole said. "But he is more like a bull dog, he never lets go."

Neal kept his mouth shut. *Post lucked into seeing him. If he wasn't behind trying to catch up, he never would have been there. I'm surprised he didn't just run into Washington.*

Richard was heading northeast as he tried to confuse his pursuers. For all they knew, he was going to go south after they met up. The Mexican border was far closer and just as porous, maybe even more so.

Richard was able to convince Remy to meet with Ms. Franklin instead of him.

"You have taken care of me over the years when you could have turned me in a long time ago," Remy said.

"You were never a threat," Richard replied. "Your work was always about people on the fringe of society and not the dangerous ones."

"Well, we are even now, or sort of." Remy said.

"Yes, yes we are," Richard agreed. "Where I'm going I don't expect to need you again so watch yourself and thank you."

Richard knew Remy would honor the transaction with Ms. Franklin but he was disappointed that he could not see him one more time.

Moonbaby and Moe were getting close to the meeting place with Richard's contact. They would be a little early but this was okay with her. As she pulled into the parking lot, she saw a highway patrol car. This gave her chills as if a possum had run over her grave. She cut so hard to the left, she almost threw Moe from his seat.

"Sorry!" Moon called out. "Check out the cop car. I don't want him to see us so I'm going around to park on the side toward the back."

They looked around and there was another fast food restaurant across the street so Moe went over there and left Moon with the meeting. They agreed that the news report had them together and they could not risk being made in front of a local cop, still, he did not feel good about letting her go alone.

"I'll be fine. You know I'm used to handling all types of people." Moon said as she walked around the front of the building.

"I'll watch you from the other side and leave when I see you head towards the bike." Moe replied.

Moon walked in the little café. It seemed to her that all the people turned at once and stared. She knew it was a little of her paranoia but she realized that people tended to do that anyway. This was a small community off the highway so there was a mixture of locals and people like her traveling the road. She found a booth and sat so she could see the front door. The waitress brought her a cup of coffee.

A highway patrol officer came out of the restroom and passed by Moon's table. He called out to the waitress as he headed out the door, "I'll see you later, hon, got to go back to the grind."

"Take care and go keep the nuts off the road," she shouted back.

"You ready to order, hon?"

The waitress startled Moon. "Just coffee, thanks."

A man walked in and looked around. He was an attractive man even though he looked as if he might be sixty-five or seventy. He was thin and had a full head of salt and pepper hair that looked as if it could use a cut and combing. He nervously glanced around the room until he locked eyes on Moon.

"Hello, Ms. Franklin."

He sat across from her, "I have what you need here but I'm not sure about exchanging right now."

Moon did not expect this. "I don't have much money but you can have most of it."

"I might have to go underground and out of sight for quite a while so I will collect what you have if you don't mind."

Moon left a few dollars on the table and they walked out together. "I'm in the back."

Remy said, "I'll be right there."

Moon walked to her motorcycle and looked across the street as Moe was coming back. She motioned him to stay a moment.

Remy came up behind her, "Have him come on."

Moon motioned Moe to come on as she dug into her saddlebag to retrieve her cash.

"I have $25,000. I would like to keep $5000 for the rest of our trip if that's okay."

"That is fine, thank you. You know it costs much more than this normally," Remy said.

Moon shook her head, "Frankly, I have no idea what something like this costs. I have never had the need before. Thank you for all your work."

Remy handed her a file folder. "Everything is here. Richard's included." He turned and walked away as if he never knew them.

"Strange little man," Moe commented.

"Yes but he had what we needed. I expected someone different. Another time and place, he would be an interesting one." Moon looked serious. "Now let's get the hell out of here."

Richard was leading his followers up through Fresno and then on through the Sierra Nevada mountains. His thought was if a drone had him in sight, it would have to re-fuel sometime after Fresno and he could lose whatever tail it had on him in the mountains. It was a sound plan unless they thought he was deliberately steering them off course and he had no intention of meeting up with Ms. Franklin. They would most likely cut their losses and move in, hoping to beat information out of him. That was not a pleasant thought so Richard had to be careful not to look as if he was doing anything except driving to the meeting place.

Richard was also thinking *they know all the tricks so I'm going to have to find some they never thought of.*

Richard was so deep in thought, he realized he wasn't paying any attention to where he was going or where he had been. It seemed as though he lost ten miles somewhere.

Moon and Moe were traveling on the highway and struggling with the motorcycle. It was not the best choice for a long ride for two and Moon was thinking they had a long way to go. Moon pulled over in a small town.

"Why are we pulling over?" Moe asked.

"We have to face it. This is not going to work for the distance we have to go."

"Okay, what do we do about it?"

Moon looked out at the town, "Over there, it's a small car lot. We could trade the bike in on an older car that would get us where we need to go. And there's a motel. We could trade in the bike tomorrow morning."

"Won't buying a car let the authorities know where we are?"

"Maybe, but it's a little lot, and I'm hoping he has to do his paperwork himself and maybe it doesn't get done every day. That could buy us some time, hopefully."

Moe thought that through, "Yes that might work. Plus they are looking for a motorcycle and not some random car at the moment. That solves some of our immediate problems."

They decided that this was a good plan. They pulled into the motel and checked in for the night. The next morning Moon walked the bike over to the car lot. It wasn't easy to negotiate with a motorcycle to trade. They ended up with a 2003 Subaru Baja that had over 100,000 miles but looked reliable and it was going to be more comfortable for Moe than the back seat of the BMW.

As they drove away, Moon felt a twinge of sadness when she saw the salesman wheeling the BMW back into the garage. She knew that she bought the bike for an emergency but she couldn't help remembering that first time, riding up in the hills. It was one of those magical days when she felt free. Losing the BMW almost felt as if she would never have a day like that again.

They were much more comfortable now and could trade off driving. Moon also felt more relaxed about running into the local law as they wouldn't be looking for a car. As long as she kept at or under the speed limit, there was no reason for scrutiny, or so she hoped.

It was late afternoon when Richard pulled into Carson City. He checked into an old motel on the outskirts of town and parked his truck as far around back as possible to keep it out of view.

Richard spotted a honky-tonk bar and grill across the street and proceeded over for some food before he crashed.

It was a western theme; a few locals were sitting at the bar and a couple were shooting pool. Richard took a booth at the front window. He wanted to see if he had any follows coming in late.

He ate and drank in relative silence until a fairly drunk woman came over and tried to make time with him but he wasn't paying attention so she gave up and went to bother some other lonely guy.

Richard did not see any late comers to his party so he was thinking it was safe for now. He figured they would not move in on him until he met with the others. He knew they weren't going to wait forever. He would not underestimate Cole but he needed to meet with Ms. Franklin so he could get on with their plan to get out of the country.

Moonbaby and Moe settled in for the evening at a motel. Moon was in a better mood now. She guessed it was from the fact they could talk now as they were driving and that always had a relaxing effect on her.

They had passed a sub shop called Port of Subs so Moon wanted to get them some dinner. Moe didn't like Moon going out alone but she told him he would attract more attention than she would in Carson City.

He was not convinced, "If there are men in the restaurant then I'll be noticed much less."

"I think I can handle locals in a sub shop," Moon said as she walked out the door, thinking about how cute Moe was to be so protective.

Moon got in the Subaru and started to drive back down the street when a text came in from the secure number, "Here in Carson City, may have a tail, waiting till tomorrow to be clear, contact then."

Moon got back with two subs. "Richard texted me that he's here in town somewhere. He is waiting to see if he was followed before contacting us in person. Good thing we didn't go out."

Moe smiled, "Yes I was so looking forward to enjoying the fine dining and ambiance in Carson City."

"You will just have to be satisfied with looking at me for your ambiance," Moon replied.

"I'm hungry, pass me a sandwich."

"Well I guess the magic is over!" Moon laughed.

Cole was not happy. The drone had to cut off surveillance to re-fuel. Marty was pretty far behind and was not sure he could catch up or if he could determine where Richard was going.

Cole was looking at the GPS maps and with the last known location, he determined that Richard was going in the general direction of Reno. He told Marty to head to Reno and stay the night and they would have the drone do a sweep from Carson City to Reno at dawn. Cole decided he would also put pressure on the subjects and release the names and photos to the local media. *Let's see how well you hide when all the world knows your name and face.* Cole laughed aloud at the thought. Neal just looked over at him and thought *That guy has problems.*

Charles awoke at three in the morning and could not get back to sleep so he went downstairs and made a cup of soup. He turned on the television and the local news.

Three people shot overnight, a Beverly Hills convenience store is robbed, and Hollywood connection to terrorism has a face, story in ten minutes."

Charles got a panicky feeling and couldn't eat. The story was as bad as he could believe even at 3:30 in the morning. A reporter stood outside Moon's office reporting, "Hollywood power attorney sought in connection with terrorist plot." The report showed the photo of Moon from the law firm website.

They talked about a traitor in the Department of Homeland Security and showed a photo of a man Charles had never seen. Finally they showed a photo of a man described as the principal in the terrorist investigation.

Charles could not believe his eyes. His first inclination was to awaken Anita but he thought he might as well let her sleep. He knew she would be a mess after this came out. He wasn't going to sleep tonight.

Moon awoke to the sound of the TV. Moe was up early and had turned on the morning news out of Reno. Moe noticed Moon was awake, "You need to see this, it's disturbing."

"Breaking news story out of Los Angeles. A high-powered entertainment attorney is being sought in connection with an Iranian terrorist. The Department of Homeland Security has issued a report on a terrorist plot and is seeking information on the location of a Ms. Elizabeth Franklin and an Iranian national known as Sheikh Mohammed Abdallah Waseem. They are presumed to be dangerous and should not be approached. If you have information...." Local phone numbers flashed on the screen.

They just sat there with blank stares, not knowing what to do. Tears started to flow down Moon's face and Moe put an arm around her. "I know it has been serious but now that it's public, it's just too much," Moon said as she wiped the tears from her face.

As she wiped the tears her face got harder and she looked out the window, "It's time to go public with what we have and see how Cole likes it."

Moon got out her phone and signed on to the secure site Sam had set up. Sam's face appeared on the screen, "You've seen the story I take it?"

"Yes we have, so it's time to let our information out of the bag," Moon replied with a blank stare. "Take it all to my friend Jan and send it to the *LA Times* to a reporter named John Lew. He will be much interested in all of it."

"And Sam, tell my family I'll be okay but I won't be able to see them anytime soon, not until I stop the people responsible and trust me, I will."

"It's going to be hard on your sister and parents," Sam said.

Moon sighed, "I know, but this is the hand I'm dealt so I have to play it out." Her eyes welled up with tears. "I wish it was all different, my family and friends don't deserve this at all."

"Don't worry about us," Sam reassured her. "It is you we worry and care about. We will all be alright."

"It will take time, Sam. Thank you for all your help. I know I have put you in danger."

"No, you haven't and I'll get it done. See you later Moon."

Her screen went black and she looked up at Moe, "We have to get out of here and we have to get to Richard."

Moon went out to the local drugstore and came back with a bag. She had red hair dye for her and blonde dye for Moe.

Moe looked at the blonde hair dye, "I don't think this is going to fool anyone."

"We have to do something to change you," Moon argued.

"I'll shave my head. That will be better. I can look Hispanic or Italian with a bald head," Moe replied.

Richard saw the news that morning and texted Moon, "Time to get in gear. Meet me at Davis Creek Park at noon."

Cole got a call from Michael first thing in the morning.

"We got a report called in from a small used car dealer just south of you that Ms. Franklin traded her motorcycle for a silver 2003 Subaru. He reported she headed north."

"Okay, got them!" Cole said with satisfaction.

Cole called Marty, "Start heading back this way and check every motel off the highway for a 2003 silver Subaru and of course Richard's truck. I think we have them now. We can funnel them into a trap."

Later that morning, the story had made it to Fox News and Moon's face was in a square next to a reporter standing outside the law firm.

They interviewed Bamberger and he was already distancing himself from her. This hurt Moon even more than any other news. For him to believe this insane story gave her pause.

She looked over at Moe, "They are out to publicly ruin you now and unfortunately people will believe it. I've had dealings with this type of misinformation my entire adult life. We will get your name back and we will have justice."

"I hope so, but I don't know anymore." Moe replied sadly.

Moonbaby and Moe were at the meeting site at noon. They parked in a lot close to the park entrance and waited for Richard. They waited about ten minutes when a text came in, "Come up the road, take fourth left about a quarter of a mile in. I'm there."

"Okay, we've got our location," Moon said as she handed the phone to Moe.

"I wonder if he thinks he is being followed."

"Probably is," Moon replied.

They made their way down the road and it was not far, maybe a half a mile from where they were and up the foothills. There was Richard standing by his truck.

Moon hugged Richard as if he was a lost brother.

"Here is a contact who will get you out of the country, Ms. Franklin, but it's only for one."

"One? But I have Moe with me. I can't leave him," Moon protested.

"I have another plan for the Sheikh and me. You have to trust me. It is much more risky but the way I have arranged for you is almost fool proof."

"No. I won't go without him." Moon said as she clutched Moe's arm.

Moe turned to her, "You have to go. Your safety is the most important now."

"No, I won't go without you!" Moon protested louder.

"We don't have time!" Richard yelled. "They are soon going to be on my ass. You've got to go!"

Moon looked at Richard's face and it was not to be argued with.

She looked at Moe with tears in her eyes, "I'm going to find you again, I promise."

Moe squeezed Moon's hand, "I'll find you as I did before. God has brought us together and I do not believe He is ready to separate us. This is a test we will pass."

"Now go, Ms. Franklin, now!" Richard insisted. "This road will wind up and around the hills and take you to a main road and then the highway. Follow these directions to this address and my friend will take care of you." Moon got in the car with tears streaming down her face and drove off north through the foothills.

Moon got about a quarter of a mile out when the road turned back on itself and she could look down at Richard and Moe. She saw another car pull up and two men get out. Her heart sank and she thought about going back but what could she do. She was helpless as she watched Richard and Moe drop to their knees.

Moon heard a plane and thought it must be the drone that had been following Richard. The sun was in her eyes and it was hard to see but it looked like a plane was flying up and over the hills.

Suddenly there was a loud crash. Moon saw flames in the sky and pieces of an airplane falling to the ground.

She looked back at the men below. There was a flash of gunfire and then a shot. Her heart stopped and she panicked.

Moon did not know what to do but her instinct was to run. She floored the gas and flew up the road as pieces of the plane crashed around her. Her mind was racing as much as the car was racing up the road. *Who was shot? Who had the gun? Oh, dear God, please don't let Moe die.* She realized it might be Richard who was shot and that was not any better.

Cole was watching the drone's screen when the image began to pixelate and then went blank. The pilot audio crackled, "Shit, shit, shit!"

chapter twenty one

Back to the Start

Moon felt the truck start again and heard some muffled voices coming from the front. The truck picked up speed and she started to feel the bumps again increasing in intensity as if they were on an old road. She tried to stuff the old smelly rags and blankets under her to pad and cushion some of the bigger bumps but this was not really a solution.

It was a good sign that they were moving again as she could not remember when they had stopped but it felt like hours. It had in fact been hours that she had been trapped in the back of this hiding place and the thought of freeing herself was almost orgasmic. Moon was never cut out for all of this and she was still worried about what had happened to her love and Richard.

She was almost panicked at the thought that she could be stuck in Canada all alone. She could not let herself think it could be possible that Moe and Richard would not meet her. If she did, she might just give up and end it all today. Moon spent her life telling people that she could never kill herself. She'd never be a suicide. If she turned up dead, it would have to be murder. But today was different. Moon was so worn out, mentally and physically, that she could not see an existence without Moe.

Moon jumped at the sound of the hatch opening.

The driver stuck his head inside, "Honey, it's the end of the line for you now. You can come out."

Moon climbed out to a bright sunny day. She had been in darkness for so long, her eyes watered in pain against the light.

"Thank you so much for your help," she wanted to hug the driver but she realized she did not smell all that good.

"Tell Richard when you see him that we are even now and I hope to never see him again."

Well okay, that seems rather harsh, "I'll convey the message," Moon replied. The driver turned around without a word and hopped back in his truck.

Moon stood alone at the side of the road and looked around. She was in an industrial complex that looked as if it had been abandoned for some time. She wandered out to a main road and started walking north. She had no idea where she was except north of the border in Canada. She could see a town in the distance and very few cars on the road.

She'd been walking about ten minutes when a mini-van with a family pulled over. A woman leaned out and asked if Moon would like a ride.

"Oh, yes please my car broke down back there and I was just walking to town to get a repairman," Moon replied.

As Moon climbed into the mini-van, the driver introduced himself as Jack and the kids all said their names.

"Why didn't you just call for help?" Jack asked.

Moon thought good question, "Well, I would have but I seemed to have misplaced my phone, isn't that silly?"

The kids laughed. Jack turned around to the backseat, "Not polite to laugh at people's mistakes, kids."

"It's alright," Moon said. "It was a silly mistake and laughing is probably the best therapy."

"Funny how you carry a phone around all the time and when you need it the most is when you lose it," Jack said.

Moon smiled, "Yes isn't that life in general."

They drove on for a few miles before reaching town.

"Is there a specific place we can drop you?" Jack asked. "We are going to stop for lunch before we head further north."

"You can drop me wherever you are stopping for lunch. That would be fine, thank you." Moon said.

As they were driving Jack asked, "Oh, I've been so rude. We all introduced ourselves to you and we never asked your name."

Moon had to think about that a moment, "Kat, that's my name. Sorry I did not properly introduce myself."

"I know a girl named Kat," the littlest girl announced. "It's short for Katrina." A big smile came over her face and she beamed as if that made her more important than the other kids.

They stopped at a café in a small strip shopping center that also had a bank in it. *This is perfect,* Moon thought. But she realized she had a problem when she went into the restroom. She looked in the mirror and saw that she looked like a homeless person. She wondered if Jack and his family really bought her story because by the looks of her, she wouldn't have.

Moon tried to clean herself up in the restroom. She still wasn't used to the red hair color and when she looked in the mirror, she almost thought it was another woman staring back.

She walked out of the restroom and fumbled through her bag and pockets in hopes of finding a dollar or two. All she found was 65 cents. *This is not going to buy anything except gum maybe.* That would help her breath anyway so she went up to the cashier and asked about the gum.

Jack walked up and asked her to step outside a moment as Moon was paying her last coins to buy gum. He spoke in a hushed tone, "Please don't be embarrassed but I'm sure you really did not break down back there. It seems to us that maybe you are in need, so we would love it if you would join us for lunch."

Moon's eyes filled with tears, "I'll be fine, thank you. I have put you and your family out enough today."

"No, I insist," Jack said. "It's just one meal and you look as if you could use it."

Moon smiled and followed Jack back to the family's table. The kids all smiled and clapped to see Moonbaby again.

The conversation went on with Moon talking as little about herself as possible. Jack was in finance and was currently working for a large bank. They were from Seattle and were visiting his wife Lisa's family in Calgary.

Lunch ended with Moon thanking them for the food and the company. "I hope all your life goodness comes to you and your family as you are such giving people and you brightened my day like you could never know."

Jack pulled Moon aside as Lisa got the kids settled in the van. "Are you sure I can't give you any money? I have a little cash but I won't need that today as we'll be at my in-laws' home soon."

Moon reached out to shake his hand, "No, thank you, you have been more than kind and generous."

Moon waved at the kids as they pulled out of the parking lot. Reality set in fast. She needed transportation and that required money. She looked up and there was the bank. If she could get to her offshore account she would be okay. She brushed herself off and tried to smooth her clothes.

Moon walked up to the reception desk, "Who do I need to see to get cash from an offshore account?" Moon asked.

"Have a seat please and I'll get Mr. Michaels, he can assist you with that." The woman directed Moon to a seating area.

Moon sat down and felt as if everyone was looking at her, even though they were not. Mr. Michaels came out of his office and asked her to follow him.

She handed her ID to Mr. Michaels and gave him the bank name and account number. She hoped this worked as it was supposed to; all she needed was the account number and a pin to deposit or withdrawal.

Mr. Michaels stepped away for what seemed like an eternity. Moon was thinking all sorts of bad things. *What is taking him so long? Is something wrong with my ID?* She kept glancing nervously at the parking lot for police cars but none came.

Mr. Michaels came back with a tablet, "Please enter the amount you want and your pin number." She only took out $9000 so that wouldn't set off any alarms, though she did not know if Canada had the same rules.

She asked the banker if he knew of a good used car dealer and he directed her to one about a mile away. As Moon was walking out of the bank, she thought about all the vehicles she had purchased recently. It was more than she had in ten years. *I'm going to have to toss this one also.*

Moon was smiling as she walked, looking as if she was just out for a stroll, though the clothes she was wearing were not indicative of that activity. She found the used car lot. The salesman seemed more interested in getting in her pants then selling her a car. *That's gross, buddy. You have to be disgusting to want to fuck me in the condition I'm in now.*

She found an old Ford that she could buy for $6000 Canadian. The disgusting man placed a temporary tag on it and said they would be sending the real one to her address listed on her driver's license.

Moon got in the car and realized she had no thought about an address or anything like that so she took a moment to look at all her papers as she sat in the car lot.

Moon laughed as she saw that she lived in Winnipeg now that her name was Kat McKenzie. *I had better memorize this or I could be caught in a lie and this is who I am now.*

Moon drove north toward Prince Rupert, their planned meeting place. She began to worry, *What do I do if there is no one there to meet me or what if it's only Richard?* She did not want to even think these thoughts. She had one goal, that was to reach Prince Rupert, and then she would see what life dealt her.

Charles and Anita were beside themselves. Moon was no longer available to call and texting her was to no avail. The story about their little girl being a traitor and terrorist was now all over the news. The media was camped outside their home and they had to sneak in and out at odd times just to get groceries.

Sam and Aspen did not have it better, actually Sam had it worse. The FBI hauled Sam in and questioned him for hours. He would not talk without a lawyer but that did not stop them from holding him and asking the same questions repeatedly. He would tell them he wanted a lawyer but that did not seem to matter to them. They said it was national security and they could suspend his civil rights if needed. A lawyer from the American Civil Liberties Union got Sam released but the FBI threatened they would pick him up for questioning again anytime they chose.

Jan got the documents and information to her station manager and she did several reports that quickly went national. The *LA Times* ran it as a front-page story but then it got moved to the back as it got old in just a week.

Fox News pounded it daily, comparing Moon to the Boston bombers and calling her a traitor and a "Jihad Jane." They had all the information Richard had gathered but some were saying if it was all true, the fugitives should just turn themselves in.

Moon's own law firm was divided. Some of the associates thought she could never do what she'd been accused of but others thought her new boyfriend must have perverted her mind and won her to his side.

It was hard on Moon's own family. Even Uncle Harry was hauled in and questioned about harboring a fugitive. Harry didn't care. To him, it was like fighting "The Man" all over again. It reminded him of the '60s when he cared about something.

Charles and Anita had it the hardest as they always stood solid on Moon's side. Initially, they did interviews until they realized that the media did not want real answers, they just wanted drama.

Sam had a big problem. His employer did not like the fact that the FBI had been asking questions so they fired him. It wasn't five days later that

Sam got a call from a group of Libertarians who needed a webmaster and computer genius so they hired him on the spot.

None of the family felt as if they could try to communicate now with so many eyes on them. They all felt powerless and frustrated that they could not speak to Moon and had no idea if she was even alive.

Charles kept reassuring Anita that Moon was alive even though he really did not know. He realized he'd come to know what families of lost children felt like. There was a longing to know but if he didn't, he'd hold out hope that his daughter was alive somewhere and just couldn't get word out.

Charles told his wife that this was exactly what Moon had warned them of in the beginning.

"I understand. I just did not think it would come to this," Anita cried. "I always thought it would prove to be a big misunderstanding, but now I know that isn't going to happen. If I never see Moon again that would be acceptable if I knew she was alive and happy."

Moon had been driving for ten hours and she was getting tired. She wanted to get to Prince Rupert as soon as she could but having an accident or being pulled over by the Mounties would be the worst possible situation.

She figured if Richard and Moe were free, they would take about the same time to get there as she would. If they were not free then it didn't matter when she got there. She did not like these thoughts so she concentrated on the positive and the belief that they would be there.

She found accommodations at a motel on the main road. It was much easier to do now that she was Kat from Winnipeg. She said she was a pharmaceutical sales rep and that she was traveling across the country promoting a new diabetes drug.

She checked into her room and decided that she wanted a drink so she went to the motel bar. Moon sat in silence with a martini, feeling a little more relaxed. The news was on the bar television but the Canadians didn't seem to care about what bullshit was going on in America. This was a great relief as she felt she could relax in public.

Moon ordered dinner and another drink. After eating, Moon was tired and full so she paid her bill and got up to leave. Two men who had far too much to drink came over and tried to pick her up.

The blond one slurred his words. "Hey would you like some company, honey?"

Moon tried to walk past them. "No thank you. I'm tired and had a long day so I'm just going to get some sleep."

The fat one stepped in front of her. "Oh, a pretty girl like you don't need no beauty sleep. What you need is a big fat sausage."

Moon sighed loudly. "It's been a long day and I can see by your finger you're married so maybe you should just go back to your room and sleep it off."

"Yeah Burt let's just do that, okay, come on." The blond one grabbed his friend's arm.

The fat one was having none of it. "Married? My wife is married. I can do what I want and I want to have your legs wrapped around my neck."

Moon tried to squeeze past him but he reached out and grabbed at her breasts. The bartender saw what was happening and started to come over but Moon swung around and kneed the fat guy in the nuts so hard, he wet himself falling to the floor.

The blond one looked at Moon in a panic, "I'm sorry honey. We had a lot to drink. We'll just go. Please don't call the cops."

Moon got in his face, "Just keep this piece of shit out of my way and you will be fine."

The bartender came over to apologize. "I'm sorry about that, miss. This should have never happened."

"You got that right, mister. Maybe you need to be more selective about who you let in this place." Moon started to walk out but turned back to the bartender. "Sorry, it's not your fault. I have just had a long day and I don't want any trouble."

Moon got back to the room and thought about leaving since there had been trouble but she figured the drunk guys didn't want her to call the Mounties so they probably would keep quiet about the incident.

Moon had gone to bed when she was awakened by a knocking on the door. Panic rushed through her as she dressed. She peeked through the peep hole and saw two Mounties. *Shit.* "Just a minute I'm getting dressed," she called out.

Moon answered the door and the Mounties looked her over.

"Ma'am, were you involved in a confrontation in the motel bar?"

"Well I would hardly call it a confrontation," Moon said, trying to defuse the situation.

"Well ma'am, that is not what the bartender said. He said that two men approached you and one sexually assaulted you."

Moon realized they were more concerned about the men's behavior than her kicking the fat one in the nuts.

"Well, they were very drunk and as I was trying to get by, one lost his balance and he reached out and brushed against my chest."

"That is about what they said. So you don't want to press charges?" the Mountie asked.

"No, all forgotten, in fact you woke me up." Moon said as if it was old news.

The two officers tipped their hats. "Sorry to awaken you. We just had to check out the complaint. Have a good rest of the night, ma'am."

Moon closed the door and with a deep sigh, she leaned against it, *This is going to take years off me. How can life get so fucking complicated?* Moon sat in the dark for quite a while before falling asleep again.

Morning came too early. She did not feel as though she even slept. She drove away from the motel realizing that she had another ten hours until she reached her destination. Moon found herself on a two-lane country road that did not resemble the type of roads she grew up driving. A major east west highway had no resemblance to the American version.

The countryside was pretty and dotted with small communities and farms with little traffic sharing the highway. The ten hours seemed to fly by with each mile sending Moon into a trance. The fact was, a couple of times Moon realized she was in a kind of self-hypnosis. She wondered how she got through the trip without running into anyone.

Prince Rupert was on an island. There was another small community named Port Edward nearby but not much else. Seemed like this part of the world was cut off from the problems everyone else knew about. That suited Moon just fine. She could go about her business as Kat with little notice.

Moon found a quaint hotel that advertised luxury rooms overlooking the water. She thought it would be perfect and checked in.

The front desk clerk greeted her with a smile and asked how long she would be staying.

Moon thought a moment, "Two, maybe three days."

"Vacationing?"

Moon was caught off guard a moment. "Oh, yes, just a little holiday alone to enjoy by myself," she said, stumbling through the words.

Moon started to pay in cash. "Could we put a card down on the room for security deposit," the clerk asked.

Moon stumbled and rummaged through her bag. She found the envelope of forged documents and felt relief. She thrust out a credit card with Kat's name on it to the smiling man. "Of course, but I will pay in cash. I have a budget and I don't want any credit debt."

The man nodded, "Very prudent of you. Cash will be fine."

Moon found the room and thought *I have to start doing better at this spy type stuff. I'm just not cut out for it.*

The room was nice but it was an old hotel. She opened the curtains and there was a beautiful view of the water and the barrier island across from Prince Rupert.

This will do, she thought to herself, and then reality started to set in. She was not on vacation. She was there to meet two people that she had no idea if they would show. One or both of them could be dead and Cole could be here waiting for her.

Moon collapsed in a chair in front of the window and just stared. She awoke from her stupor and looked at her phone and wanted to use it but could not get over the fact that Cole might have found it and was waiting for her to expose herself. She again had tears in her eyes, torn between what she knew was right and what she wanted to do.

Moon woke early the next morning having gone to bed early and having the first uninterrupted sleep in a while. She was ready to explore. She put on some running shoes and ventured out into town.

Prince Rupert was a quaint fishing community. Moon had no idea of the population but she estimated that it couldn't be over 20,000. It was an old town by the looks. It almost had an old western feel except for the docks. She ran down by the docks and saw the only people out this early were busy loading commercial fishing boats with gear. No one gave her a second look and if they did, it wasn't because of any news broadcast.

Moon ran for an hour and got a good lay of the land. She saw the ferry that went to the airport. She ran past two banks and a little grocery.

Moon was walking through the hotel lobby when the front desk clerk called out to her, "Excuse me, Ms. McKenzie. I have a message for you."

Moon panicked, her eyes darted around looking for a trap. Moon took a deep breath and calmed herself.

The clerk held out a note, "It was a friend. Said he knew you might be here on holiday."

Moon took the note and quickly made her way back to the room. She locked the door and closed the curtains. Suddenly, this relaxed, almost vacation feel she'd had changed into panic.

What if it's that agent or any other of his henchmen? she thought. *How would anyone know I'm here?* Her mind raced and her heart pounded. *Just open the note and read it, then I'll freak out and prepare to run.*

She opened the note, "Meet me at 1:00 at the Prince Rupert marina."

Damn, could it be a trap? No, if it were that agent, he would just grab me as soon as he knew where I was or would he? She could not think straight. This was not in her plan. Actually, she did not know what her plan was but this was not it.

Moon drove over to case the marina before 1:00. She was determined to have the upper hand this time. She was not going to let them trap her if she could prevent it.

Moon went first to a bank and withdrew all she had left in her account. She knew that it would set off alarms but she felt that if she was walking into a trap this would be her last chance to get away and she would need all the money she could get her hands on.

Sitting there waiting for the manager to retrieve her cash, she could feel the eyes of the bank employees burning holes in her. This was a small town and Moon had no doubt that the news would spread of some out-of-towner withdrawing a large amount of cash. It didn't matter. Moon had decided that good, bad, or ugly, the outcome today would require she had access to as much money as she could and she was not expecting to stay here long.

Moon went by a thrift store on the way back to the hotel. She laughed to herself as she bought a bunch of second-hand clothes, *okay, now the town really has reason to talk.*

She could hear it now in hushed tones, *Did you hear about the girl with all that money, bought clothes at the thrift store? Why would she do that?*

Moon went back to the hotel and dressed in her new old clothes. She was practically unrecognizable. She looked like an old homeless woman.

Moon parked her car a safe distance from the marina and wheeled over a cart from the grocery store. On her way to the meeting place, she filled her cart with cans and bottles as she walked along. She had her eye out on the marina and the boats tied to their slips.

The marina was not busy at this hour. The morning and evening were the peak times. All the boats were out for the day and they would not come back until later.

A large fishing boat looked as if it was being repaired and cleaned.

Moon saw two men come out and shake hands with who looked to be the captain and disembark. They stopped and talked a minute; Moon tried but could not make out if she recognized them. It frustrated her that she could not tell if they were friend or foe so she decided to get closer. She dug through a trashcan close to one of the docks so she could watch the two men talk.

"Get out of the trash you old hag!"

A voice from behind made Moon jump. She started to pull her Glock out of her pocket but stopped and resumed character, "Sorry I was just looking for some cans to sell."

Moon walked the other way trying to find the two men but she lost sight of them. *Damn, where did they go?* She started to panic but pulled it together and pushed her cart up and around the marina, acting as if she was leaving.

Moon walked around a corner and spied the two near a dumpster so she pushed forward with her cart. One of the men turned and looked at her for just a moment. He had a hat on and his collar was up around his neck so she did not get a good look but for an instant, it looked like Richard. *Could it be?* She didn't dare let her guard down because it could very well be one of the others. She was relieved to see it was definitely not Cole.

Moon circled around out of their sight. She pulled her gun and quietly snuck up on them from behind so all she had to do was reach around a wall and stick the gun in the one guy's back. She figured that she would know what to do after that.

She crept up and stuck the Glock into the man's back, "Keep quiet and don't move or I will shoot you."

"This is my treatment after all I've been through to see you again?"

Moon's eyes started to flow tears like a waterfall as she recognized Moe's voice instantly. He turned around and she almost dropped the gun as she flung her arms around him in the biggest bear hug she had ever given anyone. Moe put his hands to her face and kissed her on the mouth, wiping her tears off.

"I can't say I like the new wardrobe or the smell but it is so good to finally find you."

Moon could not speak. She looked over Moe's shoulder to see Richard smiling like a Cheshire Cat.

"Ditto to that young lady," Richard said. "It has been a journey but now we need to get out of here and then you two can take your time with your reunion."

Moon awoke from her trance, "I have a car. Let's go!"

The three of them went to Moon's hotel where she cleaned up and changed back into the person she was, discarding the homeless woman in a pile of old clothes.

Moon was curious how they'd made it to Canada, "How did you get away and not get hurt? The last I saw of you, an agent had a gun on you and then that plane crashed and there was a shot. I had to run as the sky started raining debris from the crash."

"It was Post," Richard said. "We were goners. After you pulled away, we were caught for sure."

"One of us would have thought of something," Moe interjected.

"Nope, it was all your boyfriend here," Richard insisted. "He's the one who saved the day. Post had the drop on us and he was fuming with hate. I could tell he wanted to rip my head off for sure. He ordered the other agent who'd been driving to get the cuffs and secure us."

Richard described what happened, "The driver started to walk to the trunk as Post hobbled closer to us."

Moe interrupted, "That was when Richard decided to rub salt in Post's wound, so to speak and say 'Lovely crutch, now you can get a handi-capped parking sticker.' Post really didn't like that."

"No, Post did not like that one bit and said, 'Washington, you mother,' well you get the idea. 'You did this shit to me and I'm going to make you pay.!'"

Moe laughed, "Yeah that's when Richard said, 'Well, hobble your way closer, gimpy and take care of business.'"

Richard became annoyed, "You want to tell the story or shall I?"

Moe made a motion of zipping his lips.

Richard continued, "Yes, Post was inflamed by then and did stumble closer, about the time that plane exploded in the air. We don't know what happened but we are guessing that a small plane collided with the drone that had been following us. That is when your boyfriend jumped into action and kicked Post in the same leg that was injured already. He screamed in pain and went down like a big sack of potatoes, shouting obscenities. Post pulled the trigger on his gun but missed. He was in-tending to kill me. Moe jumped up and took the gun and then we had the upper hand."

"We had forgotten about the driver until he closed the trunk and saw what was going on. Moe pointed the gun at him and told him to come back around the front but he just up and ran in the opposite direction. Post thought he could use this confusion to his advantage and he had pulled another gun from his good ankle and was about to shoot me," Richard said. "Moe saw this and turned around faster than I thought possible. He pointed the gun and shot Marty right in the chest. His eyes went wide with shock and disbelief and he slumped back to the ground like a big bag of flour and died on the spot."

Moon took a deep breath, "You did what you had to, Richard. He would have never stopped and his hatred had taken him over."

"Moe saved my life because Post was going to shoot me first."

Moe smiled and looked over at Richard, "He would have gotten to me soon enough."

Moon looked thoughtfully at the men, "So, what do you think came of the crash site and do you think it will be in the news?"

"It was in the news already," Richard said. "The man who died was a government contractor. He was very wealthy and his people are pitching a fit or so we saw before we lost contact with the rest of the world."

"So how did you get out and eventually get here?" Moon asked.

"I have some contacts with commercial fisherman and we signed on as hands going back up north," Moe answered.

"How did that work out? Either of you get seasick?" Moon laughed.

Moe raised his hand. "After a day or so there wasn't anything to throw up anymore so I got over it, but it is not my favorite way to travel."

They all got a chuckle out of that and soon they all sat in silence. It seemed no one knew what to say.

Moe turned and looked at Moon. "We have told you about our trip here but yours could not have been pleasant."

Moon took a deep breath, "It wasn't that bad now that it's almost over. It is almost over, right?"

The three of them sat there as reality kicked in as a mule would, kicking the crap out of a cart he did not want to be attached to.

"No, it's not but almost," Moe said. "I got a message to my family and they are sending a plane here. The problem is I am not sure when. We need to keep a low profile for another twelve to twenty-four hours.

"Twenty-four hours?" Moon said with a tremble in her voice.

Moe took her hand, "They will get here and we will be safe from that madman and we can work on our defense."

"We will never be rid of this trouble until we expose all who are responsible," Moon replied. "I did get us some money as a headstart though."

"What?" Richard asked.

"I got your note and did not know that it was you so I took all the money I had out of my offshore account," Moon explained.

Richard looked concerned, "When did you do that?"

"This morning," Moon replied. "Yes I know it will set off alarms but that will take time and we should be long gone by then."

"Yes, I suppose I would have done that also. Doesn't matter. What is done is done," Richard said.

Cole was back at his office dealing with the media and now Marty was dead. He was trying to pin Marty's death and the drone crash on the terrorists but the media was not accepting that as the simple answer. As if his life wasn't going bad enough, he got a call earlier that day that the person Washington was sending had arrived and was coming to the headquarters for a briefing on the situation.

Cole knew that this wasn't a briefing; it was more of an indictment of his leadership and decision-making abilities. He knew that he would be losing command to this person. He wasn't about to let some bureaucrat wannabe from Washington come in and take over. *That's never going to happen,* Cole thought.

He was still in denial over how serious the situation had become. The national networks were now talking about drones and their safety and the need to use them on American citizens. They seemed to have forgotten the plane shot out of the air and another 9/11 thwarted by Homeland Security. Instead, they fixated on the drone accident and what it might be doing to spying here in the US. One small town was even issuing licenses to shoot down drones.

The crash could not have come at a worse time. The records that Richard leaked had just about run their course and now with the crash, the media was in a frenzy trying to connect the two. Reports of the crash opened all the old cans of worms and photos of Ms. Franklin and the Sheikh were back in the news. Cole was growing more and more desperate to find his missing people. That way he could squash them and finally put this whole episode away.

Cole buzzed Michael in the Geek center, "You have anything popping up on the Franklin case?"

"No, not yet," Michael reported. "I would have thought we would but it seems they may have new identities and cash."

Cole was getting more annoyed. "Didn't Ms. Franklin have an off-shore account?"

"Yes, but she closed it a while ago and transferred the money to an-other account that we have not been able to access."

"Why the hell not!" Cole screamed.

"It was transferred to a country that is not friendly to our cause and they are becoming increasingly obstinate with US requests for informa-tion about their account holders," Michael explained.

Cole hung up abruptly, "Fucking incompetents! I'll just have to do this myself."

As Cole was preparing to contact the bank himself, his door opened and in walked a woman. Cole looked up and started to say, "Who do you think you are..."

"I think I'm here to clean up your mess, Mr. Hargrove. Washington sent me. I am Sayna."

"Sayna, who?"

"That is all. Sayna. Now let us get to the business of fixing your fuck up." Sayna closed the door.

Sayna was a tall woman. She was at least six feet tall. She wore a tight-fitting vest around a very voluptuous bosom with a pencil skirt that had a hemline about three inches above her knee and a pair of black pumps with a four-inch heel to finish it off. Her feet started the rise of some very long legs. It seemed to Cole that she could cover his office in only two steps.

She was beautiful with chiseled features but she had a hard, cold look. She had black hair and a light caramel color to her skin. It was hard to pin down her ethnicity as she looked like many. She could have been from the Middle East, Africa, India or even the Far East though she lacked some of their basic features. She seemed to be a mix of the world physically but her personality was far distant, almost alien.

As she sat, she crossed her legs over and Cole could not notice one ounce of fat anywhere from her foot to her thigh. Her skin was very tight and her muscles tightened underneath. She seemed to look right through Cole and that gave him an unsettled feeling.

She had makeup on but not very much. She seemed to have no need of it, physically or professionally. What makeup she did have on seemed as if it was to hide her real face and mask someone truly dangerous.

Cole tried to put all his decisions in a good light. Sayna just sat and listened as if she was not interested but she let him speak without interruption. The next few days went by with Cole explaining himself at every turn and Sayna taking more and more control. This was torture for Cole, it was as if he was her assistant and everyone in the office saw it this way. Cole's ego could not take much more but he was going to have to.

Sayna called Cole into his former office, now her office and he gave her an update that she was not very happy with. When Cole seemed to be finished confessing his incompetence, Sayna got up.

"I have a helicopter waiting for us."

She walked out of the office.

"Where are we are going?"

"Ms. Franklin made a sizeable bank account withdrawal in Prince Rupert, British Columbia."

Cole was puzzled, "We believe she isn't using her real name so how do you know this?"

"She used the account number and withdrew it all."

Cole followed Sayna out the door. He stopped at the front desk and tried to tell the secretary what they were doing but Sayna did not wait. She would have left him behind so Cole barked orders as he left the building.

chapter twenty two

Confrontation

Moe looked out the window of the hotel room. "I'm not even sure who or what is coming for us but I am sure they are coming."

"The earliest is about ten hours from now and the latest is twenty-four," Richard replied. He turned to Moon, "Did you use your new identity or your real one to get the money?"

"No, I got rid of all my old IDs and had to show my new one to the bank manager. I used a number to identify myself to the offshore bank," Moon replied.

"Well that means they may know your new name if the banker wrote it down or remembers you," Richard pointed out.

Moon looked more concerned, "I did not see him write it down. I just showed it to the manager and what does that mean? Does it mean I can't get out of here and to another country?"

"No, it will complicate things a little but I can handle anyone we encounter where we are going," Moe said.

"We need to get out of here and someplace where we can get to the airfield at a moment's notice," Richard said.

"You have to take a ferry to get there so I suppose that will take time," Moon observed.

"Yes, I suppose that is our only choice. The problem becomes once we are out there, we are kind of trapped," Moe turned to Richard. "But if we stay here until the last minute, aren't we trapped here with the ferry ride looming?"

They all sat quietly pondering their choices.

Richard stood up, "We go and wait. And we have to get rid of the car."

Moon found a lot and sold the car. The salesperson was a little curious about what she would use for transportation but she said she was on her way home and would not need it. He bought the story and the car.

The trio got tickets for the ferryboat and arranged transportation to the airport once they were on the island. They hoped that the people coming for them would start looking back in town first.

Cole, Neal, and Agent Ruth Dwyer followed Sayna to a helicopter that flew them to the airport where they boarded a Gulfstream. Cole was puzzled. *So what agency does she work for that she has instant access to a Gulfstream?* This woman's connections must go higher than he ever thought; Cole was going to have to be careful around her. They were in the air in minutes, passing as priority above all other air traffic.

Sayna directed the agents to sit as she went forward and would not appear again for a couple of hours. When she finally returned, she asked Cole to follow her to a small conference room.

Cole started the conversation, "Okay, why are we here?"

Sayna looked at him as if he were a child. "In this room or on our way to Canada?"

"I know why we are going to Canada. Why are we in this room?"

"Really, I would think you would know that answer after the way you have fucked up this operation from the beginning. You have endangered surveillance operations around the world with your stupidity and now I have to straighten out your mess."

Cole started to say, "But I..."

"But you what? You went after a high-profile target who had nothing to do with any security risk and now you made them a huge risk that frankly we can't afford to have running free. Our target was never the Franklin woman. It was Waseem all along. I read all the correspondence and the reports. You ignored your own primary investigator's reports." Sayna opened a folder but did not read the documentation she had in front of her.

"His findings and I quote, 'This subject is of no security risk. She seems to be going about normal legal business operations. The so-called connection in her past to a current subject on our watch list seems insignificant.' That is what your own investigator wrote."

She didn't even read that, Cole thought. *She must have some kind of memory.*

"Does that ring a bell to you?" Sayna looked coldly at Cole.

"Yes I remember reading that but I felt that the investigator had personally involved himself with the subject," Cole replied.

"As in sexually?" Sayna asked.

"No, but I felt he was swayed by his personal feelings for the subject."

"Well I'm here to make sure that we erase these three people and create a story to keep the media satisfied. The hard part is going to be the families, the Franklins and the Waseems. They both have influence in their respective communities and governments. This will be far from over even after we eliminate them."

Sayna walked out of the conference room and left Cole sitting there.

They arrived at the Prince Rupert airport. Cole was looking out the window thinking *The Canadians are so backwards, this has to be fifty years behind the rest of the world. Every town in Canada is so remote I do not understand how can people live this way.*

As they got off the plane, a local customs official approached Sayna. They spoke a moment and he used his radio. "Will you need any other assistance?"

"No that will be fine," Sayna replied with her usual indifference.

A car appeared from around the corner. A man got out and handed Sayna the keys. "Use it as long as you need."

Sayna got in the driver's seat and instructed Cole and Neal to come with her.

Cole thought the road to the ferry was almost dirt. It wasn't but maintenance was far from adequate as far as he was concerned. The people of Prince Rupert would have been insulted with his opinions but Cole would not have concerned himself with that. To him, the Canadians were just people who would get in the way.

The ferry was arriving and Moon and Moe were sitting in the passenger waiting area. Richard was watching the boat approach the dock when he thought he saw Neal on the deck.

Damn it, Richard thought. *We have to get out of here.* He immediately got Moon's and Moe's attention and they all hustled out of the building and around a corner where they could look through a window at passengers getting off the ferry.

They saw Cole get off the boat and walk towards the cars driving off the ferry. "Do you know that woman driving that car?" Moon asked.

"No, I have never seen her before," Richard replied. "Although she could be sent from Washington to look over Cole's shoulder. Probably a low-level agent just reporting back to Homeland Security or she could be from the NSA to monitor their progress. We have created quite a stir."

The trio watched the agents as they drove off into town. Richard was concerned. "We need to watch ourselves. Can you get a message to your pilots, Mr. Waseem?"

"No, not at this moment, but the time is getting closer for the plane to arrive," Moe replied.

Richard sighed deeply. "Okay we have no choice. We have to get on the ferry and try to stay out of sight once we are at the airport. We will tell the officials that we are waiting for travelers to arrive. We will not tell them we are going to leave. We do not want a record of these new aliases leaving the country because they could track us later," he warned.

The next group of passengers started boarding the ferry. There were only six other people. Richard was uncomfortable with the small numbers as it would not allow blending in.

Sayna drove through town and dropped Neal off at the cruise line office to check it out. She and Cole went on to the seaplane air facility.

As they drove through the small town, Cole wondered how and why the fugitives would end up there. "It is so remote. I always wondered why they didn't just make for the Mexican border."

"Looks perfect to me. Big enough not to call question to yourself, remote enough that you could get in and out easily and it's a tourist stop of sorts. People traveling to and from Alaska. It's perfect cover," Sayna said. She laid the out possibilities. "There is a good chance that they are going to blend in with the cruise passengers or they will try to make it out with a seaplane pilot to another more remote location. Or they could have a plane coming in at the airport to pick them up. In any case, we will have all options covered. They may have left the area already. Ms. Franklin did withdraw a sizable amount of money and I assume she knows that would call attention to herself."

They investigated the seaplane flight docks; most craft were gone for the day. Sayna looked around the office, "How quaint."

An old woman came out from the back, "How are you folks this afternoon?"

"We are fine. We are looking for three people." Sayna laid three photographs out on the counter.

The woman looked them over, "Sorry I have not seen them here. Why are you looking for them?"

"You're telling me that they have not secured air transport in the last twenty-four hours?" Sayna asked.

The woman looked at Sayna, "No, I have not seen them. Now that doesn't mean they haven't spoken to somebody else."

Sayna frowned. "How many others work here and how long have you been on duty?"

The woman laughed, "On duty, that's funny. I have been running this establishment for longer than you have been alive, young lady and no others are ever here except the pilots and they can't think unless they are in the air."

Sayna squinted her eyes. "This is a dead end, let's go." She turned abruptly and walked out.

"You take care now!" the woman hollered. *Silly bitch, that one could be a problem.*

"They have either taken a cruise, driven off back east, or they are going to the airport," Sayna said as they headed back to pick up Neal.

Neal didn't have much to report from the cruise line office. No one with the fugitives' descriptions had purchased tickets but the desk clerk also informed him that tickets could be purchased online and at other ports of call.

"Interesting, we can come back later if necessary," Sayna said. "We will go back to the airport." Cole followed behind her, looking and feeling as if he were a child following his mommy.

Moon, Moe, and Richard reached the island and took the transport to the airport. It was a single paved airstrip that ran northwest to southeast and was long enough for medium jet service. There was a small terminal building, a couple of out buildings, and a hangar.

The trio entered the terminal and were greeted by an officer of the Canada Border Services Agency. "Good day, how can I help you folks? Off on vacation or heading home perhaps?"

"Hi. No, nothing of that sort, we're just waiting for a relative to fly in," Richard replied.

"That will be fine just make yourselves comfortable in our waiting lounge." The officer smiled and went about his business.

The three of them looked around. Richard told Moon and Moe to relax and sit as if waiting and he was going to scout out the place.

Moon and Moe found seats and tried to calm down. They both felt on edge, being so close to escape and yet so far.

Richard looked around the restroom and found an exit through a side door. Security was not exactly tight. He decided it would make it easier to scout the area without interruption. He walked out to the hangar. He saw the Gulfstream but no activity and nothing unusual so he headed back to the terminal.

Richard came back to the waiting area drying his hands as if he was coming back from the restroom. He took a seat next to Moon. "Have you seen any other people here since I left?"

"Nobody. Do you think they are watching?" Moon asked.

"I don't know I could not find anyone. There is a Gulfstream parked out in the hangar but I did not encounter a single person. I would think there would be a crew for the jet but they may be hanging out on board."

A fuel truck drove by and out to the hangar. That was the only activity at the entire airport. "I think the two of you need to hide out at the hangar while I sit and watch from here," Richard said.

"Why do you want us to do that?" Moon asked.

"Because they will be looking for the two of you together and not one of me. In addition, when the jet arrives it will be easier for the two of you to run out and catch it as it pulls in. I will catch up with you. There's no one out in the hangar. I believe that you will be safe there."

Moon did not want to leave Richard by himself. "What happens if you need help?"

"If I need help then you are in trouble and need to stay clear of me," Richard insisted.

Moon did not like the plan but she had no better one. Moe and Moon walked out to the hangar. There was an office, a couple of closets, and a workshop. They made themselves comfortable in the office where they could hide if they saw someone coming.

Richard sat down and started to read a paper. The border officer strolled by. "What happened to your friends?"

Richard hadn't expected to be questioned. "Oh, they had to go pick up her aunt at the ferry. She is old and we told her not to come but you know the elderly. They don't pay any attention and don't follow instructions well."

"Yes don't I know it," the officer agreed. "My mom is old and getting very forgetful and she won't do anything I ask her to do. She has turned into a big child. I say please don't go out at night and that is what she does. I catch her over at her friend's house playing poker and drinking.

Can you imagine at her age, drinking and gambling, not very lady like, don't you think?"

Richard just sat there and let the officer keep rattling on about his family. After a while, he stopped babbling and said he needed to take a break and would be back on duty before any air traffic arrived.

"Can you do that? Richard asked. "Is there another officer to take your place while you take your break?"

"No, just me today. We usually have two border officers here and two at the ferry but half of our staff is down with the flu. Bad bug too, you know."

"Yes, flu sucks," Richard said.

"Well, best be getting along so I can be back in time to see your family come in." The officer walked away.

Richard positioned himself to watch the parking lot and the road into the airport. He sat there pretending to read the paper while scanning inside and out, parking lot, road in, and runway. He saw a car coming up the road and made a quick retreat to a corner, out of sight. He saw Cole, Neal, and the tall woman get out of the car. She appeared to be ordering the men around. Cole did not seem too happy. He turned and walked towards the hangar with Neal.

Damn, Richard thought. *Why are they going toward the hangar?* The woman walked into the terminal which forced Richard to duck into the restroom. He listened at the door, hoping to determine where she was going.

Moon and Moe were sitting in the hangar office talking quietly when Moe thought he heard sounds outside. They heard people talking and the sound getting closer.

They had nowhere to go. Moe urged Moon into the closet, "Hide in here. There is only room for one. I'll try to hide over behind that file cabinet." Moon started to protest but Moe got very insistent and she complied.

Neal opened the office door and looked in. "Looks like no one's in here or anywhere."

"Let's go in and take a look," Cole said, pushing past Neal.

Cole flipped on the light and walked right past Moe's hiding place. Moe held his breath. Cole surveyed the room, "Looks like you're right for once. Let's go, I'm tired of this."

Cole walked toward the door. He looked at Neal and pointed to his right. He pulled his gun and backed away from the file cabinet. "Okay, come out slowly. You don't want me to shoot you." Moe stepped out of the shadows.

Cole held his gun on Moe. "Where is your girlfriend?"

"I'm here alone."

Cole raised his gun to point at Moe's face. "Go tell Sayna I have one of them. The other two won't be far." He ordered Moe to get on his knees. "Come out, come out wherever you are, Ms. Franklin."

"I told you, she is not here," Moe deadpanned.

Cole just looked at him as if he knew that was a lie. "Okay Ms. Franklin! I'm going to count to ten and then I'm going to shoot your boyfriend if you don't appear," Cole called out.

Moon could hear him just outside the cabinet. She knew it wouldn't be long before he would open the cabinet door and find her. She readied her gun.

As Cole started counting, he advanced to his right toward the cabinet. He reached for the handle with his left hand to open it while continuing to point the gun in his right hand at Moe. Just then Moe jumped and rolled himself as far to Cole's left as he could. Cole had the door handle in his left hand and awkwardly turned towards Moe as he made this maneuver. This threw Cole off as he was opening the closet trying to look in and concentrate on his captive. The action twisted and tied Cole's arms for just a moment.

"Oh, no you don't, buddy!" Cole yelled as he let go of the handle turned and swung his gun towards Moe turning his back to the cabinet Moon was in. The cabinet door opened and Moon stepped out.

"Not again, you're not going to get away now," Cole said as he started to aim and pull the trigger.

Moon placed her gun to Cole's head and said, "Oh, no!" and she pulled the trigger pointblank.

Richard was hiding in the restroom and he heard the woman go into the ladies room. He could hear her walking around and opening stall doors.

Richard backed into a corner but thought she was just going to come in anyway so he was going to be proactive. He started for the door, opening it, and stepping out into the hall. Just as he crossed the threshold, he didn't see the foot until it slammed into his face, sending him back into the men's room again and almost losing consciousness. He felt a pain at the top of his nose and the wet feel of blood streaming down his face. He looked down to see the spots appearing on the tile floor.

All Richard could think was *What the fuck* and as he looked up, barely holding on to consciousness, another foot swung around and hit him on the side of his head. He did not have another thought after that. He regained consciousness, looking at a tall woman standing over him.

As Richard started to pick himself off the floor, Sayna turned from the mirror to face Richard. As he started to stand, she spun around pivoting on her foot as her other foot rose in an arc and landed on the side of his head. This time he saw it coming, not soon enough to stop it but enough to dodge it just a little or Richard would have been knocked unconscious all over again.

Richard wiped blood from his eyes, "I'm really getting tired of this shit."

"Really?" Sayna said. "I'm just getting warmed up."

As Richard started to get in a defensive posture, she kicked forward with those long legs and pointed heels right into his chest, sending Richard backwards into one of the stalls, sprawling over the toilet.

Sayna laughed. "Cole's people are such pussies. You have no fight in you." She advanced to the stall door pulling her gun, "Okay, fun's over come on out quietly or I'm going to have to shoot you."

Richard opened the door as he was getting to his feet. He did not even look up as he stumbled out of the stall and fell to one knee. Sayna pressed the gun barrel into his head. She looked toward the door as a shot rang out in the distance. Richard took this chance and grabbed the gun twisted it her hand making her wrist bend violently back as he stood and came down hard on the side of her head with his fist. "I told you I was tired of this shit!"

Sayna fell to the ground in a crumpled heap, unconscious and bothering no one for a while.

Richard took Sayna's gun and felt for a pulse. She had one; so he tore off the cloth hand towel from the rack and tied her hands behind her back.

As Richard was coming out of the restroom, the nice officer finished his break and was coming down the hall, "My gosh man what was all that ruckus and look at your face."

Richard pointed the gun at him, "Sorry about this mister but I'm going to have to tie you up."

Richard took the cuffs from the officer and left him secured in the bathroom with Sayna. She was still out so she would not be much entertainment for the officer. He was just going to have to wait alone.

Richard walked out into the terminal and saw Neal running in. They both turned to see a jet landing on the runway.

Neal shook his head no to Richard, turned around, and ran back towards the government plane. Richard left the terminal, finding Moe and Moon walking back as they all watched the jet taxi towards them.

"What did you run into?" Moon asked.

"Looks like a wall doesn't it? But it was just one mean ass woman," Richard replied.

"Whose blood do you have all over you?" Richard asked, thinking about all the possibilities.

"Cole's. He was going to shoot Moe." Tears started to flow down Moonbaby's face as she finally broke down. Moe put his arm around her and they continued to try to clean her up.

"You did the world a great favor, don't worry about it," Richard said.

"It doesn't feel that way. It just feels bad," Moon sobbed.

"Trust me, you did what you had to," Moe added. "You saved my life once again. I'm going to have to stop putting you in that position."

The jet pulled up and the door opened. The stairs were lowered and the three of them scrambled up into the jet. The door shut and they took off, heading out of sight and leaving Prince Rupert behind.

At the same time, Neal made his way out back to the hangar, finding Cole's body on the floor of the office in a large pool of blood. He went up to the terminal and had a look around but could not find anyone. He checked out the restrooms and that is where he found the officer and Sayna tied together. Sayna was conscious by then and not in a good mood. "Get me the fuck untied and away from this piece of shit."

"Piece of shit, huh, you're not a nice lady," the officer said.

Sayna ignored him. "Where is that idiot, Hargrove?"

"He's dead."

Sayna did not even comment. She just walked past Neal. "We are leaving now."

"What about Hargrove and all this mess?" Neal protested.

The officer chimed in, "Yes, miss what about all that? You can't go anywhere until we have this properly investigated."

"Don't touch anything. A team will be here momentarily." Sayna said as she walked past the officer.

Neal was following Sayna but then stopped again not knowing what to do. Sayna kept walking, "Come, stay, it makes no difference to me but the jet out there is leaving as soon as I am on it."

Neal looked at the officer. "She is my ride I guess we are leaving."

The border officer just stood there with his mouth open. *Who are these people and who do they think they are? No one does this here in Canada.* He started to try to stop them but thought better of it and called the local police.

Moonbaby, Moe, and Richard were safely on the jet flying out over the Pacific. They were helping each other clean up and assess all their injuries.

Moe looked at the two of them, "I'm just glad this is over and we are out of there."

Moon looked sad. "I believe as long as that woman is still out there, we will never be safe and I will never see my family again. There has to be someone in a much higher position than Cole Hargrove and we need to find out how high this goes."

Moe and Richard realized that Moonbaby was right. "Who was that woman anyway?" Moe asked.

On the Government's Gulfstream, Sayna was verbally whipping Neal for his incompetence. Neal was used to listening to this type of shit so he just stood there and took it. "Get out of my sight! I don't have time for cowards such as you!" Sayna said as she stormed off in the other direction toward the conference room.

Sayna sat down in a huff looked at the phone and dialed a number.

"No, no sir we did not get them. They got away."

"Agent Hargrove is dead, killed by one of the subjects, either Waseem or Ms. Franklin."

"No, I do not know that."

"Yes, I will be in Washington later tonight."

"Yes, I'll debrief your team."

She hung up the phone and a blank stare turned into a hateful vengeful stare. The other end of the conversation ended with a man in a suit standing and walking through a door. "Things just got complicated," he said.

"What? I don't pay you for complicated. I pay you to get the job done. Now do it!"

chapter twenty three

Home is Where the Heart is Unless It's Broken

Once the trio safely made it to Hong Kong, Moe's Father set Richard up with a house, a boat, and enough money so he never had to work again. That seemed the least he could do for the man who saved his son.

Moonbaby sat out on a pool deck overlooking the waning light in the evening sky. She had a drink in her hand as she looked out over the ocean towards some distant point. The moon was almost full and she could feel its shadow cast upon her. There are no more visible scars from the past and her hair has returned to its normal golden brown color. From all appearances, she was still the beautiful woman she's always been but there is sadness deep inside her, barely visible only to the people closest to her.

"I have dinner ready for us." Moe called out from the house, wiping his hands with a towel.

A big smile came over Moon's face. "Paradise would be intolerable without you."

"Are you hungry? I've prepared a delicious meal."

Moon sighed as she walked into the house.

"Why are you sad my love?" Moe asked.

Moonbaby paused and looked out over the water, "I miss my family and I wonder when we will have our day in the sun. But it would be much worse without you."

She took his hand in hers as they walked in the house and disappeared from sight as the night encroached on the last of the day.

About the Author

Michael Sullivan Eddy is married to Jane and they live in Florida with their daughter, Allie, and their cat, Sunny D. Michael has two sons, Sam and Ray.

www.ingramcontent.com/pod-product-compliance
Lightning Source LLC
Chambersburg PA
CBHW061554170626
46811CB00001B/203